A BRECK DEATH

ALEC PECHE

GBSW PUBLISHING

ACKNOWLEDGMENTS

Thanks to my friends, families, and readers who have expressed joy in my prior mysteries. It's such a motivation to tell a new story!

For my editor, Chereese Graves, thank you for helping me make this story better for my readers by exposing the holes in this tale and errors that I have since fixed with this reprint.

PROLOGUE

*J*oseph Morton was skiing down the final eighty yards to the bottom of the chairlift for peak six. As usual the sky was a very pretty blue with fluffy clouds that were blowing by fast as the wind was howling. It would be even worse at the top of the mountain. Joe would just have to grin and bear it until he could drop below the peak and gain some cover from the wind. Not many skiers were on this lift today as it was mid-week, and this particular mountain wisely scared off intermediate skiers. Lots of chairs traveled up the mountain empty. It was steep just below the top of the lift and that steepness could be seen below at the lift line. Then there was the sign at the chairlift advising advanced skiers only. Colorado had more than usual snowfall for November, so the resort had opened early for the season.

Joseph liked this chair because the lines were short to non-existent and the mountain offered a challenge. He hadn't fallen on it the previous ten times he skied it, but he could increase the difficulty by increasing his speed and being more aggressive at attacking the mountain. His partner was giving his legs a break today and he was shopping in town. Usually they skied together, but today he had the mountain to himself.

Seated next to Joseph was a complete stranger. If you knew the mountain, then you liked to have someone on the lift with you as it reduced the chair swinging in the wind. At 12,000 feet of altitude, it didn't take much for nausea to hit and a swinging chair could put him over the edge. Silence reigned on the chair with each man in his own thoughts. Perhaps thinking about the ski run or maybe about a problem at work or home, or just happily enjoying good music coming through the ear buds. With all of the clothing, helmets, goggles, and gloves that people wore on the mountain it was hard to tell age and sometimes even the gender of the people on the chairlifts.

The chair hit the fiercest part of the wind and swung back and forth as they hit the last pole of the lift before the top. He had always liked the juxtaposition of the strongest wind hitting the chair while the ski resort provided the helpful signage that you could raise the restraining bar on the chair. As if you would want to do without your restraining bar, exactly when you feel like the wind is going to dump you off the chair.

Joseph exited to the right. He usually skied to the left as he loved the steep bowl, but on the right side, it was a little less steep and a skier reached the trees sooner. After this run, he was planning to head back to the intermediate runs as his legs were tired from the aggressive day. After adjusting his gear at the top in the wind, he just wanted to get below the summit. He started off heading straight down, doing just enough turns to slow his speed to his comfort zone. He would stop and catch his breath midway down since by then he would be out of the wind, but he would also be low on oxygen with his leg muscles pumping hard on the way down.

Joseph reached an area of less wind and took some gulping breaths of the thin cold air. He could see the fall line below him with the clear visibility of a sunny day. He looked over his shoulder before starting up again to avoid any collisions with other uphill skiers close by. His chair mate from the lift had stopped just above him and also seemed to be taking a break. He didn't see any other skiers around which was surprising, but then he looked over at the chairlift in the distance and it was stopped - that would certainly prevent people from reaching this path. He pushed off and descended into a lower altitude where trees actually had enough water and warmth to live and grow. Based on the pattern of tree growth, it would seem that the snow on this particular trail rarely melted enough for trees to flourish.

Joseph continued farther down to where the trees grew heavier, looking for a place to ski inside the forest. Sometimes you could feel a little like James Bond skiing through the trees flying over some bumps, ducking under branches, almost losing control, while some mad psychotic assassin was on your heels. Joseph had to smile at his fanciful imagination. Whatever motivated you to have a good time flying through the trees. He located the end of his tree ski run up ahead and thought too bad it's over, this was fun.

Those happy thoughts were pretty much his last thoughts as he felt a strong pinch in the center of his back. Given the trees and his speed he couldn't afford to look back and see what had caused that discomfort, and then it didn't matter as he felt his legs collapse underneath him. He keeled over on his skis, lying next to a tree, with his hand on his chest. He couldn't move, he tried to reach his cell phone to call for help but his arm didn't follow his brain's commands. He felt like he was suffocating, unable to draw a breath. Then the panic was over as he lost consciousness from the lack of oxygen feeding his body.

The stranger who had shot him in the back with the veterinary dart gun just waited, watching the minute hand on his watch. He unscrewed the scope of the gun in well-practiced moves, and fit it back inside his backpack. He moved closer noting the man's eyes were open and unblinking and removed the dart from Joseph's back. He wanted it to look like just another heart attack on the mountain and leaving a dart filled with curare would dispel that theory. When ten minutes had passed he sent a text to someone else, and a minute later the ski lift resumed its motion, and he continued down the mountain. He wondered when the body would be discovered, when would the next skier with a desire for tree skiing take this particular path and come upon his target?

It turned out to be about three hours. Joseph didn't appear at the cabin he and his partner, David, shared. When he didn't answer his cell phone, David contacted the ski patrol. They organized a search and rescue group up on the mountain. Since Joseph was wearing a multi-day pass ticket, the ski resort tracked every run he took and was able to identify that his last chairlift was to peak six. The group was soon searching both sides of the lift, checking close to all the tree bases as that was typically how skiers were injured. His cold body was found shortly thereafter. Apparently, no one else had had a desire to tree ski in that particular location that day, or he would have been found sooner.

CHAPTER 1

*J*ill had been home from Belgium for about two months. She had taken a small, simple, case verifying the cause of death for a widow. Her husband of fifty-one years really had died of heart failure. All the signs were there in the medical record. He was increasingly tired and in pain. The week before he died, he was very short of breath despite having oxygen in the home. He had even signed a do not resuscitate order. His widow was suspicious of her stepchildren and wanted to make sure that none of them had hastened his death.

Jill had felt more like a grief counselor than a pathologist on this case. She had refused to charge the woman since it was such an open and shut case. Even the stepchildren had felt bad for their stepmother's feeling over the loss of her husband. The County had determined there was no statutory requirement to do an autopsy and his body had been resting at a mortuary in a town close to the Palisades Valley, her hometown. She agreed with the coroner and had not wanted to do an autopsy on the man. Instead she sat down with the medical record and went through his case with the widow. This helped her see that his death had been entirely natural, and in fact perhaps he might have wanted to go a few days earlier. The hospice nurse had tried to perform the same service for the widow, but it took the assurance of a complete stranger to convince her all was according to God's plan and no-one else's.

She had been working on her vineyard in the interim, trimming the vines as they headed into their dormant season. Jill had planted another half-acre of vines that would take five years to mature and become production ready. She had nearly sold out of her first vintage of wine after five months and so she knew she needed to increase production. She would have to purchase grape juice of the varietals she planted as a stop-gap measure until she could increase her own production when the vines matured.

Jill was a part time vintner and part time private consultant in the field of forensic pathology. Grieving families and friends made calls to her to assist with autopsies and death investigations. She was averaging about one case per month. When she was on a case, she might work twelve or more hour days for a week ignoring the vineyard.

She took off her gloves, sunglasses shielding her green eyes, the hairband holding the blond hair back from her forty-something face and walked inside the house with Trixie, her energetic Dalmatian, for lunch and a tall drink of lemonade. She saw the message light was blinking on her house phone which also served as her business phone for both her consulting business and the vineyard.

She pressed the button and heard a man's voice.

"Hello Dr. Quint, my name is David Gomez and I would like to speak with you. My partner of almost twenty years, Joseph Morton died unexpectedly on a ski slope in Colorado yesterday. I understand you provide a second opinion on the cause of death and I need your help."

Mr. Gomez had provided his number and ended the call.

On the surface, the case intrigued her. She had been skiing at several resorts in Colorado. In fact she had been skiing for over twenty years. Late November was an early time to be skiing, but she had watched the ski reports and knew that the snow had come early this year. She would call Mr. Gomez now.

"Hello," said a male voice.

"I would like to speak to David Gomez."

"Speaking," the male voice again said, strain coming over the lines in just that one syllable.

"Hello Mr. Gomez, I am Dr. Quint. I am sorry for your loss."

"Please call me David and I am having a hard time believing that Joseph is dead. When I couldn't sleep last night, I did a little searching on the internet and found your name. I need professional help navigating the cause of death with Joseph."

Jill knew this was going to be a long conversation and so she settled her five-feet-three-inch frame on to one of her breakfast bar chairs with pad and pencil in hand. Jill gave an overview of her consulting service, her fees, and what her standard contract entailed. Business out of the way, they moved on to the case at hand.

"David, tell me about Joseph and yourself. How long have you been together, what are your ages, do you have extended family, what are your occupations, what is your level of physical fitness, and ski ability?"

"Joseph and I live in Boulder, Colorado, but we have a second home in the Breck area as we love to ski in the winter, and hike in the summer. Joseph has a PhD in chemistry and he is the CEO of Broomfield Pharmaceuticals which creates and sells cellular solutions like DNA modifications for Cancer treatment. I teach high school math as a substitute teacher in the Denver public schools. I work full time, but I can take a week off when Joseph and I want to travel during the school year.

"We met in college at the University of Colorado and have been together ever since which is about twenty years. We were married last year when the laws in Colorado were changed. We are both in our early forties and we are fitness freaks - we love to play any sport from tennis to softball to Ultimate Frisbee. We ski, hike, and run triathlons. I am of Hispanic heritage whereas Joseph is half Asian half black. We never adopted any children, but we both have extended families with siblings, parents, cousins, etc.

"It is because we are fitness freaks that I can't believe that Joseph had a heart attack up on the mountain, which was what was relayed to me by the search and rescue team that found Joseph. We were both in excellent health, taking no medications. It won't bring Joseph back, but I need to know what happened and I want it verified by an outside source.

"Yesterday, I took a break from skiing, choosing instead to get some maintenance done at our cabin and spend time in town so Joseph was skiing by himself. When he didn't return to the cabin within forty-five minutes of the lifts closing, I called his cell phone and the call went unanswered. I raised the alarm with the ski patrol and they found him on one of the ski runs of peak six. He appeared to have been dead for several hours and a heart attack is suspected as it was clear that he hadn't hit a tree. That was all speculation on their part of course and a coroner down in Golden is actually determining the cause of death."

"Joseph sounds like a wonderful friend and partner and I will do what I can for him and for you to give you what little consolation you might find through my evaluation. I agree with you that it is hard to believe he would have a heart attack up on the mountain, but that may be what I confirm for you."

"Thank you and I understand that this is very likely a wild goose chase, but I need to do something besides planning for his funeral."

"I understand. I will send you a contract for my services, and paperwork that gives me permission to speak to the coroner, conduct an autopsy, obtain his medical records. Once you return it to me, I will coordinate with the coroner and your funeral home to be as least a disruption as possible. If there are airline seats available, I'll be there tonight, but no later than tomorrow morning".

"I'll look for your paperwork and sign what I need to and have it back to you quickly. Let me know when you arrive in Breck."

"David, I like to communicate frequently with my clients. For types of information like my arrival, I'll text you, as well as when I complete the exam. We'll spend time together in person as necessary and I'll keep you informed of bigger topics by phone until the case concludes. Talk to you soon"

Jill ended the phone call. She had a lot to do in the next few hours. She would start by getting to David, the paperwork she needed to start moving on the case. She was pleased to hear that they were married as it made all of the authorizations so much easier. She would give Nathan a call canceling their date and drop Trixie off to stay with him. Then she would email a note to Angela, Jo, and Marie giving them advance notice about the case, just in case she needed their help.

She also thought she would notify Nick Brouwer. During their last big case in Belgium, the women had met Nick when they needed his help with security in Amsterdam. He had fit in nicely with the group and he and Angela were exploring a relationship even though they lived four thousand miles apart. He had wanted to become a member of her team on the right case to give him an opportunity to try working in the U.S. He had a potential partnership to open a branch in America, but neither had a feel for operating a business in the U.S. As she recalled, they had spoken of skiing one night, so he might enjoy this part of the country. Airfare, however, would be dreadfully expensive for a last minute flight and it wouldn't be fair to stick a client with that bill, so she doubted she would see him.

She added David and Joseph's names where appropriate to her forms and the contract and emailed them to David. Once she had a signed contract she would start making reservations for air, hotel, and car. Sometimes an autopsy provided conclusive evidence, and in other cases, she found it helpful to visit the crime scene. For now, she would hold on packing her ski equipment which she would need if she had to inspect the location where they had found Joseph. Besides as a result of the footprints and ski tracks from the rescue operation yesterday, the crime scene would be very contaminated. It might have snowed overnight which would further hide any evidence.

She picked up her phone and called Nathan. Nathan had been her boyfriend of over a year. They kept separate residences mostly due to the nature of their businesses and likely a need for personal space. He was a world class wine label artist and needed space for his studio and for the printing services for his labels and marketing materials that he designed for clients. Jill had property that her vineyards were planted on, and in one of her outbuildings she had an extensive lab for running testing for her consulting business. At the moment, the separate residences were working just fine for the two of them. He was her version of tall, dark, and handsome and his artistic personality was a nice off-set to her science based personality.

"Hey sweetie it's me. Did I get you at a good time?"

"Yeah, I was just about to break for lunch. I just finished a new label for one of the clients I visited while I stayed in Germany. What's up?"

"Is that the label for the new beer that your German wine-maker is trying to enter the market with?"

"Yes, it has been interesting to think about a glass design that will fit the beer in addition to the beer bottle's label. Wine labels are less complicated than beer labels. Are we on for dinner at seven tonight?"

"Sorry, probably not. That is what I am calling about. I just picked up a new case. As soon as I receive a signed contract back, I'll try to make plane reservations for Denver tonight or early tomorrow."

"Denver?"

"Actually, Denver overnight then probably Breck or back here depending on what I decide for processing my specimens or discover during the autopsy. The body is in Golden which is a suburb of Denver just as you head up into the mountains, but he died while skiing at Breck."

"Wow that sounds interesting. Did he hit a tree?"

"No, had a heart attack at eleven thousand feet, in his early forties and a tri-athlete."

"Hmmm, a decent way to die, but way too young. What is your gut telling you about this case?"

"Sudden heart attacks kill every day. Usually the patient has a weird arrhythmia that they can't recover from, but I am still surprised given this guy's level of fitness. A weird heart rhythm should have killed him before now or at least made him faint on occasion. So this second opinion may not be the open and shut case it appears on the surface. I'll have to give some thought to how I would disprove such a theory."

She had been looking at her computer screen while talking to Nathan and noted that David had returned her paperwork already, she would check for all the signatures and then it would be off to Colorado.

"My client just returned the signed documents so it looks like it is a go. I should be able to catch a flight tonight to Denver, I'll call you back in thirty minutes after I have made arrangements and I'll let you know my schedule. Would you and Arthur desire Trixie's companionship tonight?"

"You know I get endless entertainment watching Arthur make Trixie his supplicant. I have to marvel over a fifteen pound cat subduing a sixty-five pound dog. I'm not planning on going anywhere for several weeks so we should be good. Where will you run your tests, in Denver?"

"With the airport just an hour away and frequent eighty minute flights to Denver, I was thinking about collecting my specimens and bringing them back here to process and then returning to Breck to look at the bigger picture if I find anything that doesn't fit with the coroner's pronouncement of death by a heart attack. It would likely be cheaper and faster for my client than for me to individually contract the tests out to labs in that city."

"Sounds like a plan. If you do drop back here for a few hours tomorrow, let me know and Trixie and I will join you for a meal before your return to Colorado."

"Thanks, love you," and Jill ended the call.

She looked into flights, booked one but waited on the hotel for tonight. She would have about ninety minutes before she would have to head to the airport. She kept an autopsy kit packed and ready to take to her next location. Her kit even had a nice letter written to airport security in it since she found their inspection notice inside her kit with every flight. It didn't stop the inspections, but nothing was out of place or missing.

Next she called the coroner's office that was performing, or was scheduled to perform, the autopsy. Apparently they had so few deaths in Breck that bodies were transported down to the big city for examination. She had never met any medical examiner from the great state of Colorado, and she hoped they would be cordial.

"Hello this Dr. Jill Quint, may I speak to the medical examiner?"

"Just a moment, is this about a particular deceased person?"

"Yes, Joseph Morton."

"Just a moment."

Jill waited a few minutes and then a female voice came on the phone.

"Yes, this is Dr. Jones, how may I help you?"

"Hello Dr. Jones, I am Dr. Jill Quint. I am a former medical examiner from California and now I'm a consultant that provides a second opinion on the cause of death. Mr. Morton's partner has hired me to provide that service and so I wanted to make arrangements to attend the deceased's body tonight and perform a private autopsy."

"Um, I have never heard of such a thing in this office or even in my career. I'll have to check with someone else in this office. Tell me more about yourself."

"I am a licensed physician in the State of California. I am board certified in Pathology and sub-boarded in Forensic Pathology. I also completed medical toxicology training, but I am not boarded in it. I worked for the State of California's crime lab for fifteen years, resigning about five years ago. Since that time police departments and individual family members have hired me as a consultant. I can provide references from the San Francisco Police Department as well as the Special Agent in Charge of the San Francisco regional FBI office. If you'll give me your fax number, I'll fax those documents to you now."

"Do you have the family's written permission to examine the deceased's body?"

"Yes, I'll also send that to you. I am leaving California in about two hours for a flight to Denver and should be at your facility by eight this evening. I have my own equipment and require nothing more than access to the body and an empty stainless steel table. If you find for some reason that you cannot accommodate me, I'll attend the body at the mortuary when it arrives there, but for best accuracy, I would really appreciate the use of your table and access to Mr. Morton."

"This is a most unusual request. I'll need to run it by my superiors and I would really appreciate any and all documentation that you can email me."

"Thank you Dr. Jones. When I land in Denver, I'll call your office to see if you're going to give me access."

"Yes, please do," and the conversation ended.

Jill hated cold calls to medical examiners. She had such a rare occupation that most medical examiners would go their entire life and not cross paths with her. She had learned at the start of her career as a consultant to compile a packet that contained her credentials. The recently added recommendations from the FBI and SFPD put further shine on her curriculum vitae. She hoped that this Colorado medical examiner would not create barriers that delayed her attending the deceased.

She finished packing deciding she wouldn't even try to locate a lab she could use in Denver; she would just fly the specimens back with her to do the analysis in her home lab. It was likely where she would have the best turnaround time for results. She then sent a second email to her friends and often partners in her consulting business. Angela had huge emotional intelligence and because of that could obtain state secrets out of just about anyone. Marie was an absolute whiz at finding common and obscure facts about someone on the internet, and Jo could make financial sense of any document and find the financial ticking time bomb. Nick's talent was in security systems - hotel entry, cameras, etc. He might know how the pass system at the ski resort could be put to good use if they did have a crime on their hands. She often kept them updated about her cases, but at this point she didn't need their help.

She packed everything up, piled Trixie's bed, toys, and food in her car and stopped at Nathan's house on her way out of town. He was used to her odd hours by now, and they would likely get together over lunch tomorrow while she was running tests. She left her car in the airport parking lot and traveled through security. It was perfect timing as she arrived at the gate just as boarding began. Eighty minutes later she was touching town in Denver and arranging a rental car for her trip to the medical examiner.

She called Dr. Jones from the airport, "Dr. Jones, this is Jill Quint. I picked up my car at the airport and need to start my drive to the location of Mr. Morton's remains. What can you tell me about where I will be allowed to autopsy Mr. Morton?"

"Your call earlier created quite a conversation here."

"Why?"

"We have never been asked to allow an outside consultant into our autopsy area. There are legal questions, resource questions, and ego questions."

"Ego questions?"

"Yeah, what if you come up with something different than my ruling? It is like having an outside auditor review our body of work. Mostly our egos are on the line there."

"So you're not going to allow me to use your facility?"

"Actually, we are going to allow it. We verified your credentials and then did an internet search. We decided we might learn something from you, even hopefully if all it becomes is verification that we do good work. Do you need directions?"

"Thank you for your honesty and accommodation. I have your address programmed into my GPS, and it says I should arrive there in about twenty minutes."

"We of course have security so just hit the bell when you arrive, and someone will bring you to Mr. Morton's examination room."

"Again, thank you Dr. Jones," Jill said as she ended the call. She sent David a text to notify him of her arrival in Denver, and that she would not be traveling to Breck tonight.

She left the airport heading into the city. She had always liked the look of the tepees on the prairie architecture of the airport and corny western music that played on the tram that moved you between the boarding gates and the baggage claim. She had held off booking a hotel since she didn't know her schedule and location for the evening. She might stay near the coroner's office or she might stay near the airport. Twenty minutes later, she arrived at the Medical Examiner's Office.

CHAPTER 2

*S*he parked in the lot and pulled her testing kit out of the trunk. She wheeled over to the building entrance, and noted the bell that Dr. Jones suggested she ring.

She depressed the button and a few seconds later a voice called out, "This is the Medical Examiner Office, and how may I help you?"

"This is Dr. Jill Quint. I just spoke with Dr. Jones and she is expecting me."

"One moment and someone will escort you inside."

Jill stood in the cold darkness of the nighttime. Street lamps provided lighting to the parking lot as well as the front door, but beyond the perimeter of each light it was very dark. At this time of night most of the lot was empty giving Jill a little bit of a creepy shiver feel. However when she looked out, there were a few more cars than she might expect. Her imagination was far too fanciful to spend much time waiting. Fortunately, she heard the door snap open as someone beckoned her inside.

"Hi. I'm Al, are you Dr. Clint?"

"It's Dr. Quint, and I am pleased to meet you."

"Do you need some help carrying stuff?" Al asked peering out to the parking lot, perhaps looking for an open trunk.

"Thanks for your offer of help Al, but I have everything I need on wheels in this container," replied Jill pointing to her autopsy kit.

"Okay, come on in and we'll take the elevator to where Dr. Jones and the others are waiting for you."

"Others?"

"Yes, several pathologists that were not working came in tonight to meet you."

Great, thought Jill. She would have people in the way, being suspicious of every time she capitalized a letter in her notes for the case. That meant it would be a long night. Medical Examiners reacted differently when she indicated she wanted to review their work. Rarely was she welcomed, and often she met with hostility. She had just thought that the atmosphere was going to be better here based on her earlier phone call.

The elevator doors opened and Al directed her down a corridor and to an examination room on the right. He held the door open so Jill could easily enter with her wheeled case. A woman in green scrubs approached her.

"Hello Dr. Quint, I am Lucy Jones, a forensic pathologist with the coroner's office. Let me introduce my colleagues," and she performed introductions.

"Nice to meet all of you and please call me Jill."

"As I am sure you have run into this before, we had a variety of emotions when you first called. After researching you and some of your interesting cases, we decided we all wanted to observe and learn from your forensic skills."

Whew, thought Jill, this is going to be okay.

"Thank you and I hope I can meet your expectations. Let me describe for you my process before we begin with my examination of Mr. Morton."

"Sounds good," encouraged Lucy with a smile.

"Typically I get a call within twelve to thirty-six hours of death. It is equally split between whether or not an autopsy has been performed. In some cases no autopsy is required, and the patient's family wants one, and in other situations the coroner has done an autopsy and the family is disputing the finding on a gut level. Sometimes it is a grieving process that drives the family, and often there is a family feud. Most of the time, I do a second autopsy at a mortuary because the body has already been moved to that location. I have a kit ready to go at all times and a laboratory on my property back in California. If Denver were farther away, I would contract with a local lab to process the specimens. In this case, I'm going to fly home on the first flight and process the tests myself, which will likely give me the best turnaround time for results.

"I often approach a case with the thought that this is a murder and how do I disprove that it is natural causes. I choose to be biased; something a medical examiner can't do in their position. I believe all medical examiners are doing their best to identify the correct cause of death. Here is my reality - I will only work on this one investigation, until the case is closed. Since I was once in your position, I bet that each of you will likely go on to do another four autopsies tomorrow. I have more time and perhaps more testing resources to study Mr. Morton than you will ever be allocated given the usual workload of this office. That concentrated time gives me more time to think and pursue loose ends. I also have a team that supports me to go beyond this initial autopsy to investigating the murder itself. My average at the moment is that I agree with just over eighty percent of autopsy findings. I had a case two days ago, where no autopsy was performed by the county, nor did I do one as the patient so obviously died of natural causes. My work with that client was simply going over the patient's medical record with her as an outside stranger. So my scope and examination varies with the circumstances of the case. Any questions so far?"

Dr. Jones and her colleagues just shook their heads "no". They had their arms folded in front of their chests, a classic posture expressing that while they were listening and nodding agreement, they were really not happy to have her there.

"Dr. Jones, have you ruled on Mr. Morton's cause of death yet?"

"Yes I completed the autopsy this afternoon. I ruled Mr. Morton had a myocardial infarction while skiing at a high altitude as the preliminary cause of death. As you know, I will wait a few weeks to get back all of the tests that I conducted."

"Did you determine the cause of that heart attack?"

"No, I could see the damage to his heart muscle. I've observed that clinical finding on other heart attack victims."

"As I mentioned, I would approach this case assuming Mr. Morton was murdered. Now I need to prove that it was natural causes, so I would need to look for a natural source of the heart attack. Thus looking for that source will be the focus of my examination."

Jill could see that her statement resonated with Dr. Jones and several of her colleagues. They were slowly warming up to her method for approaching an autopsy. They now knew that it was very unlikely that she would overturn the cause of death. However, if she could not find a natural cause for that heart attack, then they would have to examine their processes in this office.

"Mr. Morton's partner called me earlier today, obviously in the deep throws of grieving. Part of the problem for him in accepting his death was how he died. I am sure I wouldn't be here if he had died in an automobile accident. The problem for David is that Joseph had no history of heart disease. He was forty-three, a triathlete, and he had been skiing for at least twenty years. His father and uncles are alive with no history of heart disease. So this heart attack came completely out of the blue for him and Mr. Morton's family. I looked up the statistics on sudden death and for men ages thirty-five to seventy-three, it occurs in 191 of 100,000 deaths. Given that wide age range, I would expect many of those 191 deaths to be in ages over sixty.

"In thinking about natural causes of heart attacks, at the top of my list are fatal arrhythmias. I'll be evaluating the cellular structure of the heart for infection, defective genes like those that cause hypertrophic cardiomyopathy. I think most genetic mutations either show up well before a patient is forty-three or they affect other parts of the body such that would have prevented him from being a triathlete.

"I'll also look for occlusions of major coronary vessels such as an acute thrombosis or atherosclerotic plaque. I'll request his partner provide me with his prior medical record, which I presume that you have also requested. I'll want to see his history and whether he has ever had an electrocardiogram. I'll complete the autopsy with a variety of chemistry and toxicology tests."

Jill ended her explanation and waited for questions.

"If your examination provides us with new or conclusive data, whom will you contact first?" asked Dr. Jones.

"If I find evidence that would lead me to think that I cannot validate a natural cause of death, I will contact you, Dr. Jones, first. While I was hired by David, I feel that I am not infallible. So I will call you with any inconsistent findings so that we can talk those through. Certainly if my collection of evidence impacts your ruling, I like to be able to tell my client what to expect for next steps, which is information I can only acquire from you."

"That is good to know. I think you have answered all of our questions. Would you like some help with this autopsy?"

"Thanks for asking. I have been working alone now for five years so I am afraid that assistance might throw me off my approach so I'll pass. I would like some help turning the body over. Usually I work in silence so I'll try to narrate what I am doing for those of you watching me. If you all want to take a bathroom break or grab something to eat or drink, now would be the time, as I will need to spend about ten minutes to gown up, unpack my kit and lay out my specimen containers. If you'll provide me a disposable gown, I'll get started."

Just as Jill predicted, ten minutes later she had her checklist ready, her specimen containers laid out and ready to be filled, and she was wearing one of their protective gowns. She wore her own face shield and goggles.

"If you'll help me flip him over on his stomach, I'll begin by examining his skin for any findings."

She put her goggles on and using a tape recorder clipped to the rim of her gown she began dictating what she saw on examination.

"Record on. No visible tattoos on the posterior side of the body, olive skin hue, lean man. No bumps to touch, no bruises on the back other than the pooling that occurred at the time of death. A minor cut on one finger, light bruise six centimeters from the spine on the right side, at the bottom anterior angle of the scapula. Record off. Dr. Jones, what are your thoughts for this bruise and what looks to be a needle hole?"

"I didn't have an explanation. I noted it in the report and biopsied the surrounding tissue in case there were any drug traces if indeed that is a needle stick."

"Interesting or maybe it is nothing at all. I'll do the same thing as you by taking tissue and blood samples from this space. I'll also draw blood from his extremities to look at the chemistry of various locations of his circulatory system. Okay, let's turn him over so I can complete the examination. How long was he estimated to have laid on the ski trail before ski patrol discovered him?"

"Two to three hours. It is hard to get an exact reading given the air temperature and high altitude. His body was very cold when the ski patrol found it. They have a ticket system at the resort, so the last record of Joseph on a chairlift is at two in the afternoon. The lift takes seven minutes to reach the top, and then he had to ski down to where they found him in the trees. So time of death might have been as early as eight minutes past two. He was discovered by the ski patrol around five-thirty."

"The ski pass time is helpful. Were there also cameras on top of the lift poles or at the top?"

"I didn't ask, but it would have affected the cause of death by a few minutes swing at best."

Jill turned her recorder back on and continued with her visual examination of the skin noting nothing of interest. She then re-opened the Y slice that Dr. Jones had used several hours ago to examine Joseph's internal organs, weighing them and looking for abnormities. His heart muscle looked healthy, ruling out most congenital defects. She was left with perhaps two avenues to pursue as to why his heart stopped - asphyxia leading to his heart not getting enough oxygen to function or an electrical malfunction.

Asphyxia might result from several sources - poisoning of the air around him with smoke or carbon monoxide. She would rule that out as Joseph was likely breathing some of the cleanest air on earth and yes the air was thin at eleven thousand feet, but unless he had low hemoglobin or a lung ailment like emphysema, he would have been fine. Since he lived in the mile high city, he already had a raised level of hemoglobin that would have helped his body deal with the higher altitude. It could also result from someone putting something over his nose and mouth to prevent air from entering his body. Usually if that was the case there would be broken blood vessels around the face called petechiae. If someone strangled him there should be ligature marks around the neck. Another source would be paralysis of the diaphragm, where he would be unable to expand his lungs to take in air. She would have to do further examination to rule out that cause.

Thinking about an electrical problem with his heart - either a complete failure such as might occur after being struck by light-ning or some other electrical current. Again he could have a rare genetic defect, but really such a problem should have killed him by the time he was twenty. Her last option to evaluate would be a problem with his ions - sodium, potassium, or magnesium. Potassium chloride was one of three drugs generally used to execute prisoners since it stopped the heart from functioning. She would check the blood levels of his electrolytes, but she was sure that Dr. Jones had already tested for that as it should be routine in a case like this. Still she liked to check readings in different areas of the body to look at how concentrations differed around the body as the body naturally broke down certain substances.

She explained this last point to Dr. Jones and her colleagues, "when I worked for the State, I would routinely send off blood for chemistry analysis. In the eighty or so autopsies I have done since I left the lab as a private consultant, I have learned to do what I would call extremity sampling. Every once in a while I find something strange that leads me somewhere."

"Can you give us an example of what you have found?" asked one of Dr. Jones' colleagues.

"I performed an autopsy on a young man who by all indications died of septic shock caused by necrotizing fasciitis. When I started that autopsy I knew and had great respect for that medical examiner. I thought I would be confirming his diagnosis. Then I sampled two different sites of infection - one on the lower leg and the other on the upper arm. The results came back as an exact genetic match with an exact growth pattern of the infection. How could that happen except by intentional exposure to the bacteria at both sites - the growth pattern wasn't Mother Nature at work, but rather the hand of a murderer.

"Early in my career, I had a gentleman with several chronic diseases whose life was cut short by five to ten years as one of his grandchildren provided him with a little extra heart medication in his daily protein shake. The extremity testing painted a picture of how saturated the tissues were in his fingers compared to blood levels elsewhere in the body. However, I will admit that most of the time this ends up yielding no new information."

Jill continued taking tissue and skin samples as she completed the autopsy. She then asked to see the deceased's belongings. She didn't think again that she would find anything but it was worth looking at. Some body fluids would have leaked out after death into the personal effects, but it was just part of a thorough exam.

Al brought a bag of stuff into the autopsy room for Jill to look at. She asked Dr. Jones, "Did you review his personal effects, or were they simply logged in?"

"One of the aides logged in the personal effects, and that will become a part of the autopsy report. They will soon be offered back to the family for collection."

Jill spread out the belongings on an empty exam table. She noted his wallet had his credit cards, money, and driver's license. There was also men's underwear, ski pants, and boots, a jacket, turtleneck, hat, and goggles. There was a tiny backpack that probably carried his lunch and had a water reservoir in it. She took a sample of the fluid in the water reservoir and swabbed its mouthpiece. There was a tear near the knee of one the ski pants, and his boots looked well used. Jill searched the pockets of the jacket and then held it up to the light. Since she had a suspicious mind she searched the jacket for pinholes, tears, body fluids. Holding the jacket up to the light she thought she spotted a tiny hole that might be the same place as the needle stick on his scapula. However, it was a long day and this might just be wishful thinking on her part.

She pointed out the tiny needle hole in the fabric and said "This may be nothing more than poor eyesight on my part or a fabric imperfection, but I am going to sample this spot of fabric to see if there is anything there."

Dr. Jones commented, "I think I'll also sample the fabric. So far, except for the extremity sampling that you did, I think we have tested the exact same areas. The water reservoir would have to be tested by the crime scene investigators if the case was referred to them."

"I don't have a perfect approach to autopsies; instead my findings seem to arise from chasing loose threads like this jacket hole. I agree that the preliminary indications are that he died from a heart attack. He was a very fit and healthy man so I have been unable thus far to find a natural reason for the resulting heart attack. Do you have any theories? "

"My theory was an unexpected arrhythmia. Nothing else makes sense as I agree that most genetic abnormalities would have killed him two decades ago. I haven't received his medical records yet or the results of most of his tests, so either one or both of those might change my opinion."

"I have to agree with you, Dr. Jones. I am done here and as soon as I pack up my specimens, I'll get out of your way. I really appreciate your assistance and cooperation in this matter. I know it is not easy having a stranger verify your work."

"If that ski jacket sample comes back with anything that gives us more information on Mr. Morton, then I have learned a valuable lesson today about the deceased's belongings."

"It may also be nothing more than my vivid imagination," cautioned Jill while she looked at her watch. "It's late, so I am going to head back towards the airport and find a hotel for the night before flying back to California in the morning. As soon as I have test results, I'll share them with you and I would appreciate if you would do likewise."

"I will," replied Dr. Jones and she escorted Jill out to the parking lot. She bet her ears would be burning all the way to the hotel as Dr. Jones and her colleagues discussed Jill's intrusion into their case. She had no complaint as they had all been very accommodating.

Using an app she had on her phone she located a hotel near the airport at a great last minute rate. She would sleep there and catch an early flight that would put her in her lab around nine the next morning. She sent David a text indicating she had completed the autopsy, and had settled in at the hotel. She had informed him earlier of how she was going to process her tests in California and that she would arrive in Breck either the next evening or the following day.

CHAPTER 3

*J*ill awoke for the early flight, arrived at the airport to check her investigation kit filled with specimens. She wanted a special discussion with security on her specimens. She was fine with the case being scanned and x-rayed. However, if they opened any tubes or tissue specimens, they could destroy the samples. She also wanted to make sure that the dry ice continued to keep the specimens cold. In a little more than two hours later she was driving towards her property thinking about the order of processing the specimens. Those that took the longest, she wanted to process first. Really though, she was dying of curiosity about the jacket. Was there something there or was it a figment of her imagination?

She had called Nathan while she was driving from the airport and they were going to have lunch together. She pulled into her driveway and went straight away to her lab. An hour later she had all her specimens being processed by her analyzers. She would soon hear the various analyzer printers typing away with results.

She had swabbed the jacket and was most interested in seeing if the spot on the jacket was a stain, a figment of her imagination, or an actual source of the heart attack. She pulled the jacket swab out of its evidence bag and went to work on it. An analysis was rarely that easy, but maybe she would catch a break. She had also cultured Mr. Morton, but she didn't really believe he had died of any kind of infection; there were simply no signs of an infectious agent. The cultures would take the longest and the rapid test method would be complete just before she headed back to the airport. If something came up, she would set in motion some testing that would take another seventy-two hours, which would require her to return to Colorado potentially sooner than she planned.

She went back to her house and packed for a longer stay in mountains, collecting winter clothing as well as her ski equipment. She loved to ski, but she didn't know if she would have time to mix work and leisure time. Next she looked at her options for lunch and decided it was best if Nathan brought over a pizza as she didn't have much in the house and didn't want a mess if she was leaving again on business.

Nathan and Trixie arrived for a quick lunch. Nathan knew Jill was anxious to get back to her lab. She was usually eaten up with curiosity about something in each case. He had been annoyed when they began dating about her single-mindedness when it came to an autopsy result. He personally had thought he was a more exciting guy than the dead people she was so enthused about. He had quickly come to realize that it was a part of her complete package. She deeply cared about giving loved one answers, blocking the escape of murderers, and the quality of her work. Once she was over a case, then that single-mindedness was turned on him and he could bask in her attention.

She went back to her lab to begin looking at the first results. The chemistry analyzers had completed the round of tests related to the jacket. Her suspicions were confirmed that the jacket had something on it - it was a paralytic agent 'd-Tubocurarine' better known as curare. Yikes, that was a lousy way to die if this was the agent used on Joseph. He would be awake and conscious and panicking about suffocating until the lack of oxygen sent him into unconsciousness. It was a very concentrated amount in a very small circle of the jacket. Next she previewed the tests around the hole in Mr. Morton's back to see if she had the same finding. Again the analysis showed his skin had evidence of curare. That wouldn't necessarily be a problem if the curare was limited to the skin surface in that one area. She would look at its concentration elsewhere in the body. If it was high throughout his body, then she likely had a homicide on her hands.

Curare was used for anesthesia in the early twentieth century until other more predictable drugs were created. If it was swallowed it caused no harm, but when it reached the vascular system it caused paralysis with no pain reliever qualities which had left some patients conscious during surgery and in agonizing pain. She looked at a few more test results and thought she had her confirmation that the paralytic agent killed Joseph Morton. Furthermore, the entry route was likely related to the hole in the back of the jacket which meant that someone had to have injected him on the ski slope. The camera at the top of the lift was increasingly important at determining the time of death. It was time to call Dr. Jones to see what she had found on her end. Jill picked up her phone and dialed Dr. Jones' number.

"Hello Dr. Jones, this is Jill Quint."

"Hello Jill, I was about to call you. I have received some of the test results back and was going to call to confirm the same finding from you."

"I presume you're talking about the d-Tubocurarine concentration in Mr. Morton's body, leading to diaphragmatic paralysis and eventually asphyxia."

"Yes I found concentrated d-Tubocurarine in the jacket swab, in his back, and in his kidneys, blood, liver, and spleen. Those levels of the drug would be enough to eventually disrupt and stop the beating of his heart when he didn't receive enough oxygen. At this point his death will be listed as suspicious, and with a little more time that ruling will likely become homicide."

"Did your crime scene staff fingerprint his jacket?"

"I don't know, if they didn't dust for prints, I'll have them do so. I have notified local law enforcement as to this preliminary ruling. This is the first homicide in a long time in that city, and they will likely involve the sheriff and the State Bureau of investigation. Requesting help is standard operating procedure in the smaller cities of Colorado."

"I have more tests that I am still running the analysis on, but I don't expect any surprises there. I'll provide a written report to David Gomez, Mr. Morton's partner. Would you like a copy?"

"Yes, you have been very helpful. I missed the jacket. Regardless, I think the chemistry results would have shown the paralytic drug. The jacket and small pinprick in his back make it pretty definitively murder."

"Would you let me know if there are any prints on the jacket?"

"Yes I will. It has been interesting getting to know you Dr. Quint. Best wishes for the future."

"And to you as well. Depending on Mr. Gomez's preferences, I may stay involved in this case. I'll probably know later today and I'll keep you informed."

They said their goodbyes and ended the call.

Jill owed David Gomez a call next, so she dialed his number.

"Hello."

"Is this David Gomez?"

"Yes"

"Hi. It's Jill Quint, calling with some preliminary autopsy results in Joseph's death."

"Okay, what have you found?"

"The results are not complete at this time, but my initial findings match the medical examiner's findings. I am afraid it's very bad news. It appears that Joseph was likely the victim of intentional homicide. My call to you cannot be considered official notification, I just wanted to give you the finding as soon as possible. The medical examiner will be ruling his death as suspicious later today which will put in motion the state police and the county sheriff beginning an investigation into his death."

There was a long pause on the other end of the phone. Jill was used to the shock of the next-of-kin upon hearing that what they had thought was a natural death, was actually murder. She waited out the silence until David began asking questions. She had found that it was best to feed someone the answers to their questions as they began to process the news, preferring to answer questions in their order rather than her own order of delivering the facts.

"What does suspicious mean?"

"It means that the medical examiner has enough grounds in her autopsy findings that she wants law enforcement brought in to investigate Joseph's death beyond what she has collected as evidence on the autopsy table. She will probably rule it as a homicide, but she must collect all testing so that the autopsy is complete. Some tests will take another week or two for her to get the results on."

"What information has she collected? Will she be calling me?"

"Let me answer your question about process first. The medical examiner conducts the autopsy and provides test results to law enforcement. An officer will contact you and discuss the results with you and question you extensively about Joseph. I would think they would be contacting you today.

"Back to the findings which I confirmed independently in my lab, Joseph appears to have been shot with a dart containing a paralyzing drug which interferes with the movement of the diaphragm which is the muscle that moves air through the lungs. Eventually when the lungs no longer introduce oxygen into the blood, the heart muscle as well as the brain quit working."

"Oh my god, he was shot with a dart while on the ski trail? How do you know that?"

"I, like the medical examiner in Golden, started with a visual examination of Joseph's skin. I noted a small needle size mark on his back around his shoulder blade. We both took samples of the skin in that area as well as performed a chemistry analysis of the blood from many areas of the body. We found a lethal dose of curare in his blood. I requested to look at the ski jacket that Joseph was wearing at the time of his death. There was an imperfection in the jacket. We sampled that area of the jacket and it also gave a positive reading for curare. You may remember stories of Indians in the jungles of South America using curare paste derived from plants to cover their dart tips when they were hunting for animals to eat. The curare generally caused the animals to drop to the rain forest floor and die. For the Indians, the animals were safe to eat as curare doesn't get absorbed by eating it. Does my explanation make sense?"

"Yes it does. Man, this is hard to absorb. This news is such a shock. Murdered? Someone actually followed Joe up the ski lift carrying a dart gun and shot him in the back. Who would do such a thing and why?"

"Did Joseph mention anyone that he was having trouble with? Was he worried about something?"

"Joe was a CEO of a biotech company and so things would ebb and flow on the job. He tried to create the perfect culture at work, but he would mention from time to time that someone was not living up to his expectations. He didn't feel threatened by anyone, wasn't worried he would be shot on a ski slope."

"David, I should probably mention that you'll be the number one suspect as spouses are usually the first person the police want to rule out."

"What? I wouldn't hurt Joseph, I loved him. I certainly wouldn't have called the ski patrol to look for him or brought you in on the case to check the work of the other medical examiner!"

"I don't mean to make your day worse, but I thought I should prepare you for the questions that will come from law enforcement.

"I am presently in my lab in California processing the remainder of the samples I obtained from Joseph," Jill disclosed. "Unless something shows up different than I am expecting, I'll complete the case tonight and provide you with a written report. As you may remember from the contract I sent you, I can assist you in a variety of ways, but it is entirely your choice as to what I do next in this case."

"Since you are the only person that has bothered to talk to me about Joseph, I would like to keep you on a retainer. If I am not satisfied with the cops assigned to this case, I'll need you to help me navigate this new terrible world in which Joseph has been murdered."

"David, keep me posted and I really am sorry for your loss. It probably feels like Joseph has died twice in the last two days. Changing a death by natural cause to a death by homicide is tough on you."

"You've been right in everything you said so far. I feel devastated to have Joseph's life cut short by murder. I have a lot to think about and sort out. I'll give you a call when I have major news or know where I am going with this case. Thank you very much Dr. Quint for giving me answers so soon."

"You're welcome David and let me know how I can help."

They ended the call.

Jill put in a brief call to Nathan indicating she would be staying put in California. She would join him at his house for dinner and spend the night, bringing Trixie home in the morning. After she completed the report for David Gomez, she would go back to being a vintner. Such was the life of a second opinion on the cause of death. She would have days where she would devote up to sixteen hours a day to a case, and other days when she would relax by nurturing her vineyard and her relationship with Nathan.

She spent the next few hours concluding her testing and finishing the report for David Gomez. She verified that asphyxia caused the heart to stop beating which in turn ended the function of all of his organs from the lack of blood flow. She found no infection at work, and really nothing to deny that Mr. Morton was in perfect health as his partner had thought. She emailed David the report. If after twenty-four hours, he had no additional requests, she would send him a final invoice.

It was getting late, so she returned to her house, showered and changed her clothes, preparing to head over to Nathan's house. He was making dinner which was always a treat since he was a great cook. She had had a busy twenty-four hours and was looking forward to relaxing with Nathan over good food, great wine and awesome conversation.

She checked her e-mail just before she got in her car and noted an e-mail from Dr. Jones. Pausing to open it, she quickly scanned the attachment which was a medical examiner's report. Just as they discussed on the phone she had ruled the death suspicious and notified law enforcement at three that afternoon. David Gomez should have been contacted by the police by now. She drove over to Nathan's house thinking about what next steps she would take if it was up to her.

Nathan, Trixie, and Arthur were all happy to see her when she arrived. There was a wonderful smell coming from the kitchen. She was very thankful that her boyfriend loved to cook and was so good at it. Between the pizza at lunch and now his wonderful dinner, she would have to find time to exercise in the morning to work off this food. When she returned to her own home in the morning, she and Trixie would go for a run. Arthur made sure she properly acknowledged him as he sat on the barstool supervising Nathan's technique with fish. As only he could do, he gave a look of feline superiority and faith that his dinner that night would consist of finely cooked fish. Jill settled onto a stool next to Arthur to watch Nathan cook. He poured her a glass of Chardonnay that perfectly complemented his main course.

"Can I see your drawing of the beer label and glass? I am

curious to view your expansion into an entirely new industry and having observed the beer glasses in Belgium, I want to see your design."

"I feel pretty good about it, though the glass was harder than the label. It's out in my studio at the moment so I'll take you out there after dinner. I bought a 3D printer and so I have a real plastic model of what the glass will look like rather than a graphic on the computer screen."

"Wow, how real is it? Can I drink out of the plastic glass?"

"Yes you can drink out of it. I love this new technology; it makes it easy for my clients to visualize my design. It brings out a desire to design wine glasses and I may suggest that to a few clients."

"That sounds like a way to extend your wine brand. Some day when I open my own winery I could sell customers on the theory that wine tastes better in one of my glasses. Maybe it is something in the aeration unique to the shape of the glass."

"There speaks the scientist instead of the artist. I would prefer to think the shape of the wine glass sends signals to your brain about the sensual feel of wine on your tongue."

"Hey, you're going to get me too revved up to eat your delicious dinner."

"Maybe that is my plan."

"Certainly Arthur would be pleased if we skipped dinner. I have other plans; I am hungry and want to eat your fabulous dinner. Then, after you show me your beer glass, I want to watch you practice hapkido. I want to see your bi-directional kick that I missed in Belgium. Then I am going to reward you for your achievements today."

"Wow, all that? I think I am up to that and what I want following your reward. Sounds like a great night ahead!"

Indeed it was a wonderful night. They enjoyed their companionship, and the antics of their animals. Jill was impressed with the glass, and even more wowed by Nathan's demonstration of his hapkido skills. Now she understood how he had taken down the man in Brussels so effectively. She didn't know why she hadn't asked to see this before now.

Much later Jill lay curled up next to Nathan. Her last thoughts before she drifted off to sleep were they both had gotten rewarded that night.

CHAPTER 4

*J*ill returned to her house before Nathan awoke in the morning. Their body clocks would never synchronize over the early hours of the morning. She took Trixie out for that promised early morning run. Even though it was fall, the morning foretold the warm day coming in the central valley of California. She was checking her e-mails as she approached her driveway, walking as the cool down to the five-mile run. She noted the usual e-mails related to the wine industry. She had one blog site for new vintners that she followed daily. Scrolling down she noticed the e-mail from David Gomez. She opened his e-mail first wondering if he had questions about her final report.

He wrote 'you were correct and the cops notified me of Dr. Jones preliminary autopsy results. You are also correct that I would be their prime suspect and I appreciate the time you gave me to think about my answer to the question of what I was doing at the predicted time of Joseph's murder. I had a credit card receipt from within fifteen minutes of his estimated time of death which is too narrow a time slot for me to have gotten up to the top of chairlift. I don't feel confident in the investigative skills of the officers. I have always had very accurate radar to read people's attitudes toward the gay lifestyle and I sense that the officers disapprove of my relationship with Joseph. In looking over your contract I see that you provide additional investigative services. Would you give me a call so we can chat about those services?'

She was both dismayed and intrigued by his e-mail. To feel prejudice towards him and the love of his life as he was dealing with all the questions of a funeral and an estate to settle was additional misery that he didn't need at a time like this. Regardless she was glad to be potentially called into the case. It had all the factors that made the case intriguing to her. This somewhat exotic murder of a skier would be nationwide news at some point. The killer had thought that by removing the dart from Joseph's back, that his death would look just like another heart attack. He or she had not done their research or they would have known that such a means of murder was detectable by autopsy.

She entered her house making sure that Trixie's bowl was filled with water. She went upstairs to shower with the plan to call David shortly after she was dressed with a cup of coffee in hand.

Twenty minutes later, she dialed David.

"David, its Jill. What can I do for you? I read your e-mail."

"Hi Jill. Thanks for responding to my e-mail. As I mentioned, I don't have complete confidence that the police are going to do everything possible to solve this case quickly. I thought about hiring a private detective to be my and Joseph's advocate during this investigation. Then I thought of your contract and it seems that while you are not licensed as a private investigator, that you and your team provide all the services of one. Furthermore, you've treated me with respect and dignity and answered my questions quickly. So are you available to take on this case immediately?"

"Oh David, I'm so sorry to hear that you feel that Joseph's death is not being investigated the way you want it to. I hope you're wrong about the officers as the vast majority of law-enforcement officers that I have worked with served without prejudice and had an overwhelming desire to bring justice for the victims.

"In answer to your question, I can be in Breck this evening. I'll need to check in with my team to determine their availability. They give me support both in person and via the Internet on cases that I'm working on. I'll have a better assessment of the situation by the time I arrive in town tonight. I am a skier and I have been on the ski trail that Joseph was murdered on and I'll want to reacquaint myself with that setting. I have a favorite lodge that I like to stay at and I'll text you when I arrive. Are you available to meet tonight? If your cabin is easy to find in the dark and the road is okay, I can come to you."

"Excellent. Thank you, Jill, for such a rapid response. I will be available to meet tonight but our cabin can be difficult to find in the dark. How about if we meet in the lobby at your lodge?"

"Sounds like a plan. I'm going to do some research before I arrive. Can you give me the name of Joseph's company and the names of the officers that you spoke with today? Tomorrow I'll want to talk to the search and rescue people that found Joseph as well as probably somebody in this ski resort management to discuss the ski pass system and their cameras. I'll also send you a contract extension and some authorization forms that I may need to speak to various people involved in this investigation on your behalf."

"I'll get those forms back to you and I will send you a scanned copy of Joseph's business card and those of the two officers I spoke with today. Would you mind if I accompanied you to where they found Joseph tomorrow?"

"David, how about if I asked the reverse question? Would you like me to accompany you as you visit the ski trail were Joseph was murdered? I haven't thought that you might like to see that. I may make several trips to that location, but let's make the first trip about you and what I can do to help you at that location."

There was a pause for a while on the phone and Jill assumed that David was regaining his composure. A moment later he continued in a strained voice.

"I would appreciate that Jill. Text me when you arrive. Thank you and safe travels."

They ended their call and Jill knew she had a lot of work to do. That was her life; she either had the leisurely pace of the vineyard during the dormant season or the hectic pace of her job as a forensic consultant. She had ski equipment to pack. She would need to drop Trixie off again at Nathan's, and she would have to contact her team. She was grateful she had got her morning work-out in. Heading to a town at 9,600 feet elevation was enough to make anyone short of breath. She would begin drinking a lot of water once she got on the airplane. That was the easiest way to avoid altitude sickness she had found. She would still need to take aspirin and try to get a full night's sleep that night.

Next she worked on composing an email to her friends and teammates. She especially thought she would want the assistance of Jo to look at Joseph's company's financials and Nick to get everything possible out of the security systems at the ski resort. While she packed her ski gear, her winter clothing, and her laptop, she thought about taking with her a little mini – evidence kit. She was not expecting to find new forensic evidence beyond Joseph's autopsy, but she thought she would pack it just in case there was anything to be collected at the scene or in David and Joseph's cabin.

She heard some e-mail arrival pings and walked over to check her computer. She must've got everyone at a good time since she had five responses waiting for her. She opened Nick's e-mail first expecting it to be short – an 'I can't come' message. She was pleas-antly surprised that he would be on his way in about four hours. His friend, Henrik, who is the CEO of a software company, was heading from Germany to Texas for a technology conference on his private jet. He agreed to swing by Denver on his way to

Austin. It was about an hour and a half out of his way, but on a private jet coming from Germany, ninety minutes wasn't a lot of time. All that would be charged to the client was Nick's hotel and transportation up to the town. That would be a really good deal if Nick could maximize their use of the security system at the ski resort. Next she moved on to read the e-mail from Jo; again expecting a decline to her invite to join her on the mountain. Instead Jo would give her two days as she had a sister she had been meaning to visit in a city about forty miles away.

So far this investigation was shaping up well from a resource perspective. Given that Jo had been held at knife point during their last case, Jill felt fortunate to have her back helping her on an investigation. Moving on to Angela's email, she would not be available for three days because she had two photo shoots, and Marie had wanted to ski Colorado for a long time. She had been able to reschedule her calendar for a long week-end. Wow, the only person missing from this gathering was Nathan, but he was more protector than investigator. As a world class wine label artist, she would bet he had clients in Colorado, and if he decided at some point to join her in Breck, he could drop in on those wineries if it suited him.

Jill developed a calendar that had all of their arrivals and departures. She would get a four wheel drive vehicle at the Denver airport and have her friends arrive by shuttle. She would lose too much investigative time if she was going back and forth to the airport to pick them up. She loaded her car and prepared to take Trixie over to Nathan's while she was gone which she guessed might be a week at most. Certainly if she and Marie had time to ski for pleasure she would add a few days to her stay to do that. From a client's perspective, since he had hired Jill, she couldn't vacation in the middle of the investigation, but her team members could as they were part-time contract workers.

She was soon pulling up to the airport's long term parking lot, unloading her luggage and ski gear. She was breaking a sweat by the time she arrived in the terminal between the warm temperature in California and the weight of her luggage. A little more than two hours later and she was at the same car rental, she had been at two days ago. This time she got a more winterized rental car since the mountain weather could be unpredictable and even more so this year since they had substantial early season snow.

After a thankfully uneventful drive in the dark, she was soon arriving at her favorite hotel in Breck. The rates were about half what she paid during the regular season as while the resort had snow, many skiers and boarders were unable to make vacation plans that quickly to take advantage of the conditions. While she unpacked her belongings, she called David to let him know of her arrival. As she hadn't eaten dinner yet they agreed to meet in a restaurant in town. The walk would do Jill good helping her adjust to the altitude. She felt like she had drank a gallon of water in the last couple of hours, but so far no headache and no racing heart, so she was doing well acclimating to the thinner air.

A short ten minute walk down Main Street had her walking into a little Irish pub. Guinness was one of her favorite beers, but she knew better than to drink alcohol on her first night in Breck. David arrived shortly thereafter and they settled into the restaurant.

"Hello David. How are you doing?"

"Normally I would say fine, but with Joseph's murder, I'm just devastated. I'm truly bewildered contemplating a life without Joseph. I wasn't on the mountain skiing with him as I was getting quotes for a new furnace for our cabin, one that would last us the next twenty years. Now I don't want to even keep the cabin. Shopping for a furnace on my part might have gotten Joseph killed."

Placing her hand on David's she emphasized, "You can't think that way. Murder in about twenty-two percent of cases, is random. The other seventy-eight percent the murderer knows the victim. Given that this occurred in an isolated area of the ski resort, with a dart gun as opposed to a gun or knife, my opinion is that Joseph was a target. If you had been skiing with Joseph, his murderer would have simply picked another time or location. In fact he might have murdered you as well. I will be focusing on what the possible motives are for Joseph's murder."

"Thank you Jill for that explanation. The police have not been so forthcoming. They spent most of their time with me looking for evidence that I murdered Joseph. Beyond that I was not informed of their plan on how they would conduct their investigation."

"Keep in mind David that I work for you and I am answerable to you. They answer in theory to justice and the law. I also stand for justice, but I have a duty to you as well. Can you tell me about your conversation with the police? Please describe for me every statement they made and every question they asked you."

The waitress arrived to take their order. Jill had been debating fish and chips or Sheppard's pie. Both would be heavy meals, but again thinking of the symptoms of altitude sickness, she thought she might avoid any nausea induced by a deep-fried entrée, so she went for the beef in the pie. David settled on a soup as he seemed to not be very hungry. His eyes were red-rimmed and he had dark shadows below suggesting the lack of sleep. He looked exhausted.

"Two officers appeared on my doorstep about two hours after you called. They delivered the news of Joseph's autopsy findings as murder in about as cold a fashion as I can imagine."

"Maybe they were just not used to delivering such horrible news. This county had a very low murder rate and I would guess an officer could go an entire career and not have to tell someone their loved one was murdered."

"I thought of that after they left, but then I went back to their words and behaviors and decided that was not the problem. They had no nervousness about them or hesitancy. They also had no empathy and wasted a lot of time trying to pin the murder on me. They couldn't argue about the receipt even as they went so far as to verify in front of me with the merchant that I was in the store. If they had cared they would have shown discretion in checking out my alibi."

"What else did they ask you?"

"They showed me a picture of his face taken during the autopsy, just to have me verify that it was Joseph. It was another hugely insensitive moment."

"Did they ask you if you were aware of anyone that threatened Joseph or if you were aware of any financial concerns of his?"

"Once they had irrefutable proof that I couldn't be Joseph's killer they were done. I asked them when Joseph's body would be available for burial and they said they had no idea. They didn't even give me a number to call and check. Joseph has a large family, many of whom will come from out-of-town and I need to give them a date as soon as possible, but the officer couldn't help me with that."

"It sounds like you had an awful time with these officers. At some point I will need contact names for Joseph's company as I will probably want to talk to someone there, but hold on that for now until I see the direction of this investigation. I'll have several team members arriving over the next couple of days that will have different questions for you. One of my team members is a security technology expert and I think depending on what we find in the cameras at the ski resort it could greatly influence where our investigation takes us. My financial wizard may find information that takes us on a different path.

"Tonight I'll do some computer research on Joseph and try to line up an interview with the two officers tomorrow morning. My security expert will be arriving about mid-day. I want to wait to approach the ski resort for access to their tapes until he gets here. I'm hoping that his background will convince them to give us access to the tapes."

"If you have problems, let me know. Joseph and I were friends with one of the board members of the corporation that operates the resort. I won't hesitate to call in a favor to get access to their information."

"Will do. You look exhausted, David. I'm going to walk back to my lodge and you should try and get some sleep. I'll call you in the morning after my interview with the police officers. I'm curious to see what kind of reception I receive from them."

"Thanks Jill and have a nice evening. I'll look forward to your call in the morning."

Jill enjoyed the walk in the quiet town. The air was cold but had this feeling of purity about it. She had her own fanciful imagination and thought, 'I could be passing Joseph's murderer on the street'. The few people she passed were all bundled up, chins tucked into collars. She arrived back at her lodge without problem and dialed Nathan.

"Hey, how's it going?"

"It's going well. How about you? Is there anything new in the case?"

"It's going to be a reunion of sorts from Belgium. Everyone is going to make the trek to Breck including Nick."

"Nick? Isn't it far for him to come? Can your client afford his airfare?"

"No, I wouldn't think of charging my client for Nick's airfare, except when Henrik is your friend. Henrik had to fly to Austin for a tech conference and so he is giving Nick a ride on his private jet to Denver. It's only about ninety minutes out of his way if that, so I lucked out. The client only has to pay his transportation from the airport. Nick will arrive and I am hopeful the ski resort will share camera shots as well as ski pass chairlift data with us. David said he had a friend on the resort's board if we need some insider help to get us the information."

"I may have to drop in on you then and catch up with everyone. I hate when you're having a good time without me."

"We are not here to have a good time, we're here to work on

the case for David Gomez, so it is not like Belgium when we were vacationing first and solving a crime second."

"True, but seriously you know I like to ski and I enjoy your friends' company."

"Yes, I know you do, but they are coming and going on different days. I think the one day they all will be in town on the same day is two days from now."

"Well, I'll think about it. Is there a lot of snow?"

"Hard to tell, it was dark by the time I got here. First thing in the morning, I'm going to meet the cops assigned to this case, and then I will head up the mountain with David to see where they found Joseph. I doubt there will be any evidence but I am still taking an evidence kit with me. I have never taken a victim's family back to the scene of the murder so I am not prepared for what David will need when he views the spot where Joseph was murdered, so I expect it to be a tough few moments up on the ski trail."

"That is really sad. I hope David eventually uses the ski resort to celebrate the good times he and Joseph had and not just the bad."

"I am sure he will find some semblance of peace eventually perhaps when the killer is identified. Speaking of which, I need to get to work researching this case. Love you. Goodnight."

"Love you back. Sweet dreams."

They ended their conversation and Jill went over to her laptop and began working. She started with doing an internet search of Joseph and David. This was really Marie's area of expertise, but she couldn't wait for her arrival to begin the investigation. Jill ran the various search engines on the pair collecting most of the public knowledge about them and their families from articles, images, and social media. She didn't find any hint of discord between the two partners; there were no rants or statements likely to offend anyone. Essentially she found two nice guys with no apparent reason for one of them to be murdered. Could this be random? It just didn't fit with her years on the job as so much planning went into this murder. If the killer had wanted to see if he or she could stop skiing on short notice, get his breath under control, and shoot a moving target, he could have aimed for a branch blowing in the wind or a tree. He didn't need to kill a man. Even after accidentally shooting him, he could have called for help, or done mouth to mouth, until the drug wore off.

Next Jill branched out into Joseph's company. This was an area she wanted Angela to focus on - there would be a need for great interviewing technique with his company's employees. Angela would out of necessity have to spend a great deal of her time in Denver as likely that was where the majority of the employees and board members would be found. Jo would focus on the company's financials and Jill needed Marie's help navigating all of the social media sources of information about the key members of the staff at Joseph's company as well as collecting any information about the two men personally. It was great that each member brought unique skills to an investigation. After a few more hours of research she called it quits and headed for bed.

*a*fter a great breakfast, she drove to the office location of the two officers. She had looked up the police agency for its location and names of any leaders of the department and even the chief's name. She parked her rental car and entered the building stopping in an unmanned reception area. She hit a buzzer as the sign suggested and waited for someone to appear. A short time later, a woman arrived at the desk.

"May I help you, Miss?"

"Yes, I would like to meet with Officers Johnson and Miller."

"Do you have an appointment?"

"No."

"Can I tell them what this is about?"

"Yes, I want to speak with them about the Joseph Morton homicide."

"Are you a family member?"

"No, but I have Mr. Morton's spouse's consent to speak on his behalf."

"Okay, what is your name?"

"Dr. Jill Quint."

"One moment, please," said the woman as she disappeared to

an area beyond the door.

A few minutes later the door opened and a uniformed officer stepped through a second door and walked to where Jill was standing.

"Hello, I'm Officer Miller, what can I do for you?"

"Hello, I am Dr. Jill Quint. I have been retained by Mr. Morton's partner to investigate his death."

"Doctor? Why would a doctor be hired as an investigator into a murder?"

"I am a forensic pathologist by training. I spent over ten years with the State of California Crime Lab processing forensic evidence. Since I left the lab five years ago, I have served about sixty families in a consultant role to provide a second opinion on the cause of death. Mr. Gomez originally called me when he was told that Joseph appeared to have died from a heart attack. I attended Mr. Morton's body at the medical examiner's office in Golden where we both came to the same conclusion that it was murder by d-Tubocurarine which is better known by its street name of curare. Mr. Gomez decided to further retain my services as I have a team to assist in a murder investigation."

"Are you a private detective?"

"No."

"Well this is unusual."

"Yes, it probably is. I'll likely never again have an investigation in your county. May I have a copy of your report of the murder? Here is a copy of the statement that David Gomez has signed authorizing me to speak on his behalf and since he is entitled to any reports you complete, I'd like a copy."

"He is not entitled to a copy of police reports," said a now visibly irked Officer Miller.

"He is entitled to a copy of the report under both Victims Rights and the Colorado Criminal Justice Records Act. I'm curious though, why would you not release a police report to the immediate family of the deceased?"

"How do I know he is immediate family? I just have his word to go on."

"May I view the department's policy that requires spouses prove they are married before information is released?"

"We don't have such a policy."

"Exactly!" Jill replied with exasperation. "Look, are you going to give me a copy of the report or not?"

"I'm not giving you a copy of the report."

"Okay, when you go back inside, would you tell your Chief that I wish to speak with him or her?"

He just waved his hand at her and walked back inside leaving Jill inside the little waiting area. Well, Jill thought, David was wise to call for her help with this case. This cop was a jerk and a sad representative of law enforcement. She hoped the Chief was better. She wasn't sure she had come across this problem before. She waited another ten minutes and the Chief did not appear or anyone else.

She took out her cell phone and searched for law enforcement's number and then dialed. A woman answered the phone and indicated she had reached law enforcement's office.

"I would like to speak to Chief Jensen."

"May I tell him what this is about?"

"Yeah, I would like to discuss the behavior of one of his officers with him. I am in your outer waiting area, so he can come out and discuss it in person with me if he wishes."

"He is in the community at this time. May I set up an appointment for you, or would you like to speak to his second-in-command?"

"I'll take his second-in-command. My name is Jill Quint and I would prefer to meet him or her in your lobby."

"Give me a few minutes and she'll be right out."

"Thank you," and Jill disconnected the call. She was very mad on David's behalf.

A few minutes later, a woman in a uniform stepped out

looking for her in the waiting area.

"I am Chief Jensen's second-in-command, Sergeant Young, how may I help you?"

"I am Dr. Jill Quint, a private forensic pathologist employed by the spouse of Joseph Morton, a man murdered up on peak six. My background consists of working fifteen years in the State Crime Lab in California and since leaving that office I have done another sixty or so cause of death second opinions of the deceased. About twenty percent of my cases result in a death by natural causes being overturned and ruled a homicide.

"In this case, Dr. Jones, the medical examiner who performed Mr. Morton's autopsy and I are in perfect agreement with his cause of death. I thought that was the end of my role in this case. Mr. Gomez, Mr. Morton's spouse hired me to continue the investigation into Mr. Morton's murder because he didn't feel comfortable that the officers assigned to the case would do everything possible to solve the case. I was surprised but made arrangements to continue in the investigation of Mr. Morton's murder. I just asked Officer Miller for a copy of the police report and he turned me down citing that he did not know that Mr. Gomez was Mr. Morton's spouse and then he walked off after refusing to give me a copy of the report or ask his Chief to come out and talk to me. It is interesting that yesterday, Officer Miller arrived at my client's house to talk about the murder even going so far as to verify that my client had an iron clad alibi to prove he was not up on the mountain when Mr. Morton was murdered. Why would he question him if he was not aware of the legal relationship of the two men? I want a copy of the report."

"My condolences to Mr. Gomez, and I am sorry this department gave the appearance that solving Mr. Morton's murder wasn't a top priority. May I see the authorization form that Mr. Gomez signed that you represent him? Once I see that form, if you'll give me a minute, I'll be back out with a copy of our report."

Jill pulled a form out of her briefcase and handed it to the

Sergeant. She glanced through the document and then responded, "One moment and I'll get that report for you."

Jill waited maybe another three minutes and the Sergeant returned with a copy of the report.

"Here is the report you requested, and here is my business card should you have any further questions that we can help you with."

"Thank you and good day," Jill said over her shoulder as she left the building and headed for her car. She thought the experience of the past few minutes might go on her list of top five lousy interactions with law enforcement.

She headed back to her lodge as that was where she and David agreed to meet that morning to go up the ski trail. David and Joseph's cabin was up on Boreas Pass Road so her lodge was closer to the resort. She bought a pass each year that allowed her to ski at several Colorado and California resorts so she wouldn't have to charge David the expense of a lift ticket to go evaluate the scene where they found Joseph.

She texted him after she changed into her ski gear. While waiting for him to appear at her lodge, she read the police report. She had read many in her life and this was one of the briefest she had ever seen. Still it contained the pertinent data, including a state crime lab estimate of the needle size of the dart, but they were not able to determine the dart gun's make and model. This was probably not a surprising finding. Except for the name of the ski patrol member that found Joseph, she really didn't learn anything new. She now understood David's aversion to law enforcement.

Jill received a text from David that he was waiting in the lobby, and she gathered up her gear and went down to meet him.

"Hey David, how are you doing this morning? Are you ready to head up the mountain?"

"I got a little more sleep last night knowing you were here helping me find Joseph's murderer. Let's head over to the gondola and we can talk on the chairlift."

They left the lodge trudging along in clunky ski boots, skis and poles over their shoulders. Jill always found the first day on the mountain to be one of heavy breathing. When you travel from sea level to nine-thousand feet without giving your hemoglobin time to increase its manufacturing, then you will be short of breath; added to that was what felt like five pounds on each foot due to the weight of the ski boots. Just about the time she acclimated to the altitude, she would return to sea level. They entered the gondola, distributing their ski equipment across the car.

"David, in my opinion you were wise to call for assistance in this case. I don't mean to be self-serving, but I had one of the oddest interactions with law enforcement today. I use the word 'odd' because I can't find the right word to describe Officer Miller. I'm not sure he cares that the case gets solved. He refused to give me a copy of the report which is a violation of State law. He said I needed to prove you were the next of kin. I asked to see the department policy that required officers to identify next of kin by producing a marriage certificate. He just walked away from me so I called the office number and told the person that answered the phone that I wanted to speak to the Chief and I was waiting in their reception area."

David let out a little laugh and Jill smiled at him declaring, "Really as if they think they can deny me a report that is mine to have by law!"

"Did the Chief meet with you?"

"No, they told me he was out in the community and asked if I wanted to speak to his second-in-command. A sergeant met me in the lobby. I showed her the authorization you gave me to speak on your behalf and she returned in a few minutes with the report. The report had little new information on it. I found the only useful piece of information to be the name of the ski patrol person that found Joseph."

"So you didn't get along with Officer Miller either?"

"No, I thought you said there was another officer that visited you along with Officer Miller? Was he a problem as well? I could not read the sergeant to guess whether she was surprised or annoyed by Officer Miller."

"Like your difficulty in assessing the sergeant's reaction, I couldn't read the other officer to guess whether he agreed with Miller's behavior toward me or not. Like you said earlier, I'm glad I hired you as I lack confidence as to whether catching Joseph's killer is a priority with this law enforcement agency. When they don't get the little things handled correctly like giving me a copy of the report, then I doubt that the big things are handled well either."

"I agree with you," replied Jill as the gondola reached the top. They gathered their skis and poles heading to the chairlift.

"You know, David, if someone wanted to murder you up here, how would they find you on the mountain? It is a big place. It makes me wonder, how Joseph was located; how would someone find him up on the mountain? I know when I ski with friends, I usually won't see them unless we have a specified meeting area."

"Yes, you're right. Even Joseph and I would know of friends that were up on the mountain and we wouldn't see them unless we arranged a meeting time at a particular restaurant on the mountain."

The first chairlift was approaching the top and they needed to take an additional two chairs to reach the run where Joseph had been murdered. Jill reached down and tightened her boots. She usually liked to warm-up on intermediate slopes before heading over to peak six but she would forego those runs to keep pace with David. Where they were headed was an easy advanced slope, so she shouldn't have a problem.

"David, I'm not used to this altitude so I'm going to need more oxygen breaks on the way down," Jill cautioned. "I don't mind if you go straight to the wooded area that you think was where they located Joseph. We may need additional runs to find the right spot. Our only sign may be a lot of boot imprints in the snow. I can't imagine that Officer Miller has been up here nor will we see any yellow crime scene tape."

"Yeah I was thinking of that when I couldn't sleep last night. Joseph liked to tree ski when he could find the right trail. The trail needs to be not too steep, and not a single loop around just one or two trees. That not too steep part should eliminate most of the tree runs that we will see."

"Okay that is helpful information. Let's go back and think about how the killer found Joseph. He might have followed him from your cabin in the morning. However, I think that is unlikely as he would have had to tail him for the next six hours. Maybe the killer had a lot of patience or he just spent the time looking for the perfect place to kill him without anyone seeing it, so he would need to find an empty ski run."

"Our cabin is on an isolated road. We would have seen someone parked at the end of our driveway. I suppose the killer could have waited at the scenic overlook vista point for Joseph's car to go by and then tailed it. We get an annual parking pass for the base of the gondola, so he could have followed the car to that lot."

"Maybe the killer got close to Joseph sometime over the past several days and dropped a tracker in one of his ski jacket pockets? Did Joseph have a distinctive jacket, or were there a hundred like it on the slope?"

"He always wore a black jacket. It had a sheen on it that could look burgundy in bright sun, but generally you saw a black jacket. I guess you saw that jacket at the medical examiner's office. I need to stop by there and pick up Joseph's belongings. He wanted our skiers and boarders to be able to see him, and he also thought if he ever got caught in an avalanche, that a dark color would be easier to spot. There are lots of black jackets on the ski hill, so while the color caught your eye because the black was a sharp contrast against the white snow, it didn't stand out from the other black jackets. His helmet was white and his ski pants black, so again nothing distinctive. You would have to concentrate hard to pick him out of say thirty other skiers on a slope."

"So some other ways to track him would be by his cell phone if the person knew how to triangulate it, by social media if he was updating his day on Facebook or Twitter or on the ski pass website, or by the lift pass. The lift pass would be an approximation as it only has the last chairlift a skier used, but it doesn't tell you whether they went left or right at the top, and you would need reaction time to get up there."

"I have been so involved planning for Joseph's funeral and dealing with a hundred other details that I haven't thought through some of these questions you're asking. They are all really good questions that will give me something to think about to take my mind off the fact that Joseph is gone forever."

"David your mind is filled with many more important details. I would advise you to think of your happiest moments with Joseph rather than pondering who followed Joseph over the past few days or weeks. I'll be bouncing ideas off you not because I expect you to solve this crime, but rather to gain insight into Joseph's behaviors, habits, and routines. This helps me to understand where there were opportunities to harm him and where I might look for a killer stalking him which might help me identify him or her."

"Her?"

"It is early yet in this investigation and considering a dart gun with poison was used, the killer could be either gender as size and physical strength wasn't required. Poison homicides are more often connected to female killers."

They exited the second chairlift and there was only one short ski run to reach the third and final chairlift that Joseph took before he was murdered.

"David, I don't have the trail map for this mountain memorized. Is this ski run the only way to reach peak six from other parts of the mountain?"

"Yes, unless you are willing to hike uphill."

"I always avoid hiking. If I remember correctly, you can see the next lift from the top of this chair? Let's pause and look around a bit before we get in line at the next lift."

"Ok, meet you close to the entrance line."

They soon exited the lift and dropped down the ski trail about seventy or so feet to the next ski chair. Leaning on their poles, Jill tried to catch her breath and soak in the atmosphere.

"Tell me about this chairlift in terms of you and Joseph. Did you ride it frequently? What did you like about the lift? Did you have a favorite ski run?"

"Good questions. Joseph and I were divided on any given day as to whether we liked this chair or the T-bar better. We liked the runs off the T-bar, but the lift was a drag - you can't relax on it. You have to actively maintain your skis in the track and your posture leaning back. However, there were more trails off of the T-bar. Joseph and I never hiked from the top of this lift to the bowls above the lift. We didn't need that kind of thrill.

"We loved skiing and since we had the cabin and it was a short drive into the mountains, we averaged 15-20 days of skiing each season. We were great skiers, but knew our limits. We avoided chutes between rocks and trails where we would likely lose control and slam into a tree. We raced on Nastar, loved watching the races of Olympic trials or World Cup, or the X-Games if this town was hosting those events. We never tried snowboarding preferring skis. We never strayed from this mountain region, since there are so many resorts within a small radius of the cabin.

"At the top of this chair we generally went left toward the bowl. Depending on your mood you could attack the mountain and its level of steepness. Sometimes we had lunch at this chalet," said David pointing at a large ski hut. "They don't serve food in there so it would be those days that we packed our own lunches that we stopped here."

"Ok, this ski pass reader was the last location that the ski patrol had for Joseph," commented Jill looking at the chairlift. "I wonder if there are any cameras for these chairlifts, both at the top and the bottom. Do you see anything that looks like a camera?"

They both stood leaning on their ski poles, looking for a camera somewhere on the lift.

"I don't see one, Jill. Let's ask the lift attendant as we sit on the chair. Are you ready to go up the mountain?"

Jill observed David and thought he looked both anxious to get there and hesitant to push forward. She needed to forget about the case for the next few moments and just support David.

"Yes, let's head up the mountain," Jill replied as they pushed forward with their poles to the lift. A few seconds later they were seated on the chair, zooming up the hill. Most of the chairs were empty as it was midweek, a hard to reach chairlift, and early in the season. Jill counted in her head and decided that one in fifteen chairs had a skier or boarder on it. The lift employee looked at them blankly when they asked if there was a camera on the chair.

"David, I haven't had time to interview the ski patrol employee that found Joseph. Do you have a sense of where they found him?"

"Yes, Joseph and I would occasionally go tree skiing off this lift. There was a path through a section of trees well off the peak, that under the right conditions, was a lot of fun. I have to think that was the trail through the trees that Joseph took. We'll take several breaks on the way down to give you time to adjust to the altitude. When I reach the trail that I think Joseph took, I'll stop and wait for you."

"Depending on the condition of the snow, I would just as soon pop off my skis and walk into the forest. It may have been skied on by now, but then given the few riders on the chairlift, it is possible that no one has been on that path since Joseph was found there. I will have to decide what to do once I reach the trail."

They were approaching the top of the lift and as usual the chair was rocking from side to side in the wind. The view was magnificent. As far as one could see, the Rockies were covered in snow with beautiful blue skies framing each peak. There were wisps of snow blowing off the peaks that looked like cotton candy being fashioned into puffy clouds. Then another strong gust of cold wind shook the chair and Jill was glad to be getting off. They exited to the right and as agreed upon began skiing down, taking that last route that they suspected Joseph had followed two days previously. David graciously stopped several times on the way to their destination. Jill was glad to descend below the wind and took the opportunity to breathe heavily trying to catch her breath in the thin air. David came to a stop at the top of a forested area and waited for Jill.

She braked beside him and said, "Is this the forest they found Joseph in?"

"This was his favorite tree skiing trail, so I would guess so."

Looking around the trees Jill asked, "Where is the entrance to the trail?"

"About half way down on the left."

"Let's continue to the start of the trail, but stay outside the forest."

"Okay."

Another fifty yards downhill, David was waiting for Jill to catch up. Once she came to a stop and looked around, she could see the trail into the woods.

"The snow doesn't look trampled upon from this entrance. I see a few ski tracks. Has there been any fresh snow in the past two days?"

"No there hasn't and it appears to me that the snow cats haven't groomed the snow in this area."

"On the odd chance that there is some evidence to be collected, would you stay behind me on this trail? I'm going to go very slow and stop many times, so try to stay a little back from me. First I'm going to try releasing my boots from the bindings and seeing if I can walk inside this forest."

Jill bent down and popped one of her bindings, stepping out onto the snow in her ski boot. Inside the forest, the snow coverage should be lighter, but then the snow cats would not have been around to hard pack the snow. If she sunk too deeply into the snow in her boots, she would not be able to walk very well. It could even be very difficult to get her skis back on. Her first tentative step dropped her about half a foot. That meant that walking in the forest on the snow would be doable. She took the other ski off and then slowly navigated her way downhill. With one hand dragging her skis, the other hand contained her poles and helped her balance. She stayed next to the ski trail as she went.

Behind her David called out, "I think I will remove my skis too. As clumsy as it is to walk and sink with each step, you have better control without the skis."

"Let's hope that the snow conditions stay the same, because if there is fluffy powder in our path we are sunk in more ways than one. About how long would you guess this trail goes before it exits the forest?"

"Maybe fifty yards - half of a football field."

"Are you a football fan?" asked Jill as they continued walking slowly downhill with trees and ski poles assisting their balance as each step sunk into the snow.

"Yeah, we have been season-ticket holders for the Broncos for the past fifteen years. Now I can't imagine going to a game without Joseph. One of a thousand things I will have to get used to."

Jill had no answer to give to David's statement other than giving him a sympathetic grimace. They plowed forward a few steps with Jill peeking through the trees looking each way as they moved. They soon came upon an area where the snow had been trampled by many boots. The sun was bright as it was approaching high noon and something got Jill's attention as it reacted to the bright sunlight.

"David, is that a cell phone?" asked Jill while she pointed to the glistening object.

"It looks like Joseph's cell phone. I'll go get it."

Jill reached out her arm to block David saying, "Wait, I don't want this crime scene trampled on. It has sat on the snow for two days; it can sit for another thirty minutes. Did they find Joseph in the dark?"

"No it wasn't dark, but it was dusk and with the canopy of trees here, it may as well have been dark."

"That must explain why the phone wasn't secured by the ski patrol - they didn't see it. Let's see if there is anything else that they missed."

Jill walked around the perimeter of the area while she visualized Joseph dropping to the ground as his muscles lost control in less than a minute after being hit by the dart. His quadriceps muscles in his legs would have been some of the first muscles to feel the impact of the curare. She looked up the trail at the direction he would have come from. She jumped over the ski trail which was no easy feat in her heavy inflexible ski boots and walked around the opposite side of the trail. She would have to research how far a dart gun fired and what kind of aiming accuracy the shooter needed. She took an excess of photos.

Looking over at David, Jill said "I would like to walk up the trail and examine the various angles a shooter has on someone in this area. Likely Joseph was hit by the poison dart a little above where he came to rest in the snow. David I am sorry to put you through this, but I feel that this might be the only time we might get to visit this scene before someone skis it. While it was trampled by the rescuers, it still yielded his cell phone. Sadly, I can't distinguish the boot prints and the ski trails to identify which belonged to the killer or the rescuers."

"Jill, what do you need me to do?" asked David. The tone of his voice spoke to how desperately he wanted to help Jill find clues inside this forest.

"Would you mind standing here, I would like to get a sighting of where Joseph would have been standing when he was hit by the dart. Were you about the same height?"

"He was an inch shorter than I. Where would you like me to stand?"

Jill looked at the clearing and guessed where Joseph had dropped. It helped having the cell phone as she knew the body had to be close by. She then moved David uphill to where she guessed Joseph had been hit by the dart. He would have traveled downhill a little distance before the dart felled him. She took measurements of the approximate distances, as that would eliminate weapons, suspects, and even locations based on the circumstances. Curves in the ski trail or trees blocking a view gave her a strong estimate of where the shooter had to stand. He also would have to be in good shape, able to control his breathing. Jill had watched the Olympic Biathlon and knew how hard it was for those athletes to control their breathing and maintain accuracy in shooting. She now imagined the shooter would have had to follow Joseph closely, stop, quickly aim, and fire the dart gun. He or she could have fired several darts depending on one of them hitting the target. The killer would have then stood in the forest waiting for the paralytic drug to take effect. It now seemed like Joseph had pulled out his cell phone to call for help, but had become incapacitated before he could dial any number.

Jill finished with the scene and looked over at David and asked, "Would you like a moment alone here? Some more time here at the scene?"

"Thanks for asking, but no I am done here. I thought this would become sort of a shrine for me. You know - Joseph's last moments alive were here. Now that I have visited this site, it has none of the emotions I thought I would associate with the site. I don't 'feel' Joseph here at all. He is not in my mind in this location. I would follow him here on occasion to this trail but it is not one of my top memories of our years together."

"Okay, let's put our skis on and continue down this trail and stop where the trail exits the trees. I want to ski to the bottom and come hit this spot a few more times. Did you want to break at the chalet to review Joseph's phone?"

"I can't, it is dead. It will have to wait until I get home to recharge it as long as there is no moisture inside the phone. I may have to take it to a retailer if water got inside the phone or if anything cracked with the cold temperatures. I'll join you on a few more runs."

"Okay sounds like a plan. Remember that I am struggling with the altitude. So I'll be taking frequent breaks, but I will catch up to you at the forest if you want to take a speedy run down the hill."

"I might do that. The mountain has a very soothing effect on me," David said and indeed it seemed as if some of the weight of the world had been lifted from his shoulders.

They continued to ski to the base of the lift and rode up again. David skied ahead of her to the forest and they again stopped where Jill thought the shooter might have stopped. She concluded that the killer had to be an excellent skier to be able to stop on a dime in amongst the trees. She repeated the experience one more time having asked David to ski at his normal speed. She then stopped on the spot in the forest where she thought the killer had taken aim and held up her cell phone looking through the camera lens. Her breathing was heavy, her heart racing, and even when she held her breath she couldn't steady the phone. This exercise told her that the killer was either in great physical shape and acclimated to the altitude or he or she had been very lucky.

She and David would break for lunch and then she planned to head over to the ski patrol offices to hear from them what they had found up on the mountain. She was going to then walk over to the administration offices to see if she could get a contact person for the cameras and ski pass system.

CHAPTER 6

They sat down to lunch on the mountain. Jill was going over in her head the details of the crime scene and then she couldn't help herself, the statement just burst out of her, "I can't believe the police have not been up on the mountain inspecting the crime scene. We know they haven't been up there because Joseph's cell phone was up there. It really goes against every forensic principle that I have ever operated under. You never let a murder go by and for two days fail to visit the crime scene. No detectives, no crime scene investigators! It's gross negligence."

"Yeah, I am pretty surprised too and thankful I hired you. Even if the officers didn't ski, surely someone in the department does or at least a crime scene investigator should have gone to where they found Joseph."

"I guess I won't look for any help from them, and for the first time in my career, I will ignore law enforcement.

"My associate Nick Brouwer arrives this afternoon. Let me tell you a little about him as he was not in the biographies that I included in the original personnel information in my contract. My team and I met Nick while we were on vacation in Belgium and the Netherlands. He is from Amsterdam and helped us solve a crime there. He runs a hotel security company that provides security people and processes to hotels in Amsterdam and Brussels. I think he will be helpful in reviewing the security system of the resort as well as the ski pass system. You don't need to worry that you're paying for his last minute travel from Europe. He is arriving for free thanks to the client we helped while in Belgium. He was on his way to Austin and so he is detouring to Denver to drop him off."

"I'm not worried about the cost. It's good to know you have an expert coming to assist. Does he ski?"

"Yes he skis, and since he spent some time employed by the Dutch police, he'll have crime scene eyes to view the forest. I assume he is an advanced skier and can handle the slope. Since Amsterdam is below sea level, he'll probably have some altitude sickness in addition to jet lag, poor guy. I was hoping to have him meet the ski patrol folks and security staff this afternoon. I'll take him up the mountain in the morning after he has had a little time to acclimate."

"I should head home to Denver and take care of issues related to settling Joseph's estate and the funeral plans, but I am feeling more purposeful assisting you with this investigation. I'll plan to return tomorrow to meet your team in the afternoon."

"David, please take all the time you need to make arrangements. Anything I need from you can be handled by phone. Mostly I am picking your brain about Joseph - you knew him best. If there is a convenient time, we can make arrangements now to chat by phone every day, or we can set up a time on a day by day basis based on what is going on."

"Many of the arrangements I need to work on are with nine to five businesses. Would an eight in the morning call work for you with your schedule?"

"Yes, we'll talk tomorrow and after you recharge Joseph's phone, I would love to have Nick take a look at it. If there is personal or private information on the phone, you should know that it is secure with me and my team. Let me know after you have taken a look at the phone. Also if you would forward all emails to your account, as we may want to look at them later."

"Will do and we'll talk tomorrow."

They cleared their table of lunch debris and parted ways, David to return to his cabin to pack and return to Denver and Jill to talk to the Ski Patrol. She paused a moment to check on the progress of Nick's travels. He should have arrived in Denver by now. Scrolling through her email she saw a message from Nick. She opened it and read, 'made it through customs, and the shuttle just left the airport. I should be there between two and three this afternoon.' That was an hour at the earliest from now. She would go over to the Ski Patrol, and then return to her lodge to meet Nick.

She did an internet search of where the Ski Patrol was head-quartered on the mountain. She figured it was near first aid and headed that way since she hadn't found anything on her internet search. She saw an ambulance parked near the first aid sign. She hoped that was its parking space rather than they were loading an injured skier to take off the hill. There was a little reception area that she approached.

"Hi, how may I help you?" inquired the young woman staffing the reception desk.

"I would like to speak to the supervisor of the Ski Patrol," responded Jill hoping to provide as little information as possible.

"Sure, can I tell her what this is about?"

"Yes, it is about someone that the Ski Patrol cared for about two to three days ago."

The woman looked puzzled and concerned likely thinking this was a complaint. She might be even more concerned if Jill told her it was a murder investigation. She returned a few minutes later and announced, "she is up on the mountain; if you'll have a seat she'll be here in about fifteen minutes."

"Thank you," replied Jill as she took a seat. She pulled out her phone and was soon engrossed in checking her emails. She looked up as a ruddy faced woman walked in with snow still clinging to her boots.

She approached Jill and said "Hi, I'm Kate Crenshaw, how may I help you?"

Jill stood up and introduced herself, "Hi, I'm Jill Quint. Is there somewhere we can talk privately?"

"I have a small office and I may be subject to interruptions, but otherwise, it is a quiet place to talk. Follow me," and Jill followed her down the hallway, both of them walking heavy in their ski boots.

They were soon seated in a small office and Jill passed her business card to Kate.

Kate read the card and looked quizzically at Jill, "You're a physician?"

"Yes, I am a Forensic Pathologist. I have been retained by Mr. David Gomez to investigate the death of his partner Joseph Morton. The Ski Patrol found Mr. Morton on a trail off of peak six."

"Yes, I remember that now. We don't have that many deaths on the mountain so I remember and I was personally on the scene for most of the time either here or up on the mountain. What are you investigating?"

"Were you aware his death was ruled a homicide?"

"What! We have never had a murder in the history of this mountain. I was on the scene on peak six, it didn't look like I envision a murder looking; there was no blood anywhere around where we found Mr. Morton. Look I am a little over my head here, let me notify mountain management and see if they want to join this meeting. Are you a part of the police?"

The woman picked up the phone before Jill could answer any of her questions. She had obviously reached someone in management who asked Kate several questions most of which she couldn't answer, Jill gleaned from the one-sided conversation.

Shortly she ended the call, and remarked to Jill, "Tom asked that we head to his office. It is in a building close to the base of peak nine. We'll need to take the lift over there and ski down. Can you ski an intermediate run?"

"I was just over at the top of peak six examining where Joseph was found. Does that tell you something about my ski ability?" asked an indignant Jill.

"Not really. I see people over their heads all day long up on the slopes. Did you ski down the mountain or tumble down the mountain?"

"I skied down it in a few minutes with breaks so I could suck in oxygen. I just arrived from sea level. Not a single fall on that run or indeed at all today," replied an affronted Jill.

"Just checking. I don't want to take you anywhere on the mountain that you're not comfortable skiing on. You could take the long way to the office by riding the town shuttle."

"No thanks, I think I'll mostly be able to keep up with you. As I mentioned, my biggest problem is this altitude. Before we leave if you have a file on your rescue of Mr. Morton, I would love to look through it. I have his spouse's permission to view those records on his behalf. If you take the record with you, we may be able to go over it together once we reach your supervisor's office. I just hate to waste time and doubling back here seems like a waste of time."

Kate paused a moment to think about Jill's request, then went and retrieved the file and placed it in her pack. They exited the building walking to the lift. Two lifts later they were heading for the base of peak nine. Jill left her skis on the rack outside the building. Her skis were ten years old so they weren't likely the target of any thieves. Clumping up the stairs they reached a suite of offices and it was clear that Kate was expected. They were gestured towards an office. Jill was still panting from the walk.

A gentleman stood up and introduced himself with a title that Jill soon forgot. He seemed mostly curious about Jill and why she wanted to speak with the ski patrol.

"I am a forensic pathologist that families hire to review the cause of death of a loved one. I have been doing private death investigations for five years and prior to that I spent nearly fifteen years in the State of California Crime Lab. As you now know, you had a skier die on the mountain two days ago. I was hired by that skier's spouse to provide an opinion on the cause of death.

"He had been told that a heart attack killed his partner and he couldn't believe that conclusion. When I arrived at the Golden medical examiner's office, the autopsy had been completed but the tests had not returned. The next day both the medical examiner and I, through separate investigations, came to the conclusion that the skier was killed by a poisoned veterinary dart. The spouse asked me to continue with an investigation into this murder as that is a separate service I provide. As a part of my investigation I would like to review the paperwork and speak to the ski patrol staff that located the skier on a trail off of peak six."

"Why haven't the police been by to speak with the resort? I find this most odd to be approached by a private citizen."

"Good question, but I can't speak for them," commented Jill. "I do have a document that allows me to speak on David's behalf and make inquiries about Mr. Morton's death. As this is a case of homicide, the Breck resort would likely be held harmless unless the killer is a resort employee. You can check with your legal counsel on that. I want two things from the resort. One I would like to speak with the ski patrol staff that found Mr. Morton. I have already been to the scene of his death; I just have a few questions about how they found him, what the position of his body was, etc. The second thing I would like is access to your ski pass records. I would like to see who rode up the lifts that Joseph had taken the day of his death.

"I have an expert in radio frequency ID tags arriving in town within the hour and I would like a contact person that he can do some research with to determine the behavior of Mr. Morton and anyone around him on the chairlifts."

"I am going to need to run this by our general counsel located in a Denver suburb. Give me a minute to see if he is available." With that comment he looked up a number and was soon dialing. At first it seemed that he was speaking to someone other than who he called. Then there was a pause and a reintroduction of the problem. Obviously questions were being asked and answered. Then the call was placed on speakerphone and Jill was invited into the call.

"Hello," said a male voice with what sounded like a Texas accent, "I am Michael Stout, General Counsel for the resort. If you would send a copy of your authorization form from the next-of-kin, I'd like to review that language. After I do that I see no reason not to allow you access to the ski patrol report and staff. I am genuinely puzzled by the lack of law enforcement interaction so far, but I understand that you cannot comment on that. Tom will be checking with our local police to verify that it was a homicide.

"Regarding access to the ski pass information, that is a much more difficult request. We have personal information, credit card information, photos, etc., contained within the system. We cannot give you full access rights to the system. We would be willing to review with you and describe the capabilities of the system and run reports for you. We will redact personal information."

"Thank you. I appreciate your help in finding Mr. Morton's killer. Depending on what we find in the ski pass reports, we may want to look at your camera footage on the hill. Some of your cameras are posted on your website and are thus already in the public view, but I suspect that many are not. I would like to request that any footage collected over the past week be saved and give you some time to think of how you would allow me and my team access to that footage."

Jill heard a sigh as Michael queried, "Your team? I thought we were just talking about you."

"The authorization provided by David Gomez gives the same rights to my team which will be arriving over the next few days. In total, I have four additional people arriving to assist in this investigation. Most of it will have nothing to do with the resort and will be focused on the personal background of Mr. Morton. I do however have a security expert arriving within the hour that will understand your camera and pass system."

"Dr. Quint, this is getting more complicated. It would be easier to comply with your request if you were the police."

"Mr. Stout, understand that the resort's role in Mr. Morton's murder is happenstance. He was a planned target. The resort's bad luck is this is where the murder occurred, but if it had not happened here, it would have occurred elsewhere. Your small piece in this puzzle is helping me see if there were any clues left at the crime scene that your ski patrol staff might have noticed and helping me sort through your pass and camera data to determine if the killer stalked Mr. Morton over the past week. After I look at those two factors, my investigation will be done with the resort. I'll also provide you with my resume and references from the San Francisco FBI office. I also have a copy of the police report of the homicide investigation. All of that should establish the legitimacy of my requests."

"You have a copy of the police report?" and there was a long silence while the attorney mused about that. "That will help, and as soon as I see those documents we can move forward. Do you have them with you at the moment? Tom could fax them right away."

"I do have them with me," responded Jill as she opened her backpack and brought out a portfolio containing her credentials. She almost always carried them with her while she was on a case. The investigation went much faster. Tom had left the room faxing them to Mr. Stout.

"One more question, have you said anything in town about the murder? I may have our PR people release something as soon as I have the death verified as a homicide."

"I have not said anything to anyone other than Kate here. Certainly my client's friends and family know of the murder."

"Ok. I am looking over your documents now. Thanks for faxing them so quickly. Everything looks in order. With this copy of the police report, I think we can move forward with your requests, Dr. Quint. Kate, go ahead and provide Dr. Quint with full access to the ski patrol. Tom, I would like to be kept posted on this investigation, keep me updated. Any other questions or requests?" and after a brief pause he continued, "Then, I'll thank you for perhaps the strangest call I have had this year."

Kate pulled the file out of her backpack and placed it on the desk in front of Jill.

"As I mentioned, I was a part of the search and rescue operation. Let me give you an overview of that operation and what we found on the mountain and what is contained in this form. Tom, we could go to the conference room or continue the discussion in your office. What is your preference?"

"I mean no disrespect to Mr. Morton, but my favorite kind of book is murder mystery so please let's continue the conversation in my office. I'll also facilitate your meeting with our IT department to discuss your technology request. I'll do what I can to help you solve this murder."

"Thank you. I appreciate your help and cooperation." Looking at Kate, Jill inquired, "tell me about the search and rescue operation. Tell me how you were notified and walk me through from beginning to end what happened."

Using the paper report to refresh her mind, Kate began describing the search for Mr. Morton.

"We received a call from his partner and your client, Mr. Gomez, close to five in the afternoon. Most of the employees had left as the lifts were closed. We sent a text out to our employees checking for interest in participating in the search and began the search about ten minutes later. We had employees returning to the mountain over the next twenty minutes to assist in the search. Then I put a call into our IT staff at our corporate headquarters to see if they could tell us what the last chair was that Mr. Morton rode."

"Had you led a similar rescue like this before?" asked Jill wondering how often people failed to come off the mountain at the end of the day.

"Yes it happens once or twice a month during ski season. This is the first time there has been a dead body at the end of the search. Usually, it is an inconsiderate kid that forgets to tell his friends that he is meeting someone at a bar or private residence. We'll start to marshal resources for the search, be looking into the lift records, and we'll get a call that calls off the search. Friends will use social media to find their friend. We occasionally have to do a search after an avalanche, but that is extremely rare, it only happens about once every five to ten years."

"Okay, so you were quickly putting together a search team."

"Yes, fortunately we had only one Joseph Morton in our database. We knew his last run was the peak six chairlift, so we started our search there."

"Do you routinely notify law enforcement when you start one of these mountain searches?" asked Jill.

"Yes, they usually assign an officer to join us. Sometimes the officer goes up on the mountain, other times they wait in the area where my office is to monitor the situation."

"Did an officer join you on this search?"

"No, we were pretty quick getting up the mountain. Once we discovered Mr. Morton and recognized that he was dead from an apparent heart attack, we notified the police. To my recall, they were never involved on-site, which was probably appropriate as we knew on the ski trail that it was an apparent heart attack. They made arrangements for the medical examiner to get the body and that is all I really know about law enforcement's role."

"So when did you decide which ski slope to point the search to?"

"Almost immediately. We have had the ability for at least five years to check ski passes in this manner - checking the location of the last pass scan. So even as I spoke to Mr. Morton's friend, I was typing in his name and coming up with the last chairlift that he rode."

"So what did you do next?"

"I dispatched staff to re-open the lifts necessary to reach that area. We can take snowmobiles and reach the area faster but on really steep slopes and for a larger number of searchers, the fastest way up is to turn the lifts on high speed. Also, it may take more than one run down a slope before a person is found. I also sent a snowcat with several ski patrollers aboard up to the top of the mountain, but they didn't find him on the first pass down the hill. We needed additional searchers and multiple trips. Once we found the body, the snowcat took him down to the base."

"Let's back up and talk about when you found the body. How many trips down the mountain had you all made before you discovered Mr. Morton?"

"It was our third trip. The first two trips were spent looking at the tree wells on and off the main trail. On the third pass, we widened our search to several groups of trees and started skiing through them. One of my staff and I took the tree group where we located Joseph. We could tell before we knelt in the snow that he was dead. I connected with all of the other searchers stating that we had found him. Some folks left the mountain; others came over out of curiosity or a desire to help."

"Did you recognize everyone in the area?"

"If you're asking if someone could have joined the search who wasn't supposed to be there, I doubt it, there should have been someone at the base guarding the lifts making sure everyone had employee identification. I don't know all of the employees on the mountain and so there were faces I didn't recognize, which I would have expected. This is the way that searches go; you need manpower on the ski slope conducting the search."

"What was the lighting like when you found Mr. Morton? Was it dusk? Did you need flashlights?"

"Dusk was fast approaching. We were not using flashlights at the time of the search, until we started looking into the tree clusters. The trees don't let much light in so between the sun going down and being inside a mini-forest, the lighting was dim. Fortunately with white snow as your backdrop it is easier to see things. Since he had dark clothing on it was even easier to spot him. Here is a piece of advice - never wear white on a ski slope; it is much harder for us to see you against the snow. Wear a fluorescent orange, yellow, green or pink."

"I'll keep that in mind the next time I update my ski clothing. So you spotted a dark spot on the snow and as you got closer, you saw it was Mr. Morton?"

"Yes, we were moving slowly shining the flashlight back and forth, when we got sight of a large black lump with a white top. His jacket was black and his helmet was white, his goggles were still on his face. We ran forward but could quickly see that he was dead. His lips were blue, his face a pale white. We checked for a pulse and found none, then reached under his clothing to find no body warmth whatsoever. He was wearing his ski pass so we knew it was Joseph Morton."

"What happened next?"

"I discussed the options for moving his body off the mountain. We could have skied down, but it was getting dark and for the safety of all involved we decided to put him in the snowcat and head to the base. I wanted to give my ski patrol staff who had participated in the search the opportunity to make sure the mountain was empty and that all of the searchers safely reached the base. I wasn't really sure what to do about notifying Mr.

Gomez. So I waited until we got the body down to our first-aid station, and with Tom's advice, we asked for the resort's on-call physician to pronounce Mr. Morton dead. He then made the call to Mr. Gomez."

"Can you describe the position of the body when you found it?"

"He was lying on his back and a little on the left side, head uphill, skis still attached, eyes were open behind the goggles, and one arm was sort of stretched out. We wondered if he had been reaching for something,"

Jill was trying to think of all the questions she should ask about the body's position, and after a pause she asked, "Do you think Mr. Morton fell that way to the ground, or did it look like he had been placed in that position?"

"I am no expert on how a body should fall to the ground, but it looked natural and comfortable. He wasn't grasping a leg or anything like that."

"Is there anything else that I haven't asked or that you have thought of while we were discussing the rescue operation?"

"Mostly I hate the fact that someone was murdered on my mountain. It had seemed to be the one violence free zone left in the world and now that pristine mountain is gone for me."

"If you think of anything else, here is my card. I'll be staying in town for another four to five days at a minimum. Thank you for your time," said Jill as she stood up to leave the building. Looking over at Tom she asked, "When my security expert is available to study your data, should I contact you? He could be ready as soon as within the next few hours."

"Yes that would be best. The people at headquarters will assist with pulling data, but I warn you, they only work day shift, so unless the company clears this as an emergency and the employees are willing to stay and work on the data, you have about two hours of time before that function closes down for the day. I will put in a request to use overtime, but it is not under my control. I would guess that the company would want to cooperate and would authorize the overtime."

"Thanks Tom I appreciate your help," replied Jill with a wave as she left the office heading for her ski equipment. She was soon putting on her skis and taking the chairlift to go up the mountain from one peak to the next so she could reach the gondola to get back to that base. Traversing a mountain was more than reading a trail map. Occasionally a skier could get caught by an uphill trail that didn't appear to be uphill on the map. Jill was lazy when she was on the mountain so she always avoided uphill efforts.

CHAPTER 7

When she arrived at the base on the gondola, she checked in with Nick to see if he had arrived in town. She texted him 'have you arrived?' A minute later, she got a text back, 'yes just checked into my room.' She texted back, 'awesome! heading back to the hotel now see you in fifteen.'

A few minutes later she walked into her hotel. She wanted to get out of her ski gear and enjoy the lightweight feeling of her regular shoes. A few minutes later she finished changing and asked Nick to meet her in the lobby bar. She wanted to drink lots of water while she filled him in and encourage him to do likewise. She was soon giving him a hug and they were seated in the bar area.

"Nick, how do you feel? Have you ever been at this altitude before? Did you get any sleep on the way here?"

"Hey Jill, you still have that staccato fire questions at people trait, I see. I got some serious sleep on the plane so I am well rested. I have been at this altitude before but only at the top of the mountain, I haven't tried to live in it. In Austria some of the peaks are the altitude of this town, it will be a new experience for me to go higher to ski. Regardless, I have been at sea level for several months so there is no avoiding the effects of the altitude. I am up to chasing after any bad people, but I think I'll run out of steam after about one hundred meters."

"You and me both. Let me catch you up on the case and then I would like to take you over to the Ski Resort Management offices so we can begin working on the security tapes. They close in about an hour and a half so we need to leave soon to drive there. Tomorrow I would like to take you up to the location that they found Mr. Morton just to see if your police brain sees something that I missed."

"Sounds like a plan. I took some time while on the plane to sketch out a few reports that I would like to retrieve from the ticket pass system. Since we have limited time to speak with those folks, why don't you tell me about the case while we travel to the resort's offices?"

Jill notified Tom that they were on their way to his office. Like Jill, Nick was dumbfounded that Jill and David found the phone at the crime scene two days later. He had watched many American cop shows on television and had expected that they would be far more aggressive in investigating Joseph's murder. This newest case of Jill's was getting more interesting by the moment and tomorrow he had Jo and Marie's arrival to look forward to. Angela would be arriving the day after. Since meeting in Belgium, Nick and Angela had stayed in touch through videoconferencing, emailing, and texting. They were taking their friendship very slowly as neither had figured out a future given the distance between their two homes. He was very fortunate that he had been able to hop aboard Henrik's plane to the United States. It was a nice break to his usual routine; he was grateful that he had good supervisors in place that allowed him to leave on short notice.

They arrived back at Tom's office and introductions were made. The resort had agreed to put an employee at Nick's disposal to pull data. Nick had a short list of data needs and depending on how quick the employee was to write the reports that Nick needed, they might be done by close of business this afternoon. Nick learned he would need to deal with a different person for the cameras sprinkled around the resort. Henrik had connected Nick to an engineer of his company that would do any facial recognition software searches that Jill's team needed with him so he could do some data manipulation with the camera feeds.

An hour later Nick walked away with a report about the skiers that had ridden the chairlift with Joseph over the past week. Naturally at the top of the list was David as they had spent several days skiing together. He also had the pass ID of the last person to ride the chairlift with Joseph. As the person did not purchase a multi-day pass, there was no name associated with that skier. Whoever had killed him had to ride the lift up with Joseph or be no more than a chair or two behind. Otherwise by the time the chair got them to the top of the mountain, he had too many choices of where to go next on the mountain. The killer had to have been one of the ski passes around Joseph's last ride; the logistics and terrain of the mountain required this close proximity.

Nick noted that Kate Crenshaw said the ski resort had an interesting mechanical failure shortly after Joseph had reached the top. The chairlift had stopped four empty chairs later and stayed inoperable for a little more than fifteen minutes. The resort maintenance had just about decided to begin manually unloading the lift, when it started up again.

"That lift failure was odd. I have never been on a lift that stopped for more than about five minutes, and that lift was stopped for sixteen minutes. It is likely that the stoppage occurred during the time that Joseph was murdered. I think we should ask the resort to look at whether something was introduced into the chairlift system's computer to cause that failure," Jill suggested. "I don't like the coincidence of the timing of this failure."

"They may not have the technical expertise to do that kind of evaluation," replied Nick. "Henrik might have an engineer that could evaluate the failure. I'll ask him if he has that kind of engineering talent in case the resort needs some help and is willing to go outside for it. I agree with you that it is an odd failure. Like you I have never experienced a delay of more than about five minutes on a lift."

"Did you see that pass used on any different runs at the resort or on different days? Was it a single day pass or a multi-day pass? Do they know when the pass was purchased and is there a camera on the ticket booth?"

"Fortunately they gave me the data in an Excel spreadsheet so I will be able to sort it and look at the activity of the skier wearing that pass. It was a pass paid for with cash, so there is no credit card record of the purchaser. I'm going to look into the cameras at the resort tomorrow. There are a lot of cameras all over the resort and I felt like I needed to narrow down time periods or specific camera locations before going back and asking for camera activity recordings."

"Good point; there are a lot of cameras around this resort. So at the moment you have three avenues that you are investigating," said Jill as she counted off with her fingers. "One, you are looking at the ski pass activity; two, you're looking into the chairlift failure; three, you're looking next at the cameras to see if we can get a visual identification of the person with the ski pass in question."

"Yes, that sums up the next few hours for me. What are you working on? We don't seem to have a clue as to why someone needed Joseph Morton dead."

"You're correct, I don't have any kind of a motive yet. I wanted to glean all of the information from the crime scene knowing it might disappear with weather changes on the mountain, or in people's memories as time passed. I really need the skills of Jo and Marie to help me with a motive. I need to take a deep dive into Joseph's company. I need to dive deeper into his immediate family, but something in the way this murder occurred; it doesn't feel like someone close to Joseph. It's just a feeling that I'll have to have validated by Marie's research. The behavior of local law enforcement confuses me, but at this point I don't believe it's connected to a motive. What are your thoughts about the motive?"

"I haven't met David Gomez yet so it is way too early for me to rule out family involvement in this death. I will say it is very exotic for the murder to have occurred where it did. Certainly an ability to ski an advanced slope reduces the pool of suspects. I agree with your approach to concentrate on Mr. Morton's business. What I have learned from your previous two big cases is that there may be more than one layer of murderers involved that may reveal themselves as the investigation expands. When do Jo and Marie arrive and how long will they be here in Breck?"

Looking at her watch Jill replied "they should be here by lunch tomorrow. I have given them David and Joseph's names as well as the name of Joseph's company and they will have internet aboard their flight tomorrow so they will start their search en route to Denver."

"Sounds like a plan. Why don't we have dinner now and then we can go our separate ways. I'll be reviewing the lift information and you can begin your search for motive."

"What kind of food are you in the mood to eat? I don't believe there is a Dutch restaurant in this town. There are several good microbreweries but I would advise against alcohol tonight. Give yourself twenty-four hours to adjust to the altitude and then you can drink."

"I am in the mood for one of your famous American cheeseburgers and I'll follow your advice on the alcohol. I have a little time zone disorientation – I feel rested, but I also feel we should be eating breakfast. I am sure that having a cheeseburger will help orientate my mind and body to this time zone."

Jill had the perfect restaurant in mind and they exited the hotel to walk to the restaurant. It was below ground level and had a family-style eating area on one side and a huge bar area on the other side with the same menu. They were soon slipping into a booth with Nick finding plenty of tasty varieties of the American cheeseburger. Over tea and burgers they caught up with each other's life. Nick had done more investigation into expanding his business into the United States. His operation was running so smoothly in the Netherlands and Belgium that he had been able to travel to Colorado with little advance notice to assist Jill with this case. Nick was pleased to hear about the success of Jill's first wine vintage and Nathan's beer glass design.

Soon they had finished dinner and were sauntering along the streets towards their hotel. Jill appreciated the thin, crisp air. It was still fairly hot and dry in California with the rainy season just starting - the hills were still brown and parched looking. Colorado was a nice break. It was pretty deserted as most of the skiers taking advantage of the early snow were day trippers from Denver. They heard a snowmobile turn the corner and head down the street behind them. Jill looked over her shoulder as she couldn't remember the last time she had seen or heard a snowmobile in town. People either walked or drove cars. All of a sudden she knew this was no casual snowmobiler.

The snowmobile sound was getting louder as it got closer. Jill yelled over the noise at Nick, "Be careful, this guy is trouble!"

But Nick had quickly come to the same conclusion himself. Rapidly taking stock of the situation, he grabbed a loose picket fence board in one hand and used the other hand to shove Jill over a snow bank. When the snowmobile got closer Nick took a swing at the man's chest with the board. It splintered in pieces from the impact, but it was enough. The snowmobile whirled off and disappeared.

Jill climbed back over the snow bank and complained, "If Angela had been here we would have had a picture of that snowmobile. Damn, I was too slow with pulling out my cellphone to take a picture of that snowmobile driver!"

"Should we call the police?" asked a worried Nick.

"Given my interaction with them this morning, I think we would be wasting our time. Besides I don't have a description of the snowmobile; I didn't notice the color, make or model. I don't even know if the driver was male or female, do you?"

"I was so busy trying to take perfect aim at the snowmobiler that I didn't catch any details of the driver either. I guess I had forgotten how you seem to bring an avalanche of bad people down upon you when you take on a case."

"Ha-Ha. If the going is too rough for you here, you could always join Henrik and hide behind him for a few days in Austin."

"Ouch! And miss the entertainment value of one of your cases? No way. Besides I like how you face harm or death with a sense of humor. Seriously, I guess we better keep a watch out for trouble on the way back to the hotel. Who knows you are on this case? Much like Mr. Morton's death this was a very targeted attack. Someone must have been watching us at the restaurant. Thank goodness we didn't have to run to get away from the snowmobile or I would now have snowmobile tracks going down the center of my back. I was breathless just from grabbing the board and shoving you over the snowbank."

"We had better warn the rest of the team and Joseph's partner. As to who knows I am on this case? Hmmm, obviously David since he hired me and whomever he told. Next I would include the Medical Examiner's office, local law enforcement, and the resort management. Beyond that small group, I don't think anyone knows we are in town. I'll call David as soon as we reach our hotel. Do you want to have a conversation with hotel security about our needs?"

"That sounds like a plan," Nick agreed.

They made it back to the hotel without any further incident. Nick did a quick search of Jill's room to see if it had any surprises or had been disturbed, but it appeared that all was in order. They planned to talk on the phone in an hour and went their separate ways.

Jill dialed David's number. "Hey David; it's Jill. How was the rest of your day?"

"Mostly I spent the afternoon receiving condolences. It's been a very draining day. How about you? Did Nick arrive as planned?"

"Is this a good time to talk or am I taking you away from something?"

"No you're not taking me away from anything; this is a good time. Our conversations give me something else to focus on. Did you find anything new?"

"Yes I do have progress for you, but first I wanted to alert you. Nick and I were walking back from dinner and were attacked by someone on a snowmobile. We are both fine, but David, you might be at risk."

"Oh my gosh! What happened?"

"We had just left Main Street and had turned onto one of the smaller streets – I couldn't tell you the street's name, when I heard the sound of the snowmobile as it turned onto our street. I looked over my shoulder because I've not heard a snowmobile in that part of town before and that was when we determined that the driver was aiming right for the two of us. Nick shoved me over a snow bank for protection and grabbed a wooden picket from someone's front yard to whack the driver. The board splintered when it hit the driver's chest. The snowmobiler drove off."

"Did you call the police?"

"No, for two reasons. I wasn't impressed with law enforcement this morning and both Nick and I could not come up with a description of the snowmobile."

"I guess I understand your hesitation. So why do you think I need to be careful?"

"Much like Joseph's murder, the snowmobile incident was targeted precisely at me. Someone is unhappy that I'm working on this case and they may be equally unhappy that you hired me."

"I see your point. I have a friend in law enforcement that lives close by. I think I'll see if I can get her to spend the night at my house. I'll tell her I would appreciate her company at a time like this. I hate to lie to her but I think that's the better route than telling her the truth. In the morning, I'll talk to my security firm about increasing my home protection. What is your other new information on the case?"

"As you know I had planned to meet with the ski patrol. The resort has not been notified that Joseph's death was a homicide. They were quite surprised that the police had not visited them. I ended up talking with an executive in their offices close to peak nine and their general counsel located at their world headquarters and gained full cooperation from the resort. Nick met with their IT department this afternoon and has data on what other skiers were around the two of you for the past week. Tomorrow he's getting camera information from the resort. Around the time of Joseph's death, the chairlift stopped for about sixteen minutes."

"Sixteen minutes? I have never been stuck on a chairlift for that length of time."

"That is exactly what I thought. I don't like the coincidence. The resort has not found the source of that shutdown. Nick is checking with an engineer friend that owns a company to see if he might have an engineer among his employees that could look at the lift failure and determine its source."

"This is getting complicated very quickly. I think back to what you said about Joseph being a target and as you gather more evidence, it sure points to that theory. I'm sorry that you've been put in danger, but at the same time I'm happy I hired you."

"Thank you David, and please make sure you take care of your own safety immediately. I'm starting to think that there are professionals at play here and the only amateurs in this case are law enforcement. Talk to you in the morning."

Jill ended the call and thought about the snowmobiler. How would the driver know where they were in town? Had someone been in the restaurant and called someone else? Given their new information on the lift failure, it appeared that at least two people had coordinated Joseph's murder. Maybe that was why she had this feeling that the family contained no killers. Typically you only had one mad family member not two at the exact same time. Looking at the clock, the conversation with David had taken very little time and she still had nearly an hour before she talked with Nick. His conversations would take longer and he might be examining the hotel for security. She decided she would begin her research on Joseph's company, and for the next hour or so she was so immersed in learning what she could about the company that she was startled when her phone rang.

"Hey Nick what did you learn? Are we safe here in this hotel?"

"Actually their security is state-of-the-art and I think we will be very safe here. One of the investors in this hotel and several other hotels operates a gigantic security company. He insists any property he invests in must have a high level of security. Because of that security system, this hotel pays a lower insurance premium and attracts a secretive clientele that stay on the top floor. I learned about security features that I had only read about up to this point. Because you are a repeat customer and this is the shoulder season before their occupancy begins running at full capacity, they offered to move all of us to the suite on the top floor for the same room rate that we are presently paying. I agreed and so we can move now or in the morning. The suite that management offered has five bedrooms, a living room, kitchen, and a beautiful view of the mountain. Do you want to move now?"

"I'm not tired at the moment and I don't have my stuff spread around this room so it will take me all of five minutes to pack. I've learned not to take my own security lightly so if the suite offers better protection, let's move now. If indeed a second party hacked into the ski lift computers, then we have a sophisticated murderer at play in this case."

"I'll call the front desk and notify them of our decision. Why don't you meet me in the lobby in ten minutes?"

"See you in a few," replied Jill and she ended the call.

Ten minutes later they were met in the lobby by an employee. She gave them five room access cards, aware that additional people would be arriving over the next two days. She offered them assistance with their luggage, but they both would've been embarrassed if they could not have carried it. Along the way, she pointed out the security features. When they arrived at the suite, she demonstrated its features. Jill had never stayed in such a nice hotel suite and was awed about everything in it. Each bedroom had its own en suite bathroom with a Jacuzzi tub. Normally when she stayed at this hotel, she had hard days of skiing and would have appreciated the tub. Nick had also never stayed in such a fine suite. He thought to himself that except for evil snowmobilers that this trip to Colorado was proving to be a great experience. A few minutes after the employee left, Jill returned to the living room with her laptop and Nick joined her a few minutes later with his own laptop.

"I had a wonderful hotel room, but this suite is amazing. It will be much easier to work here."

"Yes I agree that we'll be more productive here. I was thinking about how the snowmobiler found us tonight. Someone must have been in the restaurant watching us and made a call that we had left. I didn't hear the snowmobile long before it appeared on our street. Perhaps it had been parked there, but I admit I didn't pay attention to that. I am going on the assumption that there are at least two people involved in this murder; one that fired that poisonous dart and the other to stop and restart the lift. Again at the restaurant tonight, one person to watch us inside the restaurant and the other to operate the snowmobile. What are your thoughts?"

"I have been replaying the snowmobile's arrival in my mind and like you I don't remember hearing it much before we saw it. What was the intent of the snowmobiler? To scare us? To harm us? I don't recall seeing any weapons – no knives or guns. I think the purpose was to scare us as I didn't have to jump from the path of the snowmobile to swing at the driver with the board. For a minute, I even thought maybe the snowmobiler wished us no harm but that street was wide and there was no need to get so close to us."

"Do you think that you hurt the driver? The board splintered easily and there was the padding of the jacket. The driver left so quickly I couldn't tell if the person was hurting, and like you, I didn't see any weapons. I think we have analyzed this event to death. Have you had time to look at any of your reports yet? "

"No I was planning to come out here and start my review. How about you? Do you have any news about Joseph's company?"

"In this first review, I'm trying to locate the names of the key players – board members, senior leadership, etc. Next I am going to be going through their press releases as you would be amazed at what you learn about a company through press releases. Then I'll focus on any filings they have had with the Securities and Exchange Commission. The SEC is really Jo's area of expertise, but you can learn a lot by reading 'Management Reports.'"

"It sounds complicated. Well, don't let me distract you. I'll be studying the data the resort gave me to see if I can find any patterns of skiers around Joseph."

They worked in silence over the next hour. Jill decided to add the local police to the list of people requiring a deeper dive for information. Nick had seen some patterns of skiers around Joseph. He would need the resort's help deciphering the data. Jill was ready to call it a night and headed to her bedroom to get some sleep. Nick stayed awake another hour and then all of a sudden the time zone difference caught up with him.

They were both awake at an early hour the next morning. Jill because she was an early riser no matter what time zone she currently inhabited and Nick because he was coping with coming from a time zone that was seven hours ahead of where he was at the moment. Their plan for the day included another visit to where Joseph had been murdered, and a meeting with the IT staff to review questions that Nick had from examining the data. He would also be presented with the camera footage from the resort. He had spoken with Henrik last night and Henrik would be able to help with this case on two levels. He had an engineer that would be able to look into the chairlift failure to see if someone had hacked the resort's computer that operated the lift. Henrik also had a fabulous beta version of facial recognition software and that would help identify faces of people that had been around Joseph over the past few days.

Soon they were changing into their ski attire to go up on the mountain. Twenty minutes later they were riding the gondola to start the journey to peak six. Jill had checked with Nick to make sure he could ski at an advanced level. Shortly they had arrived at the same place that Jill had visited yesterday with David. With lots of breaks to acclimate to the altitude they approached the mini forest where Joseph had been found a couple of days ago. Jill took the lead to the location of Joseph's murder. Jill discussed with Nick her thinking about the killer – the fact that he needed to be an expert skier and control his respirations enough to steady the dart gun and fire at Joseph. She also mentioned finding the cell phone and again he was shaking his head over the lack of police involvement at the crime scene. Nick was unable to find any new forensic evidence or develop any theories beyond what Jill had already considered. Finishing up on the mountain, they headed to the resort office that managed over a hundred cameras across the ski resort. At the end of the meeting, they returned to their hotel expecting the impending arrival of Jo and Marie. Nick had a huge amount of data to start sorting through in the hotel room.

Soon after they arrived back in the suite, they received a message that Jo and Marie were in the lobby requesting Jill's assistance to get into the suite. Jill had not seen her friends since their vacation in Belgium two months ago. Even though they had full time day jobs that limited their hours for Jill, she couldn't think of anyone she would want to work with more than her best friends.

"Hey girlfriends, welcome to Breck and thanks for coming. Wait till you see the lovely suite the hotel has placed us in. Nick is waiting upstairs and we have lots to talk about," said Jill after she hugged her friends and steered them towards the elevator. Marie was a brunette and Jo a blondish redhead, both of them at five feet nine towered over Jill's shorter frame.

Jo and Marie were soon in the suite renewing their friendship with Nick. Jill immediately began doing her best to force liquids on her two friends to help them deal with the altitude. Jo was prone to migraine headaches which was sometimes a side effect of altitude sickness. Jill brought Jo and Marie up-to-date on the case including the incident of the snowmobile.

Jo looked a little alarmed and exclaimed, "Even in this small town you have people wanting to harm you! It's strange that you went five years as a consultant with no one trying to kill you and yet in the majority of your recent cases you've become a target. Maybe I should refine that to we've become the target. I'm glad you didn't have to face the snowmobiler by yourself last night. Thanks, Nick, for being here and assisting our dear friend."

"Jill noticed the problem before I did," remarked Nick. "I just gave her a shove over a snow bank thinking the snowmobile could not reach her there."

"Is anyone hungry for lunch right now?" asked Jill. When she got affirmative nods of their heads she suggested, "after all of this travel I'm sure you guys would rather walk somewhere to get lunch. There is a cute café in town that we can walk to. On our way back we can stop at the supermarket and purchase some supplies for the kitchen in the suite."

Leaving the hotel, Marie and Jo got an update from Nick on his business plans for expansion into the US. They also enjoyed his description of the ride on Henrik's plane. None of them had been on a private jet and could only imagine the enjoyment of the trip. They soon arrived at the café and ordered lunch. A short time later they were back on the street heading for the grocery store. Since Jill had left her car back at the hotel they could only buy what they could personally carry for several blocks. They also discussed what Angela might want upon her arrival and took care of her four favorite foods - tea/beer, red licorice, dark chocolate, chips and salsa. They returned to the hotel suite, groceries in hand. Despite the encounter with the snowmobiler, they planned to eat lunch and dinner at the many good restaurants in town.

With the bigger suite and a box of freezer paper, Jill started creating a murder board in the suite's living room. She had pictures of Joseph, David, the logo of the biotech company - Broomfield Pharmaceuticals, a veterinarian dart gun, the chairlift that was Joseph's last, the building representing local law enforcement, and a stock photo of someone on a snowmobile. Her investigation would start in this town, but at some point she might move her base of operation to Denver and she wanted the murder board to be portable if that occurred.

Soon Jo and Marie were engrossed in their searches. They had performed some work on the plane, but that only scratched the surface for the both of them. Comfortably ensconced in the suite, they were both most productive if allowed to work in silence. Jill had turned over her initial research on Broomfield Pharmaceuticals and they would build from there. Jill and Nick left the suite to go and meet with Tom to discuss their IT needs and to offer help in locating the source of the chairlift failure. Before long they were seated in Tom's office as he listened to their data analysis and the offer of help with the chairlift failure.

"Tell me more about Henrik and his company," remarked Tom.

"Henrik is a personal friend to Jill and me," Nick explained. "She solved his wife's murder in Belgium. He runs a multinational company that provides software that senses and repels hackers or other intruders into IT systems. He has engineers whose sole duty is to break software solutions that other engineers of his company have created. As you can imagine those engineers are the best of the best and they enjoy a good hunt for intruders in information systems. Henrik is also a skier and when I mentioned the chairlift failure, he immediately understood both the IT system that operates the chairlift and likely your vulnerabilities. He felt he could have one of his engineers solve this remotely for you. He would give his considerable opinion as to whether hackers could stop the chairlift during the time that Joseph was murdered. He would provide that service to you gratis with no strings attached. He felt fairly sure his engineers could hack into your system even without your permission. Are you interested in having his company try to solve this problem for you? He will not try to hack into your system if you decline his offer."

"It sounds like a generous offer, but I will have to run it by our IT leadership which I will do as soon as this meeting is over," noted Tom. "Did you find any useful information by looking at the resort's ski pass system?"

"Yes, it appears that two ticket holders had stalked Joseph and David for several days," stated Nick. "No one else had the pattern of hitting the chairlift pass system as these two people. They had actually ridden the lift with them several times. As they had paid cash for their passes and had not tried to check their performance online through your app, I have no way of identifying them, unless there were cameras trained on some of the lifts. So I have narrowed it down to three lifts and four days of footage. I would also like your ticket booths windows if you have any cameras there as well."

"Before you arrived, I spoke with our counsel regarding releasing copies of pictures to you."

Jill and Nick tensed expecting to be turned down by the resort. They were both pleasantly surprised by Tom's answer.

"We couldn't think of a State or Federal law that we might violate if we gave you the feed from the cameras, so if you'll give me the camera locations and dates, we should have that for you within the hour."

"Thank you, we really value the resort's help," said Jill appreciatively. "We don't have the power of law enforcement or a judicial order behind us; we just need to solve this homicide for David Gomez and Joseph Morton."

"We don't want any murderers up on the ski slope or indeed anywhere in the State of Colorado. If we can help you identify him or her, it is a win for all of us."

"Then we won't take any more of your time. Can you give me a call when the camera feed collection is completed and a location to pick it up from?"

"Actually I understand from our IT people that they will send it to the cloud and we'll give you a password to access it."

"That will work," replied Nick and they stood up and shook hands before departing Tom's office.

Jill and Nick set off back towards their hotel. "That was easier than expected," commented Jill. "After my reception by local law enforcement, it's refreshing to get maximum cooperation."

"If they decide to take Henrik up on his generous offer, it could be of real value to them to learn their vulnerabilities."

"Let's return to the hotel and get my car. I'd like to take a look at David and Joseph's cabin to see the potential for someone to have followed Joseph from the cabin to the ski resort. David said we didn't want to be on the road for the first time in the dark. It's nice and sunny at the moment, a perfect time to go visit the Boreas Pass Road cabin. It is a short drive and you can tell me from your law enforcement experience if you think this was where the killer began following Joseph."

"Sounds like a plan," replied Nick.

A few minutes later they left the hotel garage and, using Jill's GPS, followed the directions to David's cabin. The day was bright and sunny and the view was spectacular. Jill reminded herself to send Angela up here with her camera. Sure she could take pictures with her iPhone, but they wouldn't have the balance or beauty of Angela's camera.

Jill pulled into the driveway to Joseph' and David's cabin. It was elevated above the road, so David was right that anyone waiting there would be seen. It was a beautiful stone cabin. It was a reasonable size, not an ostentatious mess like some of the newer homes built in the last decade and a half. Not seeing anything else to investigate, they turned around to return down the hill to town.

CHAPTER 8

One moment Jill was admiring the view and the next she was staring into the rear-view mirror at a large SUV on her bumper. The closeness of the Hummer had Jill remarking to Nick, "What a moron, I can't believe that person is driving so close to my bumper. I'll pull over at the next opportunity and let him pass."

"Ah Jill not to raise the alarm, but I think the Hummer is out to do us harm and I think we are about to find out how good a driver you are. If that Hummer hits us hard enough, we will go straight off the road."

"Crap! Any suggestions?" Jill could feel rivulets of sweat on the back of her neck and under her arms.

"If I wanted to push the car off the road, I would accelerate into our bumper at the start of any curve and catapult you straight off the cliff, so you need to fake him out. Slow down a lot and accelerate at the top of each curve. I'm hoping his reaction time will be slow enough to get us through each of the curves."

Thankfully the road was dry so their only real worry was the SUV rolling over on a curve. Since it was late fall, the snow banks on the side of the road were low and would not stop a vehicle from driving off the cliff. Jill had the smallest SUV and it appeared that the Hummer on her tail was the largest SUV. Nick was right in that the larger Hummer would be more prone to rolling over and so she should be able to take the curves a little faster than the car behind her. It would all depend on her driving skill and composure. She did as he suggested and was able to stay away from the Hummer's front grill on the first three curves. She asked Nick to call 911 and report their situation to the police. Her timing was off on the fourth curve and she felt a jolt from the Hummer. Fortunately she had room to accelerate and pull away but she knew time was running out and fortunately so was the hill. They had one or two more curves before the road largely flattened and straightened out as they neared the town.

It was hard to keep her eyes on the road yet check the position of the Hummer. On the fifth curve she swore she could feel the heat of the engine of the SUV behind her, it seemed so close. On the sixth curve she lost it. She'd been staring into the rearview mirror and hit the curve too fast so she could not accelerate away from the Hummer's bumper.

Jill yelled at Nick, "Brace yourself we're going off the road!"

As soon as the words were out of her mouth she felt the Hummer ram into her SUV's rear end, sending them into the air. She had planned to brace her hands on the steering wheel, but the airbags exploded at the moment of impact. They were flying through the air and all Jill could see was the white of the airbag in her face. She heard Nick saying something which she suspected were profanities muttered in Dutch. Seconds later there was a thunk and they were catapulted forward as the SUV made contact with the ground. The many low fir trees and soft snow served to slow down their vehicle and they came to a stop, moments later. Jill turned the engine off.

Jill looked over where she thought Nick would be beyond the fabric of her airbag and asked, "Nick are you all right?"

Seconds later she heard him mumble, "I'm fine, Jill, how about you?"

Just then the airbags started to deflate and they got a look at each other. After the adrenaline rush of the last five minutes all she could do was laugh at the powder deposited on Nick's face, sure that her own looked equally ridiculous.

Nick grinned back at her and asked, "Am I covered in as much powder as you?"

"Yep."

"See, Jill, these last five minutes were that entertainment factor I mentioned in connection to you. That was a wild ride and you did well. Great driving!"

"If I was such a good driver then why are we sitting in the middle of a forest?"

"If that Hummer had got your bumper on the first curve, I doubt we would be laughing at each other's looks at the moment."

"Okay the fun is over. Let's call the local police to report this accident, and I'll need to call the car rental agency to get a replacement."

"Okay here's your cell phone, but I think I hear sirens coming our way. That must be in response to the call I made a few minutes ago."

"I guess we should hike over to the road so they can find us, though I would've thought I left brake marks on the pavement before we were airborne."

They both got out of the car and walked around it looking at the damage. The rear bumper was quite dented with black paint affixed in parts. The front hood fared better with no visible dents. She had no idea what the undercarriage looked like.

Jill suddenly thought of something, "Do you think the gas tank could explode?"

"No if it was going to explode it would have done so on impact. I smell burnt brake pads, but not gasoline."

They looked over at the road as they saw two police cars

arrive, as well an ambulance. Jill waved them over. The EMT yelled "where are you hurt?"

"We were saved by our airbags, we have no injuries. I am a doctor and we're both fine."

"That's good news, we received a call that a car was trying to push you off this road. What happened?"

The officers had been walking toward Jill's rental SUV during this shouted conversation. She was pleased to see this was not the officer she had spoken to yesterday to get a copy of the police report concerning Joseph's murder.

Jill pointed to the rear bumper and said "see the black paint there. That is where the Hummer hit our car sending us over the embankment. Fortunately it wasn't a bad drop and we had airbags."

Nick held out Jill's phone that he had used to call 911 and said "here is a picture of the car, no license plate, you can't see the driver, but you can see how close he was to our car."

As the officers leaned in to look, Jill said "Nick that was brilliant! Angela has you well trained to snap pictures."

One of the officers stepped away and pulled out his radio. He requested a 'be on the look-out' alert for the Hummer. He returned to the group and said, "I issued a BOLO for the Hummer, we should find it shortly."

The ambulance had left and the sun was getting lower over the mountain peaks. One of the officers called for a tow truck. Nick used his mobile phone to check email thinking he might have an email from the resort. He did and so knew he could get to work on the camera data when he returned to their hotel. Once the police had their report completed and a copy of the photo from Jill's phone, they waited around to see if the tow truck driver required any assistance. In the end the driver parked on the road and used his towing steel cable to pull the SUV out of the mini-forest it had landed in with the police directing traffic around the wrecker. The driver gave them the address of the vehicle's location in town and left with it.

The police dropped Jill and Nick off at their hotel, having given Jill a copy of their report so she could use that to deal with the car rental agency. She wondered how many customers made accident claims of attempted vehicle manslaughter. It was going to be an interesting call to say the least. The agency would need to bring her a replacement vehicle and take away the damaged SUV.

Jill and Nick returned to the hotel suite. Marie and Jo looked at them seeing the airbag powder still on their faces.

"What happened to you two? What is the white stuff on your face and in your hair?"

"We were run off the road by a Hummer and the airbags exploded as soon as it rammed our bumper."

"Do you two have any injuries? What happened to your car? Were the police involved?" asked Marie in her usual rapid fire style.

"No injuries, the car may be totaled or not, and yes the police were involved. Let Nick and I have our hot showers and we'll be back out to discuss the event with you. Don't open the door to anyone," advised Jill.

Her adrenaline rush had carried her through the last hour, but suddenly, she was ready to drop to the floor and bawl her eyes out. Give her a hot shower, and a few minutes alone and she would have it all back under control.

Twenty minutes later she returned to the living room and she could tell the other two had peppered Nick with questions. Looking at her friends she asked, "So was Nick able to give you all the details?"

"OMG, yes! What a terrifying adventure. You were lucky that the road was dry, that your SUV had airbags, and you used evasive driving until the final curves!"

"I was lucky to have Nick with me providing me evasive

driving techniques. Whew! I need a glass of wine," announced Jill. "Does anyone else want something to drink?"

The other three joined her in toasting their good fortune.

Taking a big swallow of wine, Jill asked, "Did Nick show you the picture? Angela would be proud after all the pictures she took in Belgium of the creeps that were after us there."

"No he didn't show us a picture! Whose phone is it on? Let us see it."

Jill went over to her purse and searched for her iPhone then she leaned in and showed it to her friends.

"Wow that is so real. We are so lucky to have you alive and well," said Jo and soon a group hug was taking place.

"This is really getting scary. I was grateful to have someone in the car with me on that mountain and especially one that could quickly give me a driving skill to focus on and get us down out of the higher cliffs. Thank you so much, Nick."

"I'm starting to think that you need a bodyguard when you start one of these cases."

As the three women stared him down, he tried to think of a way to backpedal and get back in their good graces.

Finally he said, "Don't tell Angela I made that stupid remark." And with a laugh breaking the tension they knew they were back on solid footing with him.

"Someone must have a tail on us between the encounter with the snowmobiler last night and now this road rage problem," mused Jill." How else could they have found us?"

"I've been thinking about those same questions. I think we should eat in this evening as there have been two attacks less than twenty-four hours apart. At least we should maintain a low key existence until we figure out how these people are following us or perhaps until they find the Hummer. Furthermore, I have plenty of work and we haven't even heard from Jo and Marie as to what they have found in their searches."

"You're right, Nick. We'll eat in or at least you and I will. Marie and Jo, you should go explore the town; there are many great restaurants, and I don't think your faces are known here. Why don't you tell us what you found, and then take off for dinner?"

"I would like to see the town and I think our faces are not known," agreed Jo. "Let me start with what I learned about Joseph's biotech company.

"Broomfield Pharmaceuticals has been around for almost two decades and has had a few blockbuster drugs to treat cancer. It went IPO two years ago so there is a lot of public information on the company. There are three divisions within the company - one that does clinical trials, another performs the research and development that creates the drugs, and the third arm manufactures its therapies. Sometimes their clinical trials branch did trials for other companies and sometimes they would collaborate with other companies for the research."

"What is the size of the company?" asked Jill.

"Six hundred million based on this morning's stock price," Jo calculated.

"Ok that is a considerable size," commented Jill. "If there is a problem with the company, protecting that company value might drive some sicko into murder. What is the news from the last six months? I can't imagine someone that plots this kind of murder taking longer than that if something angered them."

"The most recent management reports hint at a problem with a bio-therapeutic developed in collaboration with another company."

"What kind of collaboration?" asked Jill.

"This report doesn't elaborate beyond the statement that there were problems that might affect future operating income margins. If you could look into the FDA from your medical view Jill, they might have additional information. There is mention here about interactions with the FDA, so there should be a paper trail."

"I'll work on that tonight. Would you add that other company to your list of things to review? Thanks. Marie, what have you found?" asked Jill as she added Jo's information to her temporary murder board.

"I started by concentrating on Joseph and David. David is a well-regarded teacher in the Denver area. All of the school districts at one time or another have offered him a permanent job which he has turned down. Students love him, they have a wide circle of friends, and really there are no red flags in any of the data that I looked at for David.

"Joseph has a far bigger public presence due to his position of CEO. He was a leader in his field speaking at many events. He had been on the quarterly earnings presentations; he chaired a regional committee for biotech companies, lectured at both high schools and universities, and provided several lectures on research findings at large cancer meetings. He was well respected. His personal life for the most part stayed out of the spotlight. His marriage to David, while not a secret, was rarely photographed or spoken about. It appears to me that he didn't take his partner to most corporate events. I really didn't see any negativity toward Joseph or his company in my search. Even sites where employees talk about their companies seem to be full of respect for Broomfield. I'm moving on to that second company that Jo mentioned as well as the board members."

"Thanks Marie and Jo," said Jill. "It's about time we break for dinner. Would you guys like directions to a particular restaurant or would you rather just have directions to downtown and pick whatever restaurant catches your eye?"

"Are you sure you don't want to join us for dinner?" asked Jo.

"I'm very sure that I want to stay within this room for dinner. I really think I would be risking your lives if I accompany you into town. I also think that Nick is as big a liability as I am."

"Well I'd much rather dine with you two, but I guess I have to agree," noted Marie.

"If you point us in the right direction we will just stroll into town and choose a restaurant," said Jo.

"Listen for any snowmobiles. You shouldn't be hearing them in town or really at this time of year," advised Jill.

"Will do." Then looking over at Nick, Marie asked, "Any advice on how to stay safe from you?"

"Actually, take this," Nick handed Marie a small cylinder. "It's pepper spray. Since I was coming to America, I armed myself," said Nick with a grin.

Jo and Marie rolled their eyes, as Jill said, "So why didn't you use it last night?"

Looking chagrined, Nick replied "umm because I forgot I was carrying it."

"We won't tell Angela about your pepper spray either," remarked Jo. "You know we like you since we're so willing to harass you, right? You get American humor? We really appreciate you being here and giving Jill the advice she needed to survive the Hummer up on the mountain."

"Yes, ladies, I do get American humor and I like you too. Jill saved both our lives today as I would have gone over the cliff with her. Have a great dinner."

The two women left and Jill reviewed a room service menu. She selected her choice and added a glass of wine. She wanted to celebrate being alive tonight. She passed the menu over to Nick for him to make his choices before calling in their order. She needed to talk to David and then Nathan.

She dialed David to give him an update on their research as well as a report on the Hummer incident.

"David, it's Jill. How are you doing?"

"Tomorrow is Joseph's funeral and I'm not looking forward to the day."

"If you don't mind, I would like to attend. I'd like to pay my respects to both you and Joseph, and I'd like to watch the people at the service to see if anything arouses my curiosity."

"Okay," said David giving Jill the details.

"Were you able to increase your security?"

"Yes as I mentioned I called over a friend who stayed in our house last night. It was quiet with no intruders. This morning, I've had the security company that manages this property in to increase the protection on this house. Why, what's up?"

Jill proceeded to explain the incident on Boreas Pass road. He was amazed to hear that Nick and Jill survived the Hummer with no injuries. After discussing the event a while longer, Jill moved on to update David on the resort's data. Then she ended with her team looking at the company that partnered with Joseph's company to develop the new cancer drug.

"I thought about who I had told that I had hired your company to investigate Joseph's death. I'll e-mail you that list along with an explanation of who each of the people are. Unless it is someone that you told, then I have to assume that one of the people on my list is connected to Joseph's murderer."

"David, before you e-mail me that list, would you add one more column? I would like you to add who on your list could have skied the slope that Joseph was killed on if you have knowledge of their skiing ability. Granted, it could have been a contract hit."

"Yeah I could do that Jill. I'm not sure I will know the ski ability for each person on my list, but I'll give it some thought and send you that list when I'm done."

"Thanks David. I'll see you tomorrow."

Nick had overheard Jill's conversation and asked, "Jill, how are you going to get to the funeral tomorrow?"

"I thought I would drive," she responded looking at him puzzled.

"In what vehicle?"

"Oh. Yeah, I forgot about our exciting afternoon and that my vehicle was towed away three hours ago. Let me see when the replacement is scheduled to arrive," said Jill as she looked up the rental car agency's number.

After speaking to the car rental agency, she doubted she would make the funeral. It was due to snow for the next couple of days and depending on the roads, there would be delays going through the Eisenhower Tunnel. Angela was due to arrive late morning and Jill was glad she was coming by shuttle as those drivers and vehicles were better in a snowstorm than Jill. She sent David a note about her likely difficulties in reaching the funeral in the morning. She would still make an attempt, but between the timing of the arrival of a new rental car and the weather, it seemed like the odds were against her.

They answered a knock on the door to find room service with their dinner. The waiter looked a little wide eyed at Jill's makeshift murder board. Fortunately, there were no gruesome pictures on the board, just the word 'murder' at the top. Maybe she would take it down before room service or housekeeping got a look at it. She'd have to remember to do that each morning. Since the room service attendant looked startled over her murder board, she decided to make light of it.

"Nick and I are game designers. We are working on a murder mystery app and need to keep the names straight."

That explanation seemed to reduce the alarm for the attendant as he replied 'cool,' just before he exited the room.

"That was a great explanation that you created on the fly," pronounced Nick.

"Yeah I thought it was pretty ingenuous to think up that explanation for my murder board. Remind me to take it down each morning so that I don't scare off housekeeping."

They were soon digging into their dinners. Jill and Nick toasted with their wineglasses to celebrate surviving the encounter with the Hummer. Once the plates were cleared and placed outside the room, they both returned to their research. Jill knew she needed to call Nathan, but she hadn't thought of a way to explain the encounter with the Hummer that wouldn't have him immediately heading to the airport and flying to Denver. He had wanted to come spend some time with her circle of friends, but she didn't want him getting into the habit of coming to her rescue with each weird case. So she would put off the conversation for a while and avoid an argument. She decided she'd move on to more pleasant topics.

"So are you looking forward to Angela joining us tomorrow?" inquired Jill.

"Yes, very much so! Do you think the snow will delay her arrival?"

"It's early in the snow season and therefore this is likely not such a severe storm as to be a blizzard. She is coming aboard the same shuttle you took and they're very capable of driving in bad weather. If anyone can get through the pass, it's them."

"Good to know. I am pleased to see her in person, but we haven't come close to resolving the distance between our two homes at the present. I never asked her, but does she ski?"

"She has had bad luck with skiing in that someone in her party usually breaks a bone. I'm not sure that she has even been on a ski slope or if she is sitting safely inside a ski chalet, and the broken bone happens."

"Wow, that sounds like some serious bad karma between her and ski resorts. That is amazing considering she has so much good karma everywhere else."

"Yeah, makes me scared to go skiing when she is in the same city. Back to reality, have you found any new information by reviewing the cameras?"

"Yes they have cameras on all ticket booths because so much revenue is going through the windows. I was able to view one of the two people that purchased lift tickets. Unfortunately that was not very helpful. The purchaser had so much winter clothing on, frankly, I couldn't tell if it was a man or a woman, as they were wearing gloves, a helmet, goggles and a ski mask. So I don't have enough of a face to use Henrik's facial recognition software. Instead I'm going to try to match the jacket and pants color to see if there are any interior shots in any ski lodges that show the person without the helmet, goggles, and scarf. Again the resort has cameras inside the lodges wherever they employ cashiers to take money from skiers for food and drink. So there are about an additional one hundred locations where I might see this person in the background."

"Will you manually have to look for this person of interest's clothing or do you have a computer program that can search for the clothing colors?"

"Fortunately, I have a software program that will do that for me. Despite all the cameras and all the locations, it shouldn't take more than about five minutes for the computer to give me the data. I'll still have a large number of video clips to look at but I'm planning to go back and look at the ticket window cashiers' footage to determine if there's anything original on this person's clothing."

"That's great. It sounds like with a lot of computer manipulation and a little luck we might have the names of the people that were following Joseph within the hour."

They heard their suite door mechanism unlocking and assumed that indicated the return of Jo and Marie. When Jill got a look at them she asked, "What happened to you guys?"

They had mud on their jeans, faces, and hair. Jo was walking with a limp.

"We think we met your Hummer driver in town after dinner. We took your advice and kept an ear out for snowmobile sounds. We must have heard the same thing you heard the previous day. We were about a block out from the restaurant when we heard a snowmobile engine start up and then saw it turn the corner and head our way."

Marie continued telling the story from Jo, "The sound of the snowmobile made us mad, and Nick's pepper spray made us bold. We decided we were going to get our hands on the snowmobile driver to find out who it was. So Jo had this huge purse as her weapon, and I was armed with pepper spray. But the driver coming at us was wearing goggles so we knew we needed to get close enough to knock the goggles off his or her face."

Since Jo and Marie were taking this event as an adventure, Jill decided to follow suit and asked, "Let me guess, Jo - you swung your purse at the driver and Marie you aimed the pepper spray."

"Actually," said Marie. "We did something much dumber. We took a look at our surroundings and saw a snow bank we could dive over. So with that thought we turned around and faced the snowmobile. We split apart hoping we could entice the driver to drive between the two of us. As it got close, Jo took a swing with her purse that would have done Nolan Ryan proud. The driver saw the purse coming at him or her at the last moment and took both hands off the handlebars which stopped the snowmobile. I figured I'd help the driver continue to fall to the ground so I grabbed their arm and yanked. Unfortunately the idiot landed on top of me with helmet and goggles still in place, and so we rolled around on the street. Then some other people started walking down our street and the snowmobile driver decided to give up on Jo and me. Both of us had moved away from the snowmobile and sadly that enabled the driver to jump back on and take off."

"Are you both okay, did you sustain any injuries?" asked Nick.

"No we're fine," replied Marie. "But dammit the driver got away. I think it was a woman though. All that rolling around on the ground suggested it was a lightweight person. I never saw the face and never got to use the pepper spray. So that was our adventure for the night and now I am cold in my wet and muddy clothes."

"Me too! The hotel reception staff wondered if we had slipped on the ice somewhere and I responded that we had rolled around with a snowmobile driver. They probably thought we were drunk. Oh well."

They both left and went to their rooms to change. Jill was

happy to see them taking it all in stride. She said to Nick, "How do you think someone knew they were connected to us?"

"I have been asking myself that same question. I think they either saw us at lunch all together or there is a leak at this hotel."

"I'm going to call Angela and warn her. She may choose to stay in Wisconsin, rather than join the fun and games here. Sorry Nick."

"Hey, no problem. While I was really looking forward to seeing her, I would rather she stay safe."

Jill looked at the clock and guessed that Angela was still awake so she dialed her.

"Hey Angela it's me."

Nick found himself listening to a one-sided conversation trying to guess what Angela was saying. He thought she decided to still come based on Jill's comments. He was secretly happy and thought he could protect her. A moment later, Jill held her phone out to Nick and said, "Hey you want to say hi?"

He took her phone and said "Hello, are you still coming tomorrow?"

"Yes, you guys can't have fun without me. I'll be there as scheduled."

"Jill said you have bad karma near ski resorts, that someone always breaks a bone. Maybe the person that is after us will be the one with the broken bone."

"I'll do what I can to help the team," said Angela. "Though from what Jill said, this sounds a lot worse than our little events in Belgium and the Netherlands."

"I learned from you though. I used her phone to take a picture of the Hummer that was trying to push us off the mountain. It was real convincing to the local cops to see the Hummer kissing our rear bumper."

"Maybe that will be my primary role in Colorado - to document all the bad people trying to harm us."

"Regardless, I am looking forward to your arrival."

"Me too," and shortly thereafter they ended the call.

Next Jill went into her bedroom to call Nathan. After confessing to him about the two snowmobile events and the Hummer incident, they had the first bad argument of their relationship. Nathan wanted to leave immediately for Colorado to provide Jill with protection and Jill did not want him curtailing his professional and personal life to ride to her rescue with each case. She wanted him to trust her to keep herself safe. Having him there would undoubtedly increase her protection, but the guilt of her job disrupting his with each case was not a burden she wished to carry. He was as adamant about protecting her as she was about him staying home in California. The conversation ended in a stalemate with him agreeing to stay in California for the time being. Jill had come close to threatening him with an end to their relationship, but it wasn't a conversation she wanted to have over the phone. Nathan, perhaps sensing that her breaking point was so close, backed down.

Jill returned to the suite's living room and joined the others. Jo and Marie had settled in with their computers and a glass of wine with renewed vigor to solve the mystery of Joseph Morton's death. While they were gathering details on the board members of Joseph's company as well as that secondary company they collaborated with, Nick was going through the tedious work of the camera footage with the hope of identifying the two ticketholders that frequently skied near Joseph. Jill normally would have assisted the other three in their searches, but she felt a compelling need to figure out who was presently trying to harm them and what they should do about it.

Jill had been seen in public with Jo and Marie when they had arrived at the hotel earlier that day and when they had walked to lunch. Jill was convinced that someone was stationed in the lobby watching them. It was likely not a hotel employee but rather another resident of the hotel. She decided she would go down to the lobby and observe for an hour or so. She wanted to watch the hotel employees and get a sense of whether there was anywhere that a stranger could hang out in the lobby and not be suspicious looking to the hotel's employees.

"Hey guys I'm going to head down to the lobby and observe," announced Jill.

"Why?" asked Marie.

"I want to get to the bottom of the puzzle of who knows you are connected to Nick and me. I somehow think that someone is watching us in the lobby. They know our comings and goings and they know our connection. I don't think they're using electronic surveillance to figure this out; rather, I think they have someone placed in our lobby. So I'm going to put a little bit of a disguise on and see what I can find in the lobby."

"Sounds like a plan. I was wondering myself how someone knew that we were connected to you. When we first heard the snowmobile start up Jo and I looked at each other and thought 'not again' and 'really can't they try something else?' I think that gave us the determination to try and take the snowmobile driver down. Unfortunately while we saved ourselves from injury, in the end we were unable to identify the driver. What kind of disguise are you going to do?"

"I thought I would hide all of my hair under a knit cap, then I was going to use duct tape to tape two of the decorative pillows from our sofa around my middle and cover that with a sweater from Nick. That ought to put forty pounds on my frame. I planned to wear my reading glasses and keep a scarf tied around my face. That's all I can think to do to change my appearance with the supplies that I have in this suite. You guys have any additional suggestions?"

"How about if I do your face in heavy make-up as that is not your normal look," offered Jo.

"I don't know if I have enough make-up with me to make it look heavy."

"Why don't the three of us pool our make-up and I'll see what I can do. Since I'm not trying to make you beautiful, this should take maybe ten minutes max."

"Thanks Jo; that's a great idea."

Fifteen minutes later, Jill walked out of the suite unrecognizable to herself and her friends. They had done an excellent job with her disguise. She took the elevator down to the lobby and disappeared into the restroom for a few minutes. When she seated herself in the lobby she wanted it to look as if she'd come from the restroom and not from a hotel room above the first floor. A few minutes later she was seated on the sofa close to the door as she was hot with the two pillows around her core and it was the coldest place that she could find in the lobby.

She sensed that the registration desk was eyeing her suspiciously as they directed frequent glances her way. She had been in the lobby for perhaps five minutes when a hotel security guard stopped by and asked her if she was a guest of the hotel. She showed him her hotel room key and he smiled and left. Stopping by the registration desk, the guard let them know that she was legitimate. That told her that the people that were tracking them might be guests of the hotel.

She watched the lobby for another hour but no one else seemed to be conducting surveillance. She decided to go outside to determine if surveillance was happening outside the hotel but again she couldn't find a parked car with someone sitting in it watching the hotel entrance. She spent a little more time outside considering the possibilities and then gave it up to return to the hotel suite.

"Hey, Jill, how did the disguise work?" asked Marie.

"It worked so well that the registration desk had hotel security stop by and ask me if I was a guest. I just showed him my room key and he moved on, but it got me to thinking about this hotel. I don't think they would allow any stranger to wait in their lobby for any length of time.

"I think our assailants are staying in the same hotel. Nick, I wondered if you had the ability to hack into the hotel's cameras to see if someone was stationed in the lobby and watching us as we were leaving the hotel for lunch."

"Why don't I just ask the nice security person I spoke to last night and see if he'll allow me to view their tapes? That way I won't have to do anything illegal," suggested Nick his voice loaded with sarcasm.

"You do have a point. Let me know if you get access and I'll view the lobby tapes with you."

Nick left the suite in search of the security personnel he'd spoken to the previous night. Like Jill, he had been trying to figure out how they were being followed. He needed the equipment that Henrik had used at his home to check their luggage for tracking bugs. Maybe he could convince Jill to invest in such a system for their future safety.

Jo looked over at Jill and asked, "What did Nathan think of our adventures so far?"

"We had a huge fight when I told him about the encounters with the snowmobile and the Hummer," Jill disclosed.

"Fight? What is there to fight over? I don't understand," said a confused Jo.

"He wanted to jump on a plane to Colorado so he could protect me from bad and evil people. I said no. We argued about it a little more and I think we both came close to saying something that we might regret."

"Why don't you want his help with keeping you safe? I think I'm missing the point here," said a bemused Jo.

"The guy is a world-class artist for wine labels. It feels wrong and inconsiderate of me to have him at my side whenever anyone tries to harm me. It is like I tell him to put his life on hold with careless disregard for what he might be doing at that moment," explained Jill.

"Did he complain to you about dropping everything and having to come to your rescue?" challenged Jo.

"Well. No," replied Jill.

"Was he mad that you had gone and got yourself in a dangerous situation for the third time this year?" Jo continued to challenge Jill's line of thinking.

"No he wasn't mad and now I'm feeling like a fool. You're correct he's a big boy who can make his own decisions. I think I better call him and apologize," said a chagrined Jill.

"I think perhaps you need to not worry or apologize about putting any of us in danger. We're here because we love you and enjoy the work you throw our way; you help pad our vacation accounts and it allows us to share in the adventure. We're all adults in this venture and we can opt out at any time. In my day job I just don't get attacked by snowmobiles and so at the moment it is a refreshing change," observed Jo.

Jill walked over to hug Jo. Jo was right; this is what they had all signed on for, Nathan included. After a fabulous hug from her friend she entered her bedroom to call Nathan. She hoped he would take her call.

"Hello," said Nathan and then added as he squinted at her on Face Time, "You look rather strange. What is wrong with your appearance?"

"Oh, sorry I forgot I was wearing a disguise. Just ignore my looks as I called to apologize."

"Depends on what the apology is for."

"For not trusting you to manage your own life."

"Huh?"

"I was trying to make decisions for you. By banning you from coming I could control your safety."

"True."

"Jo reminded me you were an adult capable of making your own decisions and I should stop trying to make them for you."

"Next time I see Jo, I'll have to give her a hug as I agree with what she says."

"You're not making this easy."

"True. However I was really upset that you were trying to make decisions for me. I know that some of these investigations result in you being in danger and I accept your occupation. I'm proud that you're able to bring justice to families that might not otherwise get it. But I also want to help and maybe the only way I can help is by trying to provide protection for you."

"You don't understand how bad I feel when I pull you away from your world of wine label design. I feel bad that your life is at risk, I feel bad that I'm taking you away from design and you're so brilliant at that. The guilt is killing me."

"You forget my martial arts background. And I don't mean my black belt in hapkido. I have trained for two decades to be a warrior in hapkido, and protecting you allows that warrior to exploit everything I've trained for. So while you feel terrible when I am dragged into dangerous situations, I actually feel fulfilled and master of the universe."

"Really? Master of the universe huh? Well okay. Umm, there is room for you in our hotel suite if you have a desire to take on snowmobiles and other dangerous winter activities."

"That was the lamest invitation to join an exciting murder investigation that I've ever received. Despite its lameness, as soon as I make arrangements for Trixie and Arthur, I'll head your way. Perhaps I can catch the shuttle with Angela."

"You just want to socialize with all my friends. I don't think this has anything to do with being master of the universe master black belt hapkido champion."

"I do love your friends. Besides I need to add some testosterone balance for Nick against all you women."

"Do you at least have some wineries to visit while you're in the great state of Colorado?"

"I do have clients in Colorado. However many of the wineries are closed now; some close when snow hits the ground as tourists are no longer thinking of visiting wineries. So you will have my full and undivided attention."

"Let me know your travel plans when they are finalized. Love you."

"Love you back and see you soon."

After ending the call, Jill sat for a few moments thinking about Nathan's desire to be the hapkido warrior of the world. Then she stood up to head to the living room shaking her head. She still didn't understand the male psyche.

Nick looked up as she entered the living room and motioned her over to his computer.

"Hey Jill take a look at these pictures from the ski resort and from this hotel's lobby."

Nick pointed to four pictures. "These are the three ticket booth purchases of one of the two people that spent a lot of time near Joseph. The fourth picture is of our lobby as we walked to lunch earlier today."

"Wow, looks to me as though it is the same person. In the hotel lobby, you get a better look at his face without the helmet and goggles blocking your view. That is a very distinguishing scar on his lower cheek. It's very helpful to us for future identification. Did you look for the scar on the faces of the Hummer driver or passenger?"

"Good idea, let's look at your phone."

Jill returned to the bedroom to grab her phone, pulling up Nick's picture of the Hummer from this afternoon. Between the glare of the sun and the tint of the windows, the picture was too fuzzy to be able to tell much about the driver and passenger.

"I don't think this picture is of any help," Jill said handing the phone over to Nick.

"You're right. Oh well. At least we have the guy on two of three locations. I'm emailing the picture to one of Henrik's engineers to see if their facial recognition software will identify the man. It's coming up on five in the morning in Germany so we'll probably have to wait a few hours for an answer."

"As soon as you get an answer back, forward it to me even if it is the middle of the night. I would like to start my search of this person as soon as possible."

"Will do," replied Nick as he stood up and stretched. He was also from that same time zone as Germany and his body clock was confused. With only one night in America, he was more on a European time zone than Colorado. He was crashing hard and fast and couldn't concentrate on the camera video. "Sorry to be a party pooper, but I am too tired to watch the video footage at this time, so I am heading to bed."

"Nick, we know what jet lag is like. Go and rest, we'll see you in the morning. I am sure the altitude is not helping your acclimation to this part of the world," affirmed Marie.

"Goodnight all," and he heard their echoed replies as he left the room.

"So is Nathan arriving tomorrow?" asked Jo.

"Yes, he thinks you're a very wise friend and he owes you a hug. Apparently protecting me satisfies his ninja warrior master black belt hapkido king of the universe urges."

"Wow, all of that! Far be it for a mere girlfriend to stand in the way of a guy wanting to be a ninja warrior master of the universe and those other titles you bestowed on him," suggested Jo.

"I think I must have missed an earlier conversation," declared Marie. "I'm sensing that Nathan wants to be master of the universe? That doesn't really sound like him."

"Nathan and I had our worse disagreement earlier and Jo helped me see the light. I called to apologize to Nathan and he admitted that providing me protection during our dangerous cases makes him feel like a master black belt Hapkido warrior. Who am I to stand in the way of such fulfillment?"

"Ok, now I get the picture. Did you really try to block him from being your protector? That should have resulted in a colossal fight, but now you saw his view and he is arriving tomorrow," voicing the steps Jill had gone through. "Such drama going on under my nose and I missed it all! Darn you're never a source of relationship drama, I'm sorry I wasn't there to help and I'm glad you have found peace again with Nathan. I really like him."

"Not to throw a wet blanket on your enjoyment of my idiocy, but have you guys found anything new on this case?"

"It has been a real eventful day between traveling here and our encounter with the snowmobile. I've not had the best concentration, but I found a thread that I am teasing out on Rocky Mountain Clinical Trials or RMCT as it says on the company logo," explained Jo.

"RMCT?" questioned Jill.

"Yeah, it is really too many words to say repeatedly."

"I like that nomenclature; I'm going to add that to the murder board," approved Jill. "What is the thread you're chasing with RMCT?"

"I don't know yet, it is just a feeling at the moment. I'll sleep on what I have learned today and start fresh in the morning."

"Sounds like a plan. Thank you my friends for cheerfully supporting my consulting business, and for putting your lives on the line for a client you have never met. Can I just say thank-you for being here?"

"Of course you can say thank you but it isn't necessary," said Jo supportively. "So far we have had an acceptable level of risk. I feel in danger but not like I was lucky to escape with my life. So life around you is scary and exciting and very tolerable. If I get hit with a bullet that might be my line in the sand and I might refuse to help you on-site, but I would still work for you behind the scenes."

Jill walked over to her friends for a group hug; she was lucky to have such wonderful friends. They said their goodnights and settled in for the night.

CHAPTER 9

*A*fter breakfast and well fueled with coffee they got to work on their searches. Given Jo's itchiness over RMCT she wanted to start her FDA search with RMCT rather than Broomfield Pharmaceuticals. Angela and Nathan were due to arrive in the late morning. The rental car company was delayed getting Jill a new car so she would miss Joseph's funeral. She sent David an update but indicated that he should focus on Joseph and himself today and ignore Jill's existence.

She had a moment's thought about what to do for meals.

"Hey what do you all want to do for meals? It seems that leaving the hotel results in the snowmobile from hell chasing us." Jill speculated. "I bet I could have the concierge deliver groceries to us and since Nathan loves to cook, he could be our chef but then I would think we would all eventually go crazy not getting out of this very nice suite."

"How about if we eat dinner in if Nathan is willing to cook, but we go out for lunch," suggested Marie. "I don't think these guys will be so bold during the daylight. Besides we're talking a few days before we all go our separate ways. This is not like the twelve days in Belgium."

"Yeah you're right about us going our separate ways. I agree with Marie," said Jo.

"I like to cook so I can help Nathan too," Marie volunteered.

"Great sounds like a plan. Oh my gosh! I forgot the most important thing. Nick, did Henrik's engineer identify the guy with the scar?"

"I've been checking my email every few minutes and nothing so far."

"That delay is kind of weird," stated Marie. "I remember when Henrik demoed the software while we were at his house and it seemed like it took less than ten minutes. Are you sure the guy has opened your email?"

""Let me check on that. I spoke with the engineer before we left Germany, so he should have been expecting my email. Let me call him."

They soon heard Nick speaking German and the women listened with envy at Nick's ability to speak several languages. Shortly he ended the call.

"My email got sent to his spam folder. He pulled up the picture and thought he would have an answer for me in less than half an hour. He was concerned with the scar. It could be the identifying feature or it might throw off the facial recognition software."

"Did the resort ever get back to us on whether they wanted Henrik's help with determining the source of the lift failure?"

"Sorry I forgot to mention it to you, but I received an email from Tom last night. The resort's lawyers drafted a privacy document for Henrik to sign which I forwarded to him and he signed and his engineer was supposed to access the resort's lift system this morning."

"Henrik has been a real help, I don't know what we would have done without him to figure out some of these technology questions. At the very least he has solved them faster and I am not at all sure we would resolve them without his help. Do you have a number I can reach him at? I would really like to thank him for his efforts and for bringing you here on his jet."

"Henrik feels that he is in your debt for solving his wife's murder. He'll likely want to help you the rest of his life."

"All the more reason for me to personally thank him."

After Nick supplied Jill with Henrik's number, she called him to thank him and ended up telling him about the case and everyone staying at the suite. When he heard that the entire gang was there he thought about flying his jet into Vail to join them for dinner one night. He would have to see what he could arrange. It would be good for his soul to spend some time around these people.

With Marie, Jill, and Jo concentrating on RMCT, Nick was going bleary eyed looking at camera footage. He was both looking for the scar faced man and skiers wearing his type and coloring of clothing which was very common. Finally, the email he had been waiting for arrived from Henrik's engineer.

"Hey, Henrik's engineer came through. This guy is one of yours - he is an American on the FBI's most wanted list. There is a $200,000 reward for information leading directly to his arrest. Wow. His name is Jason Derek Brown wanted for the murder of an armored car guard a decade ago. He only got $56,000 from the guard before shooting him in the head five times. He is known to be a skier, dirt biker, is fluent in French, and he is armed. He is in his early forties, 5'10" tall, blond haired with green eyes. Here is the picture from the FBI."

"Wow is right. I think I will call Special Agent in Charge Ortiz in the San Francisco office of the FBI. Colorado is not her jurisdiction but she can slice through the bureaucracy for us and validate our research and contribution to a case like this. I'm going to give her a call."

Jill scrolled through her phone until she found the agent's number and dialed. Her call went to voicemail so Jill left a message and ended the call. She would give the agent an hour to return her call and after that, she would try her luck with the local office.

Then the suite got the call from the lobby desk that Angela and Nathan had arrived. For their own safety and not wanting to appear with them in public, Jill asked the lobby to give them room keys and send them up. Once they arrived, there were hugs all around; Angela and Nick happy to re-unite, Nathan wanting to thank Jo for knocking some sense into Jill. It was coming up on lunch and so the group planned to eat in town. Before they left the suite, Jill shared the picture of Mr. Brown with everyone. Then the group debated whether they should stay together or split up. In the end they decided to stay together as they would be harder to take on as a group of six.

The group set out planning to stop at whatever restaurant caught their attention. They spotted an Irish Pub down the street and decided to make their way there. Jill's phone rang; the caller ID said "unknown" which made her pause until she remembered that it might be Special Agent Ortiz returning her call. She waved the others into the restaurant as she said "hello."

"Dr. Quint, this is Special Agent Ortiz returning your call; your voicemail sounded intriguing. Can you talk right now?"

Jill looked around her considering her options. She wanted a private conversation with the agent, but looking around her she didn't see anywhere private to talk. She might need her computer to send a picture to the agent if she asked.

"I'm in a public place at the moment. Can you give me about ten minutes to get back to my hotel suite? I'll call you."

"That is fine; you can reach me on my cell. Talk to you soon," and the call ended.

Even though Jill had indicated the group should enter the pub, they chose to wait outside, not wanting to leave any of them alone for fear of what might occur. Jill, grateful for their thoughtfulness, said, "I'm going to walk back to the hotel to chat with the agent.

You all enjoy lunch. I'll take a look at the menu and you can bring me back something to eat."

Angela replied, "I walked into the restaurant to see if they had a private room we could use while we dine. It turns out that the local Rotary Club meets at the restaurant and they have a small back room that will comfortably seat us."

"Awesome, thanks for figuring that out," smiled Jill. "Let's go inside and I'm going to ask that the restaurant employees stay out of the room until our call is over. Then we can order lunch and toast your brilliance."

After they were settled, Jill put her phone on speaker and made the call to the agent. "Special Agent Ortiz, I changed our plan on my end. I found a private location to have this conversation. On my end, I have the members of my team, plus Nathan, and Nick Brouwer. Nick is a citizen of the Netherlands and he assisted us in our last big case two months ago in Europe. He is a former member of the Dutch police and operates his own hotel security company in that country."

"Thanks for the introductions. I don't have anyone on my end. Tell me the entire story of how you think you came in to contact with one of our ten most wanted criminals."

Ten minutes later Special Agent Ortiz had the synopsis of the case including their initial difficulty with local police, the encounters with the snowmobiles and Hummer, and what role each person was taking in the investigation. In great detail she examined how they had identified Jason Derek Brown. The agent indicated she had an excellent relationship with the Denver office and would assist in connecting Jill to them. The agent would call them back after she had a few conversations within her organization.

They settled in for lunch. Jill checked with Nathan on becoming the designated chef for the group. He agreed and started a list to hit the grocery store with after lunch. Meanwhile Nick received an email from Henrik that he had rearranged his evening and was flying into the Vail airport and would join them for dinner at seven that evening.

"Did you warn him of the danger here and our connection to Mr. Brown? He would be safer in Austin," suggested Jill.

"I'm not worried about Henrik; he can protect himself," stated Nick. "Besides he is just coming for dinner in the suite. He'll be fine."

Jill was even concerned with Nathan doing the grocery shopping by himself. "Look I'll take the rental car because it would be a lot to carry through the streets of Breck." He followed that with a look that said 'don't argue'.

Just after they settled their bill and were putting on their jackets to leave, Special Agent Ortiz called back.

"Jill, I had a conversation with the Denver field office. They are on their way to Breck to meet with you and look at your evidence. I informed them of you and your team's success with your cases here and in Europe. They are taking this sighting of Mr. Brown very seriously. When they reach the town, they'll phone you. The last thing they want to do is spook Mr. Brown. "

"Tell them to wear jeans and winter coats and I'll greet them like I have done with the other members of my team as they arrived in waves," suggested Jill. "If they show up in suits, we're screwed."

"I'll pass that on to them. If you need my help, don't hesitate to call and I've asked the Denver field office to keep me posted."

"Thanks Special Agent Ortiz, you have been a great help."

"You're welcome Dr. Quint. Good luck with this newest investigation. You seem to have this uncanny ability to land in a pile of crap, but with your help we have seen some really terrible people brought to justice. Good day."

The group began making its way toward the hotel keeping an eye out for anyone that looked like Mr. Brown, and fortunately they made it back to the hotel without incident. Nathan took Jill's car to the supermarket planning for several meals even though he wasn't sure how many people would be eating. He loved cooking and it was nice to help the investigation by keeping everyone's body and brain fueled. He kept an eye out for Mr. Brown, but didn't see anyone suspicious in the store. Just to be sure he took a bunch of pictures of people that Henrik could put through his facial recognition just in case there were any other most wanted criminals in the pasta aisle.

Returning to the suite, he was unloading his groceries when Jill got the call that two friends were in the lobby. They had taken Jill's advice and were entering the hotel suite like her other team mates had done. At the time she had suggested this approach, she had not realized how awkward it would be to hug two complete strangers as though they were best friends. Oh well, she would pay-it-forward on hugs.

"Hey guys! How was your flight? Thanks for coming on such short notice. The rest of the gang is already here and upstairs. We've all been looking forward to your arrival."

The two agents murmured appropriate replies as they crossed the lobby on their way to the elevator. Once inside the elevator Jill just smiled at the agents, but didn't say anything.

"Despite the warm welcome in the lobby, if you don't mind I'd like to see some ID," advised Jill just inside the suite door. She would have asked them earlier but she feared what was being taped by the cameras in the lobby, elevator, and hallway. They hadn't yet figured out how they were being followed.

"Hello Dr. Quint, I'm Jake Porter Special Agent in Charge of the Denver FBI office," said the agent introducing himself while holding out his identification. Jill studied the ID and nodded.

Jill looked over at the other agent as she said, "Dr. Quint, I'm agent Morgan McKinsey," holding out her ID for Jill to examine and she did.

"Thank you for coming and let me make introductions," and she proceeded to introduce everyone else in the room and the skills they brought to the investigation. Nathan was quietly pleased when she introduced him as chef and hapkido warrior. She also mentioned that Henrik was joining them for dinner that evening and the skills that his firm had brought to Jill's investigation.

The two agents were very impressed. When Jake received the call from Leticia Ortiz, he had a hard time believing the agent's story about Dr. Quint and her team. But he and Leticia had gone through the Academy together and though it had been two decades, he knew he needed to trust what she was saying. Now this was quickly shaping up to be potentially one of the more fascinating cases of his career.

"So why is the Special Agent in Charge of the Denver office taking the time out to travel to Breck and get involved in our murder investigation?" queried Jill.

"Special Agent Ortiz and I go back to the Academy. She specifically said I needed to drive up here and meet with you. So here we are. Agent McKinsey has some skills that may be helpful in this case. First I would like to see the means by which you have identified Jason Derek Brown, and then we can move on from there."

Nick gave a quick overview of why he had been looking at camera footage at the ski lifts, the ticket offices, and the hotel lobby. He explained Henrik's beta version of his facial recognition software and how that had identified Mr. Brown. Agent Porter was impressed with the technology and the work of Dr. Quint's team.

"I wasn't sure what to make of Special Agent Ortiz's call to me a few hours ago. Now I understand why she was so insistent that I personally get involved with this case. I am very impressed with the information that Nick just showed me. Dr. Quint, would you start at the beginning and tell me about this murder case? I want to understand how your murder investigation crosses paths with one of the FBI's most wanted criminals."

"Please call me Jill and if you don't mind let's all use first names so that we can keep up the appearance of being friends."

Jill spent the next few minutes standing at her temporary murder board taking them through the call from David Gomez, her role in the autopsy, what she found at the crime scene, the reaction of the local law enforcement, their initial investigation of Broomfield Pharmaceuticals and RMCT, and finally the events with the snowmobile and the Hummer.

"Wow. This is a complex situation and there are several roles for the FBI. I'm going to start with assigning a protection detail to David Gomez. He has not appeared to be a target so far, but as he is connected to you, Jill, and your team, I think he merits protection. I'm also going to bring in additional agents for your protection and for manpower. I have a cabin in this area that I can assign my agents to as a base for this operation. It seems that you've maxed out the bedrooms in the suite, so I'll make arrangements with the hotel for Morgan and me to stay on this floor."

"Jake, in case you don't remember from the introductions, I'm Jo and I'm the financial wizard of this group. I work for Jill on a part-time basis when she asks for my help. I'm scheduled to leave tomorrow for Leadville where my sister lives. I won't be able to assist on a full-time basis after midday tomorrow. She is coming to pick me up and I can't imagine that I will need your protection up in Leadville."

"Jake, I'm Marie, the background search guru and I intend to get some skiing in while I'm here, starting tomorrow; then I depart two days after that. Do you have an agent that skis?"

"Okay I'll work out both of your situations."

"We all need to get back to work. Jake, we will leave you alone to organize your resources. Marie, Jo and I are looking into Broomfield and RMCT. I'm going to try and find the connection between the two companies and Mr. Brown."

As there was no one to interview at this point, Angela was going to aid Nick in looking at all the camera images. He had the technology skills, but she had the edge on looking at images for certain features. As a photographer, it was her everyday skill.

"I'm a forensic accountant," remarked Morgan, "so I'll join you, Jo, in looking at the financial data. I may end up taking over from you if we don't have any answers by the time you leave tomorrow."

Soon the room was filled with quiet conversation as Nick and Angela were working on footage, Jo and Morgan talking finances, Jill and Marie trying to figure out the people involved in Broomfield and RMCT, Nathan in a corner working out another wine label design, and Jake organizing his resources.

Sometime later, Jill asked, "Jo, do you know if there is a record of who owns which shares of RMCT?"

"Yes, the company did an IPO about five years ago which made all of their stock ownership a matter of public record."

"I think I might have found the connection to Mr. Brown."

Jo, Morgan, Marie, Angela, Nick and even Jake, as he pulled his cell phone away from his ear, said "What!" all at the same time.

CHAPTER 10

*J*ill looked at them all with excitement. "I looked at pictures of the board members of RMCT on their website as a starting place to learn about them. One of those board members looks a lot like Mr. Brown, including the scar. He has a different name, John D. White, but it looks like him. Let's put this picture through the facial recognition software to see if there is a match."

Everyone was leaning over Jill's shoulders staring at her computer screen to get a glimpse of John D. White.

"Sure looks like him," said Nick looking at the clock and calculating. "It's the middle of the night in Germany, so unless the FBI has facial recognition software, we'll either have to await Henrik's arrival or wait a few more hours for the engineer to arrive at work."

"We do have that software," replied Jake, "not as sophisticated as your friend's, but for this purpose it should be sufficient. Jill, can you email the picture? We'll have our answer soon."

Jake called the FBI's Forensic Audio Video Image Analysis Unit Laboratory at Quantico to alert them to the incoming images. Jill was soon sending a copy of the RMCT's board members to Jake for forwarding to the lab in Virginia.

Twenty minutes later, Quantico verified that the picture of John White was a match for Jason Brown. Jo, with Morgan's help, had begun examining the company documents to gain an understanding of Mr. White's financial interest in RMCT and what this company had to do with Broomfield Pharmaceuticals. Jake was excited as he believed that sometime during this case he would have an opportunity to arrest Jason Brown. Not many Special Agents could list on their resume the arrest of someone on the agency's Most Wanted list.

"Jake, I know the FBI is excited to have a Most Wanted felon in their crosshairs, but I would like to point out the bigger picture of why my team and I are involved," Jill said, correctly sensing his emotions. "Namely the murder of Joseph Morton. I have the grieving partner of Mr. Morton who is expecting that my team will solve his murder. We know that your Mr. Brown is somehow involved in it. He may be the killer. However, there is something bigger going on here that I need time to tease out. I think your agents have the capacity to locate him within the hour and arrest him, game over. What if he is part of a corporation that is cheating in some way - false financial reports, false clinical data, hiding patient deaths? Wouldn't you rather get the whole crime picture that is in play here? In my experience, someone like Mr. Brown cannot operate alone. He is smart but there are potentially many pieces in motion here. At the very least, if he is responsible for Mr. Morton's death, that would ensure that he would go to prison for a very long time."

Jake had been fantasizing about the glory of arresting Jason Brown. He had felt the thrill of his imagination upon hearing the handcuffs clicking shut on Jason's wrists. He did not appreciate Jill slamming shut the door on that fantasy. Taking a deep breath, letting go of the handcuff fantasy, and thinking about her words, he realized she was right.

With a heavy sigh, he said, "You're right, but we also can't allow him to wander free. At this moment, he could board a commercial jet to Mexico. I have a duty to the armored truck guard's family to bring him to justice. I'll put a surveillance detail on him while we let this other case play out."

"Fair enough" replied Jill. "Jo, have you found any financial information on Mr. White as he is known to RMCT?"

"You mean in the last thirty minutes since you asked?" Jo's voice tinged with sarcasm. "Yes, as a matter of fact Morgan and I have new information to add to your murder board. Mr. White at the time of the robbery had a bachelor's degree in International Business, and he later went on to obtain an MBA. He is written up in business journals as a serial entrepreneur. His initial investment of $40,000 was parlayed into ten million when the company went IPO five years ago. He has since invested in five other start-ups in the Denver area, and is a guest lecturer on entrepreneurship for several business schools. He supports local charities designed to get kids out of low income neighborhoods and into running businesses."

"Of course none of those self-written biographies mention that he got his starter cash by shooting a guard in the head five times and stealing his cash. Now, he is a regular pillar of the community." There was no mistaking the anger and sarcasm in Jake's voice. "It makes me so mad that he's been sitting here under my nose acting like a saint."

"Well you're going to get him soon, so let's focus on an examination of the evidence so that we may eventually confirm that he is Joseph Morton's killer," Jill redirected. "Jo, what else do you have for us on John White and RMCT?"

"He joined the company in its early stages and directed their clinical trials and collaborations with other companies."

"That is odd as he has no clinical background that has been mentioned so far," said Jill. "What exactly have they been doing clinical trials on? What drugs does RMCT list as having done the research for?"

"They perform clinical trials on a variety of drugs. They 'assist drug developers in identifying surrogate markers to streamline FDA approval. This is in accordance with an FDA explicit authority to rely on the marker.' I was reading from an annual report," noted Jo. "I have no idea what I just said - this FDA language doesn't make sense to me."

"Hmmm, they rely on markers. What that means is the FDA will approve a drug that, for example, reduces the chance of a heart attack using a marker rather than empirical proof," explained Jill looking around the room and seeing the puzzled looks. "So a drug that reduces cholesterol serves as a 'marker' for reducing heart attacks. Rather than the drug company proving that their drug reduced heart attacks by following lots of people for many years, they can get promising drugs to market faster by proving something simpler like lower cholesterol or lower blood pressure. I say simple because you can do before and after measurements and see patient improvement with those numbers. However, heart attacks come from many sources, some having nothing to do with cholesterol. Some people have electrical malfunctions of the heart, so lowering cholesterol won't prevent their kind of heart attack. Does my explanation make sense?"

"Yeah that makes sense," replied Jo. "So RMCT designs and conducts clinical trials that get new drugs approved by appraising a drug for markers, then they go about proving that marker through their own trials. Why don't the drug manufacturers know this information themselves?"

"It may be related to the size of the company. If you're a small pharmaceutical house with say less than five drugs developed and approved by the FDA, you may decide to outsource the clinical trials leading to FDA approval. Broomfield may lack the in-house resources to get approvals quickly and efficiently. Remember there is always someone else out there trying to invent the same thing you are and if you are delayed getting to market you can lose your opportunity to both patent the drug and get regulatory approval. I would bet that this is not the only company that does this kind of testing." mused Jill. "Let's return to the terminology of Broomfield to review what they said about RMCT. I have this impression that the word collaboration was used by Broomfield. That suggests to me that this was more than simply outsourcing the service."

"I recall that same terminology, Jill. Give me a moment to look on the Internet so I can find that section again," replied Jo as she was clicking away at her keyboard.

Jill did not want to lose track of her thoughts about RMCT so she made a few notes on the temporary murder board. Then she looked over at Nick and Angela and asked, "Anything from your end?"

"With Angela's help, we have identified at least forty frames where our suspect was close to Mr. Morton."

"Forty frames wow! Is he doing anything more than stalking Joseph? Is he talking on a cell phone, playing with gear, etc.? Did he ever speak with Joseph?"

Nick smiled at Jill's usual staccato approach to questioning of anyone involved in one of her investigations and replied, "He seems to just be stalking Joseph and David. You really can't tell which man he is watching or following. What we really need is an automated way to look at hours of camera footage, but in the end if all it tells us is the guy followed these two around, I'm not sure there is much useful knowledge in that."

"Have we heard back on the chairlift stoppage?"

"Let me ask Tom if the resort has heard anything back from Henrik's engineer."

"Can you explain your question about the chairlift stoppage?" asked Jake.

"About the time of death for Joseph, the chairlift that served the ski trail he was found on was stopped for about sixteen minutes. That is an unusually long length of time for a chairlift to be stopped and the resort had not found the source of that failure. We connected the resort to Henrik and he thought his company could find the source of failure for them and he offered to do it free of charge as it might be connected to the murder case that I am involved in. So the resort gave access to Henrik's engineer this morning and we should've heard back if he was able to locate the source of the failure."

"Your German friend seems to have an odd collection of talents that could help you on this case," observed Jake. "I'm interested in making his acquaintance this evening."

"Henrik has technology that assists us in collecting evidence," affirmed Jill. "He also has a pretty amazing obstacle course protecting his house and a server farm that both the Belgian police and Interpol are using to train their men on. You might ask him about that tonight too."

"Speaking of Henrik, he is on his way here and I'll be in the kitchen preparing our dinner to be served in a little more than an hour's time unless that timeline doesn't work for you, Jill," announced Nathan.

"That sounds like the perfect plan and thanks for cooking," said Jill.

"Marie, anything new on your research?" asked Jill.

"I switched directions a couple of times as new information has emerged from someone else in this room. While you all were chatting about Mr. White, I decided to focus my research on him. There is a lot of material. He is on his second marriage and has two teenagers from his first marriage. He is an avid skier, golfer, trap shooter, hunter. He seems to have been on vacation in many exotic locales. He has beautiful homes and what seems like a good life. He is very active in making RMCT successful. He gets a fair amount of positive press in business journals and he uses that to market to other pharmaceutical companies regarding the clinical trial services it provides," remarked Marie as she paused looking up from her notes to see if anyone had questions.

"How are he and Joseph tied together in the business community? Have they spoken together at some pharmaceutical meetings; have they been seen together at charitable events; what is the word on the street about the two companies working together?" Jill quizzed.

"Good questions, Jill. I had just started following some of the same lines of questioning as you," explained Marie. "I'm not finished looking at all my sources just yet, but there seems to be little interaction so far between Joseph and Mr. White in the public business arena. That may just be a reflection, perhaps, that Joseph was more prone to interact with RMCT's CEO rather than with Mr. White. Does anyone else have an angle they would like me to explore on this?"

Jake had his own resources at the FBI who were concentrating on fleshing out the picture of their suspect's present life and he doubted that Marie would be better than his own staff so he stayed quiet.

Angela asked, "Can you send me any pictures of his known associates? I would like to see who else is on the ski slope that we should worry about. We're looking for a second person but we don't know what they look like. It would help to place them in these pictures and unless the second person is a hired hit man, there has to be a connection between Mr. White and our second person."

"Excellent suggestion, Angela, thanks. Jo, Morgan do you have any special requests of my research?" asked Marie.

"The highest paid corporate officers are listed on the tax returns," Jo pointed out. "I would look each of them up seeking a connection between any of the officers and Mr. White. I'll email you the list so you can start looking at these people."

"Another excellent suggestion, thanks. I think I have my work laid out for me for the next few hours."

"I almost forgot I took pictures of shoppers around me at the supermarket, just to see if they were related to this case. Angela and Nick, you can add them to your list of people to identify," said Nathan as he passed his phone to them.

"Yikes, I had no idea I was making you paranoid as well!" exclaimed Jill.

"Just trying to contribute to your case," Nathan revealed.

Once again the room was quiet as everyone doubled down on their research. Jake was standing at the far corner of the room talking to his staff, looking out the window at the sunset on the mountain tops. He had worked with private investigators in the past, but none as impressive as Jill and her team. Listening to them discuss their line of reasoning, he had liked what he heard and added some tasks for his own team to do.

An hour later found Nathan opening the door to Henrik. After a brief hug and murmured words of friendship, Henrik stepped into the room reacquainting himself with the people that had solved his wife's murder. He also met two new people representing the world-famous FBI. As a security software CEO, Henrik was in his element as Jill and her team explained the angles they were pursuing to solve Joseph's murder.

"Jill, I can lend you more assistance. I brought my laptop with me that contains the beta version of my facial recognition software. No offense Angela and Nick, but I can replace the two of you and get answers in about three minutes per face. I also checked in with my engineer on my way here to find out if he had been able to locate the issue with the ski lift."

"And? Don't keep us in suspense!" exclaimed Marie.

"I can tell I am a real popular person at this dinner party," pronounced Henrik. "You should see your faces – you're all glaring at me with impatience."

"Henrik, you're just getting a dose of the ugly American," Jill laughed. "I'm happy you're here, and it's good seeing you again. But it's time to come clean and spill the beans -what happened to the chairlift?"

"Okay. The chairlift computer system was hacked and that was what caused it to shut down for sixteen minutes. The suspect in this case has deep computer skills as the resort's own IT department could not find the trace of his or her hacking. My engineer was able to determine by going back two weeks before your victim's death where he could see a tiny section of code that told the computer to stop a specific chairlift when a certain signal was sent and to restart the lift when a second signal was given and then like an Instagram picture the two coding change orders were to disappear into cyberspace after they were activated. So anyone looking at the chairlift at the date and time of the event saw nothing out of place, but by going back to the original time that the code was written he could see the code that would cause the lift to fail."

"Henrik, you and your engineer are brilliant," pronounced Jill. "What was the resort's response to your finding?"

"Considering that my engineer offered to share computer code at no cost to the resort that would prevent it from ever happening again, well let's just say I was offered a lifetime ski pass to the resort."

"Marie, have you discovered anyone in the searches that you are doing that might have these extremely sophisticated computer programming skills?" Jill queried. "This would have to be someone with extraordinary ability with the computer."

"Give me a few moments to sort through my suspect list and see if anyone is rumored to have these fabulous computer skills."

"Just a friendly warning to all of you, we will be sitting down to eat in about ten minutes. I have a red and white wine that pair nicely with the meal." Nathan made the pronouncement with a look that said don't mess with the chef. He got enough nods to know that his wishes would be complied with.

"I could use a break about now," declared Jo. "I'd like a glass of the white wine, Morgan what is your preference?" Jo was making sure that the room understood that she was on break and everyone else may as well join her for a brief happy hour.

"Why don't we all take a break and enjoy Nathan's fine wine choices and the company of friends," said Angela in earnest.

With her comment, the entire room folded. They parked their hunt for Joseph's killer and crowded around the wine bottles. Soon, everyone, with a wine glass in hand, ventured into the kitchen, curious to see what Nathan had prepared - it certainly smelled delicious! For the next hour, everyone enjoyed the sumptuous meal placed before them. Beginning with bacon-wrapped water chestnuts and mozzarella and basil topped tomatoes. This was followed by almond-encrusted sea bass, grilled asparagus and garlic-mashed potatoes. For dessert, there were three choices: a hot fudge sundae, crème brûlée, or fresh fruit in a yogurt liqueur.

Thanks to the excellent food and wine everyone enjoyed the genial atmosphere. Jill asked Henrik to describe his obstacle course for Jake and Morgan. They were soon laughing at how Henrik's course had allowed the capture of the serial killer covered in green slime. Jake was even more impressed with Jill and her team as he saw a strong instinct to solve the case and bring justice for David Gomez, deep friendships, and new acquaintances like Nick and Henrik that brought additional depth to Jill's problem-solving abilities. He would have to contemplate about how he assembled his team and what he could do to make them individually function at the highest level as Jill had done with her team.

The very enjoyable meal and camaraderie was soon over. Henrik needed to head back to the airport to return to Austin. He told Jill that he would return at the end of this conference and see if he could help her solve the case, if she hadn't already solved it. With many hugs he left the suite and their lives for the time being.

Jill came back into the living room clapping her hands like a teacher and urging everybody back to work. With a few groans at the end of the wonderful meal, everyone dispersed to their seats somewhat re-energized to do more information gathering.

Henrik had trusted Nick with his laptop and facial recognition software. When the software was out of the beta version, he wanted to be able to sell it to agents like Jake Porter. From a marketing perspective, if he got his product in front of a very important client, then it would generate future sales. It had been worth diverting his plane to Denver in order to get his software in front of the FBI. Of course at the time he made the decision to give Nick a ride, he had not known that the FBI was involved in Jill's case.

A few faces had been matched while they were eating dinner. Of the many frames they examined of people near Joseph either at the lift or on the trail, they had not found an identity for the second person that was near Joseph for most of the week. Henrik's software had also picked up a face in the supermarket near Nathan that matched a face on the ski slope near Joseph. Jake was impressed with the nimbleness and speed of Henrik's software. The software was working out the identity of the shopper/skier. Maybe this would give them the identity of the second person involved in Joseph's death. A few minutes later they had a name for the face -Bjorn Daniel Sundin.

"Hey Jake, looks like we have another one of your Yanks," revealed Nick.

"Who?" asked Jake walking over to where Nick was gazing at the laptop left by Henrik.

"Bjorn Daniel Sundin, on the FBI's Most Wanted Cybercrimes list," replied Nick. "Perhaps your office should regularly obtain footage of skiers and match faces to your Most Wanted list. What are the odds of having two of these prestigious criminals in our current case?"

"Ha ha," Jake said as he studied Nick's monitor. "It would be great to bag two of these guys off of our Most Wanted list. So we have footage of these two in the vicinity of each other, but otherwise we have no connection so far. By the way, guys, would you all like jobs with the FBI when this case is over? Your investigative work is some of the finest I have ever seen in my career."

"Thanks, but no thanks, on the job offer," replied Marie. "Remember this is a part-time job for all of us. We all have other full-time jobs, and we work on these cases because we like Jill, we earn vacation funding, and we do like bringing justice to our small part of the world. Besides, we really like our day jobs."

Jake made a note to himself to call Leticia Ortiz when he had a quiet moment to thank her for connecting him to Dr. Quint and her team. He was going to arrest some bad people and he was learning from her team's thought processes on some potential different avenues to approach future investigative work.

"If you'll e-mail me the images you have of Mr. Sundin, I'll get those to my team and set up the same surveillance on him that we have in place on Mr. Brown."

"If he is good at computer crimes, I would be very careful with electronic communication concerning him as he may have some piece of code out there in cyberspace that alerts him whenever his name is mentioned electronically," said Nick. "Certainly if I had the computer skills and wanted to evade the FBI that is what I would do."

"Good piece of advice Nick, thank you. I am not an expert in the world of computers or the Internet. I need to get his picture to my people, but I'll give them a call and rename this gentleman and put all communications under his new pseudonym."

Angela looked up and advised, "Why don't you call him Mr. Green? Since our other potential murderer goes by the last names of white and brown, why don't we stay in the color scheme? In fact if you're interested in a name for this operation for the FBI, you could call it 'operation rainbow' or 'operation Crayola' reflecting the names of the suspects in this case."

"Gee whiz, I offer you a job with the FBI, and now you're taking over my operation," remarked Jake.

"Just trying to be helpful! In the past, the FBI has kept Jill alive. Now your agency is providing us protection. The least I can do is help you name this operation."

"Okay, guys, back to the investigation," said Jill impatiently. "Jo and Morgan, would you do financial research on Mr. Sundin and Marie, would you look into any aliases that he has? If you find any, pass the names over to Jo and Morgan. Nick, will you connect with Henrik to see if his engineer can determine if Mr. Sundin was the source of the chairlift computer failure? I'm going to update my murder board with this new information and then I'll be working on a connection between these two. Jake, in case you haven't noticed that while we declined your job offer we all still feel free to advise you on how to manage your side of the investigation. So in keeping with our past behavior, I would advise that you assign your people also look for this connection between Brown and Sundin. I think it's really critical that we figure it out."

Jake sighed, gave Jill a pained look, and pulled out his cell phone to make another call to his team. He had arrived at the same conclusion that Jill had; she just jumped the gun before he had the opportunity to contact his people. Still, he couldn't complain; they were an efficient and proficient investigative team.

Soon silence reigned in the room as everyone pursued their own avenue of the investigation. Around nine o'clock Jo had had enough and called a halt. "I need some fresh air and a walk before I head to bed. Anyone else want to join me?"

After a chorus of "yes", it was decided that Morgan would join the group of six as they headed out. Jake planned to stay behind. With Nick and Nathan's martial arts skills, and Morgan's ankle gun and purse knife, they were better protected than one would suspect. After exiting the hotel lobby, they walked down the main thoroughfare. Both pedestrian and car traffic was light given the time of the evening and the beginning of the ski season. They entered a bar that offered two bar tables that they could stand around and chat. After all the sitting they had done that day working on the computers, the walk was welcome as was standing. Morgan had positioned herself so that she was looking right at the door. Nick and Nathan had positioned themselves to be looking at a back door and the door to the kitchen. With all entrances covered, they felt safe within the bar.

"You know, Jill, you warned us about the altitude, but you have to experience it to understand its impact," Marie disclosed. "I can't believe how breathless I become walking fast down the street. You know me, I readily run several 5K races a year, but my lungs still notice the thinner air here."

"Yeah thanks, Jill, for pouring water down my throat for the past twenty-four hours. I have had no headaches so far," noted Jo. "Usually when I visit my sister, I'm miserable the whole time I'm there. Since I don't stay for long, I never have the chance to acclimate. It will be interesting tomorrow if the headache comes on once we've reached Leadville."

"We're going to miss you when you leave tomorrow, and not just for the work you've done on this case. You have offered me some very sage advice," said Jill.

"Yeah Jo, I want to thank you for offering Jill that sage advice," agreed Nathan. "Especially since I've been the one to most benefit from it."

"That's my other part-time job. I'm confidante to my friends and I dispense advice when asked."

All of a sudden they noticed that Morgan had tensed. Jo, who was standing next to her, followed her glance to the door.

"Looks like trouble, and don't turn around and stare," whispered Morgan. "If I'm not mistaken, the guy on the right is our Mr. Brown. I would like Mr. Brown to remain oblivious that we are on to him." He was growing a beard which was different from the pictures on the ski slope and at the ticket booth, but the scar still gave him away.

Jill decided to perform her favorite acting job; she turned around and faked a sneeze. Anyone that knew about sneezes would recognize it as a fake because Jill's eyes were wide open during the sneeze, something that was impossible to do during a real sneeze. She got a good look at Mr. Brown and his companion, before turning back and engaging with the group.

"I agree with Morgan, it's Mr. Brown. We really need a picture of the two of them. Angela, how about if you try to take Nathan's and my picture, but you enlarge the frame to capture the two guys behind us - it will be all about getting a clear picture of those two with Nathan and I just an excuse to shoot in their direction. You could also take Marie and Jo's picture doing the same thing and it will be a better decoy if everyone's picture at the table is taken."

"Sounds like an excellent plan," said Angela. "I knew there was a reason for me to travel to Colorado! Better still, my camera has a panoramic setting on it so I'll be sure to capture them a few times."

Angela spent the next few minutes lining everyone up and shooting their pictures. She could check her camera's viewfinder so she knew she had several shots of the two men.

Jill asked Morgan while Angela was shooting pictures, "Where is the FBI surveillance crew for this guy?"

"Good question, I thought Jake had them in place. Let me text him and find out."

A few minutes later she had her answer. Mr. Brown was not at any of his usual spots so the surveillance team had been unable to track him. "They are on their way to this bar and Jake wants us to engage the guys if they try to leave."

"Engage them? Engage with an FBI Most Wanted killer?" asked Jill.

Angela suggested, "How about if I walk over to them and ask them to take a group shot of us?"

"Do you have another camera they can use? Those are the only pictures we have of the guys. If they take off or damage the camera, we'll have nothing," challenged Jill.

"I'll use my cell phone and tell them we want to upload to Facebook."

"Sounds like a plan, go for it," approved Jill.

Morgan could not believe the nerve of these women. To walk over to someone and hand them your cell phone when you know that they shot someone five times in the head was a pretty ballsy move.

Angela walked over and with a friendly smile and holding out her cellphone to Mr. Brown asked, "Excuse me, but would you take a group picture of the seven of us? We are hardly ever all in the same place at the same time. We need to memorialize it with a picture."

Angela did a silent cheer when Mr. Brown grabbed the phone ready to take a group shot. They all had big grins for the picture because they were so pleased with Angela's ploy to ensure that the men stayed in the bar. Soon the picture was taken and Angela walked back to the men pulling on her gloves as she walked.

"Thanks for your help, we appreciate the picture," Angela said to the two men as she received her phone back. Then looking them in the eye, she held up one of the gloved hands and said, "Burr it's cold in here."

Walking back to her table, she stopped next to Morgan and whispered "do you have an evidence bag?"

"What do you need one for?"

"I got his fingerprints on the phone and I'm trying very hard not to smudge them," said a smug Angela.

"OMG! Why didn't I think of that? No I don't have a bag in my possession at the moment. Let me think what I could use instead."

"No worries, I already have a solution." Angela pointed to the popcorn machine in the corner. She walked over to the machine and started to fill a bag with the freshly popped popcorn. She held an empty bag in her other palm when she brought the popcorn bag back to the table. Making sure her body was blocking any view by the two men, she slipped her cell phone into the empty popcorn bag hoping that she had just preserved the fingerprints.

"Wow, that was excellent detective work! If there was such a thing I would make sure you received the FBI's citizen's award for crime stopping."

"Just doing my job as a citizen, so I would have passed on your imaginary award," Angela disclosed.

"Okay now what do we do?" Lamented Jo. "I need to pee after all this alcohol and water, and I'm ready to return to the hotel to sleep. Is your surveillance team in place? Can we leave now?"

"Let me text Jake to find out."

"Okay, I am going to use the restroom here while you get an answer," said Jo.

A few moments later, she said yes the team was in place and they could leave. Once Jo returned from the bathroom, everyone began putting on their coats and making the motions of putting on hats, and mittens and they headed for the door. Exiting the bar, they began their walk up the street. It was about a nine or ten block walk to their hotel. They had another two blocks to go when they looked back to see a giant snowplow heading their way. The city often cleaned the streets at night after the tourist traffic ended, but there was no recent snow and nothing around them needing plowing services.

They started moving faster, discussing their options.

"How about if we run back to the hotel," suggested Marie.

"A plow can have a speed of up to twenty miles per hour, so we can't out run it," replied Nathan.

"Is there another building we can duck into?" asked Jo.

"No, just pretty much open field these last two blocks," replied Jill. "We could backtrack and duck into a doorway but we risk being crushed by the bucket on the plow."

"How about your surveillance team? Can they come to our rescue?" asked Nick.

"They must not realize what is going on and I don't have time to text Jake."

Jill had visited Breck so often that she had the town memorized, "There is a bridge up ahead. We can all run down the slope at the beginning of the bridge and huddle underneath it, even if the plow follows us off road and down the slope, the plow won't fit underneath the bridge. Follow me."

Jill had to shout those last words as the plow was getting much closer and louder. She took off on a run and stepped over the railing, and then headed downhill to the underpass. It fit the seven of them quite well. Everyone was breathing fast and their feet were a little wet and cold, but otherwise they were safe. They heard the snow plow continuing overhead. The plow driver had to have seen them take the off-road path. They waited and the plow just seemed to be idling at the other side of the bridge.

"The driver could have run off or he may be coming underneath for us," advised Morgan her Glock in hand. They listened for movement but couldn't hear anything over the idling plow. "I'm going to text Jake and see where the surveillance team is."

Angela was doing a slow motion stomping dance trying to get the blood to her feet. She had ankle high boots on, but had stepped in some kind of wetness, probably soft snow and now her feet were freezing. Nick motioned her over to a concrete wall ledge that was a part of the overpass. She hopped up and he took off one shoe, then the other and took her frozen feet in his warm hands. She almost moaned with the heat finally reaching her feet.

"Jake texted back he is on his way here," Morgan notified the group. "The snowplow driver was indeed our Mr. Brown and the surveillance team notified Jake that he left the plow, engine running at the far side of the bridge. As they were behind him, they had no idea that we were in danger. He has left the area presently."

"My feet are frozen, although not nearly as frozen as they were before, thanks to Nick! Still, I can't wait to get back to the hotel to submerse them in hot water," said Angela, as she replaced her wet sock and boot.

They all hiked up the embankment to the road where they could see Jake coming toward them.

Nick said to the group, "I'm going to get Angela home so she can get her feet warmed up. The rest of you can fill in the story for Jake," and he hustled Angela toward the hotel. She yelled over her shoulder, "Don't forget to tell him about the pictures I took!"

Jake arrived at the group and said "tell me what happened."

"Look some of us have frozen wet feet," said Jill shivering. "Let's detail what happened on this road and then let's quickly head for the hotel and we'll tell you the rest of the story."

Jake looked around the group and saw that three of the four women were shivering. Probably a combination of cold feet, adrenaline rush, and just the cold night air.

"We left the bar where Mr. Brown entered to watch us. It's about a nine or ten block walk with the final two to three blocks just open space. The snow plow came from there," said Marie pointing to where they had first noticed it. "It clearly was aiming for us. Nathan informed us the top speed of the plow was twenty miles per hour so we knew we couldn't outrun it. Fortunately, Jill knows this town really well and she knew if we went down that embankment and stood in this bridge's underpass that the plow couldn't reach us so that is exactly what we did. The plow missed turning us into asphalt by about twenty yards. The plow continued cross the bridge and then he deserted it there. Now I am too cold to stand here anymore, see you back at the hotel."

Just like that the three women and Nathan left Jake and a shivering Morgan standing there on the bridge. Jake knew when he was beat. Looking over at Morgan he said "You're shivering; let's hustle back to the hotel." He peppered her with questions on the return and he had to agree with their decision making in the bar and to avoid the snowplows. At least she had her gun ready if someone had chased them under the bridge.

Fifteen minutes later the women had changed clothes, warmed up their feet, and were sipping tea. Angela had connected her camera to her laptop, and now they were all standing around her looking at the pictures of the two men. Nick was sitting next to her on a sofa holding Henrik's laptop containing the facial recognition software. She had emailed the picture to him and now they were quietly awaiting an identification of that second man. There was silence in the room as everyone watched Nick's computer icon spinning as it searched.

"How long does this take?" said Jake impatiently.

Giving him a cool look over his shoulder, Nick said "three to five minutes. It's been forty-five seconds so far." There was a tinge in Nick's voice that said 'you idiot, do you know how lucky you are to have access to this software?'

Jill, who had huge faith in Henrik's technology, looked over at Jake, and said, "Chill".

After a few more minutes a match was found. They looked into the face of Evgeniy Bogachev. Additional photos with the man were offered for them to view. Nick brought up the additional photos and they all agreed that he was the man that had accompanied Mr. Brown into the bar.

"Who is he?" asked Jo.

"It seems that in addition to Mr. Sundin, we have a second cyber-criminal involved in this case," Nick read. "He is a Russian who has been indicted as the website administrator behind Gameover and Zeus."

"What are Gameover and Zeus?" asked Marie. "They sound like illegal drugs."

"Well no. They are actually cyber-crime software programs that send unsuspecting emails to victims," explained Jake. "Once those victims click on a link they go to a website that installs malware on the victim's computer stealing bank codes and passwords. These two software programs are credited with bilking hundreds of millions of dollars from bank accounts."

"I'm going to get this creep's name to Henrik's engineer who is searching for the source of the chairlift failure," said Nick.

"Jake, did your men say who was driving the plow?" asked Jill. "Did both men get in it to start it up?"

"They said both men got in the plow. Why?"

"Good then you have them both for attempted murder."

"I was so cold I couldn't think. I forgot to give you my cell phone. Let me go get it," said Angela hopping off the couch.

"We all forgot about Angela's phone! Whoops," exclaimed Marie.

Angela returned to the living room, cell phone in a paper bag held by the tips of her fingers. "Jake, I got Mr. Brown's finger-prints on the cell phone. I think that's just another piece of evidence of his involvement in a series of crimes. Do you want the phone?"

"As you said, this will be one more piece of evidence to iden-tify Mr. White as Mr. Brown. No one has told me the story of what happened inside the bar. You also failed to mention that you collected fingerprints. How'd you do it?"

"It was a flash of brilliance on Angela's part," Jill replied. "We wanted to preserve the pictures that we had in her camera. She walked over to him and asked if he would take a photograph of us so she could upload it immediately to Facebook and he agreed. So he reached for the phone and then held it securely between his fingers as he took the shot."

"You guys are really quite fearless and you're starting to scare me," observed Jake shaking his head. "You walked up to a man that you know is wanted for murder, handed him this phone and asked him to take a picture of you all with the express purpose of getting his fingerprints."

"Hey, you wanted us to stall him there while your team got in place. We were in a public area; it wasn't like he was going to get mad and shoot me with everyone else in the bar."

"No, instead, he tried to flatten you with the snow plow."

"I think he would have tried that anyways," Angela declared. "Especially since he has already tried to kill some of us in this room."

"Touché," said Jake finally giving up on getting the civilians to worry about their own safety.

"Guys, I am tired and I am going to head to bed," Marie announced. "Tomorrow I want to spend some time skiing. Since I'm an early riser, I'll put in several hours of research before the lifts open. If I have reception on the mountain, I'll do some more research with my smart phone on any breaks that I take, and then I'll get a few more hours of research tomorrow night. Night everyone."

There was a chorus of 'good nights'.

Jo decided to follow Marie's direction and also headed for her bedroom.

Angela and Nick decided they wanted to share a glass of wine outside on the hotel's balcony. After a little fresh air and some time alone, they might return to look at video clips or give it up and head for their bedrooms.

Jill was tired but she wanted to make a few notes of where she wanted her team to go next in the morning. Nathan, the night owl of the group proceeded to usher Jake and Morgan out of the suite with advice that they could return at six in the morning when some of the suite's occupants would be awake. In a matter of fifteen minutes, the suite's living room was cleared of occupants. Nathan debated joining Jill in bed, but he thought that she might already be asleep. He, on the other hand, was not sleepy in the least. He hadn't quite got over the adrenaline rush of trying to avoid the snow plow. He would put in a few hours of work and then head to bed. These adventures with Jill were getting more dangerous; he thought back to the time when an Albanian sniper had entered Jill's house in the middle of the night and he had dispatched the sniper with some hapkido kicks. So maybe these adventures weren't escalating in danger. Perhaps he just preferred to die from a single bullet over being crushed to death by a snow plow - it sounded much more painful. With that cheery thought he pulled out his sketchbook and began examining a wine label that was his current work in progress.

CHAPTER 11

*A*s usual Marie and Jill were the first ones awake in the suite. They had coffee and were nibbling on breakfast. A text arrived from Jake asking if she was awake yet. She sent him an affirmative response and went back to contemplating the murder board. Moments later, she heard a knock on the door.

Standing at the closed door she asked, "Who is it?" This hotel like many, had installed the peephole above the level of her eyes in her head rendering it worthless for security.

"Jake and Morgan."

"What was our main course last night?"

With a sigh, she heard Morgan respond, "Sea bass."

Jill opened the door, telling the agents the location of breakfast or coffee.

"I'm surprised you asked me those questions before opening the door."

"Why?"

"Because you seem rather reckless with your own security."

"If you're going to be snarky this early in the morning then you can return to your own suite and we will talk to each other via e-mail."

"In that case, I'll quit with the sarcasm till noon."

The three women were united in rolling their eyes. Jill was beginning to suspect that Jake was not a morning person. She would take it slow and easy until he pumped sufficient caffeine into his system.

"What happened with our suspects overnight?" Jill probed. "Did they try to plow down anyone else?"

"My surveillance team changes shift within the hour and I'll have the report shortly thereafter. Did the German engineer get back to us as to the possibility of Sundin or Bogachev being behind the ski lift breach? Tampering with a ski lift is an additional federal felony charge, so it is very critical to link these guys to the chairlift failure."

"Unfortunately he would be responding to Nick and he's still asleep. I'm sure he'll check his messages as soon as he awakens. I've been thinking about the case this morning, and I want to understand what these two computer nerds could do to assist a clinical trials company. I don't think that they were hired to take me out after Joseph was murdered. I just bet they're doing something illegal with RMCT's computers. Furthermore, I think Joseph was murdered because he discovered whatever they were doing and when he discreetly questioned RMCT, they discreetly killed him."

"That is a lot of speculation Jill," cautioned Jake.

"Yeah, but I sometimes have a sixth sense about these cases that saves us time if we focus on that avenue of investigation. So I'll direct my team to do so." What was left unsaid was that he could direct his agents to work on a different angle, but she was sure she was on the right path.

He shrugged and they both went back to their computers to follow separate paths.

Jill looked up as Nick entered the living room of the suite carrying his laptop and said "Good morning. Did you have a nice night's sleep?"

"Yeah I did. My body is still confused as to what time zone I am in, but once the adrenaline rush of escaping a snow plow was gone, I was more than ready to drop off to sleep. What's new this morning?"

"Did you get a response from the engineer as to the ski lift malfunction source?"

"I was just checking," Nick said as he was scrolling down his screen. "Yes here it is. I'll open and read it." He looked up at Jake and added, "The email is in German, so I'll have to translate for you."

A few seconds later they had their answer; Mr. Bogachev was likely the source of the shutdown. The engineer had chased the source of the code through half a dozen countries. However within Henrik's security firm they had extensively studied Gameover and Zeus and they had been successful at blocking its entry into their clients' computers. So the engineer recognized the style of Mr. Bogachev's coding. The engineer had an additional program that he ran the code of the ski lift failure through, and the software predicted a 98.7 percent chance that Mr. Bogachev was the coder.

"Can the engineer check to see if the code is still in the ski lift system and does it cover more lifts than just the one it stopped?" asked Jill.

"Why?" asked Jake who had been listening to the conversation.

"Because Marie is taking the lift today and I want her to stay safe and perhaps it suggests to us whether they have any other future murders lined up," Jill explained.

"You think they are that sophisticated?"

"Yes I do. The attack on the ski lift computer system was pure genius and I could see them doing it again. Besides the resort needs to fix their software, and get rid of this malware and maybe Henrik can help them out. I am not savvy enough about computers to know what else this bug could do."

"Jill, here is the answer back from the engineer. ' He said the malware is still on the resort's computers and it does affect all lifts.'"

"Jake, I think you had better have someone special guarding Marie this morning, especially since we know these guys can play with the lift."

"I do have someone special guarding her. One of my agents works the ski patrol at this resort on a part-time basis, so she will be in good hands. He will be armed, and he has brought a lightweight bullet proof vest and a special helmet for her to wear."

"This should be fun. I have never skied in Colorado and I'll have the perfect expert with me!" Marie exclaimed.

"You could stay home and be in a more protected environ-ment. My agent won't be able to control all of the people on the ski slope, or in the lift lines, or even in the restrooms of the resort."

"The guy probably won't recognize me underneath all my equipment. What is your agent's name and when does he arrive?"

"I asked him to be here half an hour before the lifts open to give you time to put the vest on and get up the mountain. His name is agent Michael York."

"Sounds perfect," Marie agreed. "Jill, I have another hour of work and I'll do some work up on the mountain as I am sure I'll need to take breaks. I was planning on focusing on Sundin and Bogachev. I haven't finished reviewing all my sources for Mr. Brown."

"You can work on Mr. Brown tonight. I think we'll be staying in for dinner and drinks."

"Yeah I am with you there. I did not enjoy being chased by a snowplow. It reminded me of that old movie 'Duel' where this semi-tanker- truck is sitting almost on the rear bumper of a driver of a 1960's car chasing it through a deserted and curvy road. Just like that movie, we couldn't see the face of the driver of the snowplow; we just knew he was coming for us."

"Yikes, now you're creeping me out. I remember that movie. It gave me a fear of big trucks for a while," agreed Jill.

"Nick, when you have time can you determine how someone is following us?" Jill asked. "Are they staying close to the hotel and simply following us from the hotel, or have they managed to plant a GPS tracker on us. Perhaps we would be able to tell by looking at the lobby camera film."

"Good morning everyone," said Angela entering the room. "Did you solve the case while I was asleep?"

"Yeah right, the evidence came to me in my dream and now the case is solved. Sorry, it wasn't that easy," said Jill.

"Oh well, I can always hope that the bad snowplow driver's conscience got to him and he called up the police to have himself arrested before I awoke."

"It's a little early in the morning for you to have consumed so much alcohol as to have thought up that fairy tale," Marie pointed out.

"Oh well. Are you going skiing today?" asked Angela.

"Yeah, Jake has lined up an agent who works part time as ski patrol and he is bringing both a bullet proof vest and helmet. Sounds like the perfect escort since I am unfamiliar with this mountain."

"Maybe you shouldn't go skiing. Are you sure you'll be safe?"

"I think so. While you were sleeping, we heard from Henrik's engineer that indeed Bogachev is responsible for the malware on the resort's lift computers."

"Computers as in plural?" asked Angela.

"Yes, this malware is still on the lift computers and it can affect all chairlifts."

"Well, I hope you have a boring day up on the slopes."

"Boring would be good. I have never skied such a high mountain and it's a little intimidating. Nice to know I will have the ski patrol so close by to rescue me."

"Jill, what would you like me to work on today?"

"I would like you to be on the call with David this morning. I'd like to see if anything strange was said at the funeral yesterday. From there, I would like to arrange interviews with the CEO of RMCT, and the acting CEO of Broomfield Pharmaceuticals. I'm sure that David can help us with that."

"If you arrange the interviews, I will send an agent with you for protection," ordered Jake.

"Okay."

"Good morning," said Jo blinking her eyes open. "How is everyone this morning?"

"Doing well," replied Jill. "Did you get a good night's sleep?"

"Given the terror of the evil snowplow last night, I slept surprisingly well."

"Awesome! What time is your sister picking you up?"

"Sometime just before noon. I'll get a little more work done for you before I leave and then Morgan will be your financial expert."

"How would you feel about Morgan going with you and your sister?" asked Jake. "Do you know if she has somewhere Morgan can sleep? A sofa is fine."

"You really think we could be in danger?" asked Jo. "It might be better for my sister to stay here in the suite. Let me give her a call and talk it over with her. What is everyone working on this morning?"

"Angela and I are about to get on the phone with David and Jake is planning on eavesdropping on our conversation. Then we are going to Denver to interview some people. Marie is doing more research on our two cyber creeps and then she's going to have an exciting day up on the mountain skiing with an FBI agent who also occasionally works for the ski patrol at this mountain. Nick is working on figuring out how we are being followed, and Nathan is still asleep but he will likely be working on his own business."

"Okay, once I wake up some more, and drink some coffee, I'll give my sister a call."

Jill moved to the other side of the suite to place a call to David leaving Jo to exchange pleasantries with Morgan.

"David, it's Jill. How are you doing today?"

"I'm exhausted. The funeral was so difficult yesterday and so many people said all kinds of wonderful things about Joseph that only made me miss him more. Watching his coffin being lowered into the ground was a very stark way to say 'it's over.'"

"It sounds like it was a rough day. What are your plans for the next couple of weeks?"

"It depends on what is going on with the investigation. I need closure on Joseph's murder before I plan the next steps of my life. What is the latest on the investigation? Any more Hummer chases?"

"Actually, in some ways the case has gotten a lot worse than car chases. You probably haven't noticed because your mind has been elsewhere but the FBI is providing you with extra protection at the moment."

"You're right, Jill, I hadn't noticed anyone providing me protection. Why is the FBI involved?"

"David, I'd like to put you on speaker phone if you don't mind. Listening on my end will be Jake Porter who is the Special Agent in Charge of the FBI's Denver office. Also listening will be Angela Weber who is a member of my team. We have two cyber criminals involved in this case and so I have avoided sending you anything via the Internet so that my communication with you cannot be hacked."

With Jake and Angela listening, Jill provided David with a summary of the last thirty-six hours including the identification of the two cyber criminals. When she moved on to discussing potential issues at Broomfield Pharmaceuticals and Rocky Mountain Clinical Trials, David began thinking about what he could do on his end to contribute to the case.

"Jill, there is so much going on with this case, I'd really like to meet everyone working on it and perhaps find a way to contribute."

"Actually we were hoping that you could assist us in getting interviews with the CEO of RMCT and whoever is running Joseph's company at the moment," suggested Jill.

"David, this is Special Agent Jake Porter. I would like to take a look at Joseph's computers. Do you have his cell phone, laptop, tablet or whatever he used to do work on in your possession? We don't have a search warrant but we don't need one if you voluntarily let us look at Joseph's communications."

"I have several pieces of technology that Joseph used to stay in touch with the office. I know he traveled back and forth each day with a laptop which I have. If you were to go to his office you would only find an empty docking station. I would be happy to share the technology with you if it helps to solve Joseph's murder."

"David, I think we need to meet in person. We could do that in Denver or in Breck. What is your preference?" asked Jill.

"I'll come to Breck. You folks are starting to scare me and I am glad that the FBI has been on my doorstep. Agent Porter, would you have your agents make contact with me? If you don't mind, I would like their escort to Breck and I have spare bedrooms in my cabin that I can house them in. I should be there in about two hours."

"David, I'll have my agents escort you to Breck and thank you for offering to house them."

After a few more arrangements, they ended the call as Jo reentered the living room.

"I just finished speaking with my sister and she is going to stay with us for two days. She needs to get some supplies as she is an artist. She will also need to visit some Breck stores where she has some pieces on consignment. We'll get to spend some time together and apart. We will go out to dinner so that we can have some one on one time. Jake, I assume you can have someone guard us when we go out."

"Yes I can do that," replied Jake. "You're much easier to protect if you stay in the suite rather than miles away in Leadville."

It suddenly crossed Jill's mind that she hadn't heard anything about the three suspects since the snow plow incident.

"Jake, what's the update from your men who were tailing our three suspects?"

"Bad news there. All three suspects returned to the cabin that Mr. Brown owns and my men tailed them there. Once there, they took off in the woods on snowmobiles. My men were in cars and could not follow them into the woods. Using flashlights, they followed the trail for perhaps a hundred yards but then there were so many snowmobile tracks going different directions that they were unable to determine where the three men headed."

"That is indeed bad news," Jill agreed. "Why didn't you tell us as soon as you arrived here this morning? Do either of the two other men have a cabin in this area?"

"I've had agents looking at that, but there are so many opportunities to lease a cabin for the season. Unless they are the registered property owner, I don't hold much chance of locating them through this means."

"Is Marie going to be safe on the chairlift if we don't know where these creeps are?"

"In addition to the agent who will be riding all of the chairlifts with her, she will have additional armed agents on snowmobiles, and in front and behind her on the chairlift."

Jill thought about Jake's response and said "you think they're going to go after Marie up on the ski slope and you're placing enough agents to protect her and chase down these creeps. So she is the bait to bring these guys out of hiding. That's why you didn't tell me that your agents had lost them last night."

"Don't they have a sign posted up on the ski slope that says 'ski at your own risk'? I didn't realize that was also the motto of the FBI," quipped Marie.

Jake, looking a little chagrined at being caught in somewhat of a lie said, "If you would like to stay in the suite, we will dress up an agent to look like you as a decoy up on the mountain. With the body armor that Michael is bringing all of your vital organs will be protected. The way our gear works is you will be completely covered in Kevlar except your gloves and ski boots. Even the helmet Michael has contains Kevlar and the face shield."

Given the protections they were providing her, she decided she would still go skiing. If they ran into trouble, she would have lots of help.

"I'm in. I hope I am able to draw these creeps out of the woods and your agents are able to arrest them. This is such a cute town, I'd rather be out and exploring it at night then confined under guard in this beautiful suite. We could gain our freedom if your plan works."

"Thank you," said Jake as he walked over to the suite door to allow Michael and another agent to enter. After making introductions, Marie wrapped up her computer work and began dressing in the very unfashionable Kevlar clothing. Fortunately it wasn't heavy and this opportunity to ski Breck felt like a wild adventure.

Fifteen minutes later Marie was leaving the suite with agents in tow. Michael, leaving five minutes later through the hotel's back door would be wearing his ski patrol jacket to help disguise the FBI agent and would meet them at the lift line. Her friends wanted an update and made her promise to text them throughout the day.

Nathan entered the kitchen seeking coffee. Everyone knew not to speak to him until after his morning coffee. If you spoke to him too soon you received single word replies and no memory on his part of having engaged in conversation with you. Jake and Morgan didn't know better and were surprised when they were the only two that chorused at Nathan a 'good morning'.

Jo took pity on Morgan and said "he is sort of sleepwalking at the moment. You need to give him thirty minutes beyond his first coffee before you engage in conversation with him."

"Oh, okay then," replied an amused Morgan.

"Jill, I think I'm going blind staring at the footage from the hotel cameras. I am guessing that our cyber crooks have hacked into the hotel security system and replaced the footage of the lobby with their own footage."

"How do you know that?"

"I've watched these tapes several times and I haven't once seen you, or Angela, or Marie, or Jo in a single frame yet we know that you came and went several times and greeted them in the lobby. Even Nathan's trip to the grocery store is missing. I'm becoming quite good friends with this hotel's security staff. I'm going to try and convince them to allow Henrik's engineer to take a look at the system. That may cause some flak, but that's all I can think of for a cause of why you guys are not on any of the cameras in this hotel. Even hotel security has been unable to think of any plausible explanation."

"So at least we think we have the source of how they are tracking us out of this hotel," reasoned Jill. "We should get word to Marie and the agents with her so that they know that they may be followed up to the chairlifts. Do you think the cyber crooks can track our cell phone and text usage? Is it safe to communicate with her that way?"

"I think they can eventually hack into your phone records to see who you called but not what was said," remarked Nick. "So you're safe contacting her that way. On the other hand, we need to stay away from e-mail."

Jill texted Marie about Nick's findings, and the advice to avoid e-mail when communicating anything about the case. Then she thought of a different problem.

"Not to be paranoid but did we sweep this suite for listening devices? Are we sure that our conversations inside this suite are confidential?"

"We haven't done so, but I don't think there are bugs as our cyber creeps would probably have tried to leave the country if they knew how close on their tail we are. Regardless, I will have the room swept several times a day from now on," replied Jake.

"Okay, Jake thanks for doing that. I'm expecting David at any moment. Nick or Jake, what are your plans for examining the technology that Joseph used in his everyday work to communicate with people? Do you want to split it up? Jake, does the FBI have any software program we could put the phone and the laptop through and come up with a magical answer to this case?"

"I have a command center set up in the cabin that I have outside of town. I have many agents staying there, some with the skills to look at these technologies and tell us what's on them."

"How would your men necessarily recognize a problematic communication between Joseph and RMCT?" asked Jo. "His work in-box contained perhaps ten-thousand emails. How would anyone sort through those emails to find anything distressing?"

"We have software developed by the National Security Agency to monitor emails. The initial use of that software was to catch terrorist cells planning attacks on the U.S. The FBI has found the software to be of particular use in white-collar crimes.

"If you look at our investigation into Bogachev, we found his spam scheme by our email analysis software. From there, our cybercrimes expert set up a computer and represented himself as a mystically wonderful hacker that Bogachev would be unable to pass up. This hacker promised to evolve the phishing scheme, attempting to stay ahead of any law enforcement by keeping the scheme's computer coding ever-changing."

"That is a little too technical for me; I'll just trust that you know what you are doing," said Jo.

They heard a knock on the door about three minutes after being warned by the front desk that the room had another visitor. Jill opened the door to David, giving his arm an empathetic squeeze.

David viewed all the people in the suite with puzzlement. Jill made quick work of introducing David to her team and to Jake and Morgan.

"Is this all for Joseph's murder?" asked David while he placed Joseph's technology on the table.

"Yes and no" replied Jill. "Why don't you have a seat here and I'll go over the murder board with you. I think that is the best way to explain all of the pieces of this puzzle."

A quarter of an hour later and after several questions, David understood all of the circumstances surrounding his partner's death. Mostly, he was stunned at what Joseph had likely stumbled into with RMCT. It was such a stupid reason to have to die. If only Joseph had turned the matter over to law enforcement.

"I can see the holes in your case, the points you have yet to prove. I am grateful the FBI is involved - not necessarily in solving Joseph's murder, but in the bigger conspiracy that is occurring within RMCT and these cybercriminals. To be able to take down someone that has stolen millions is very important. I wonder if they were planning on targeting the resort next?"

"David, please explain what you mean by targeting the resort," commanded Jake.

"Think of how great it would be to get into their multi-day pass system. The corporation owns about twelve ski resorts in five states and in France. Imagine the credit lines on the credit cards attached to these ski passes. There are a lot of wealthy individuals that ski and to steal their credit card information would be just a different version of Gameover and Zeus."

"I hadn't thought of that angle, but I think you have got something with that theory," affirmed Jake. "It would also explain why the software is still in the resort's computers. Nick, do you know if the resort is aware of that? Have they hired Henrik's firm to rid themselves of the bug?"

"I don't know. He mentioned at dinner, that the resort was grateful that he found the bug and that he offered to fix it, but I can't recall if they actually asked Henrik's firm to fix it. If they haven't, the FBI may want to meet with Tom and encourage them to close the gap. I think the suggestion would be more believable if it came from the FBI."

"The danger is we don't want word to get out much beyond the people in this room," Jake commented. "If these two cyber-criminals abandon an attack on the resort and decide to disap-pear, we'll have a harder time apprehending them."

"Why don't I ask Henrik if the breach is being rectified by his company or perhaps if he knows if they hired another company," suggested Nick. "If the resort is fixing it on their own, we can stay quiet."

"Great idea; let me know when you have an answer."

"I would really like to assist in this case," said David. "Although my day job is teaching math in the school district, on the side, I'm quite the computer whiz. Why don't I start by helping you with Joe's technology? Since I set most of it up, I may be able to find some key documents faster than your folks."

"We're going to use a software program that can sort through massive amounts of electronic communication. However we might be faster and more targeted if you direct us to the folder Joseph set up for RMCT and anything on clinical trials related to that company. If you don't mind, I am going to have my agents escort you to my cabin. I have a command post operating there and my computer guys are there."

"Sounds like a plan," said David. "Jill, were you able to get appointments to meet with the two company CEOs for today? Do you need my help with those appointments?"

"Fortunately, both men were cooperative and Angela and I will be meeting them this afternoon. You go ahead to Jake's cabin and socialize with the nerds."

"Hey, we nerds make the world go around," said David with a rare smile.

"Nathan is cooking something wonderful for dinner tonight,"

Jill offered. "Feel free to drop back to this suite and dine with us, or if any of the nerds cook, enjoy your time with them."

"I'll see what the day brings. Thanks for letting me help with the investigation. I really appreciate it."

Both Jake and Jill smiled and nodded. David left the suite with the technology and his agent escort.

CHAPTER 12

*M*arie had done a lot of skiing in Wisconsin and Michigan. Those hills were nothing compared to what she was seeing in Colorado simply traveling up the gondola. She had a great escort although she suspected the only reason they were up on the mountain was for her to be bait. On one hand it was very scary, on the other she felt well protected in the Kevlar clothing and with the armed escort. She had a handsome, talented bodyguard whose keen eyes were watching all around them for trouble. He had even managed to teach her about the mountain while his eye roved everywhere. The mountain was only lightly covered with skiers and snow boarders as it was still early in the season.

There were some great cruising intermediate ski runs that they had spent several hours on. Michael had offered some sound advice for improving her skiing. Despite knowing that there could be a killer anywhere around, it was her best ski adventure ever. They were going into a ski hut for their first bathroom break. Michael wanted to catch up with the other agents and the hut was much easier to secure than a large on-hill restaurant. Both he and Marie were aware that the virus was still in the ski lift system. They had both tensed over a few lift stops but each time they were one to two minutes long which was the typical stoppage when a lift operator had passenger loading problems. He had explained to her that in his pack, he had a series of ropes that they could use to get off of a stopped chairlift. He knew how to use the equipment as it was the emergency back-up method to get people off a stopped lift. To his knowledge it hadn't been deployed in at least a decade by the resort, but the ski patrol still trained on it. He hadn't had time to show his fellow agents how to use the gear, so if a mid-air departure from the chairlift was necessary, only Marie and he would be using that route of escape. The agents had been supplied with images of the three criminals including the clothing they wore the last time they were captured on the resort's cameras.

Having made use of the bathroom and re-hydrating herself with water, Marie was ready to continue skiing. Michael checked the area around the hut and saw nothing that worried him. If she did well on the run, they were going to head to the chairlift that had been Joseph's last lift ride. The route down would be very challenging and she wanted to do the run while her ski legs were warmed up, but not tired. They got to the bottom of the run and Michael checked in with her as to whether they would be proceeding.

"Do you want to try peak six? I think you're capable of skiing it, but as always just because I say 'go' doesn't mean you can't say 'no'."

"I'm game. I have had the best hours of skiing ever this morning. I couldn't imagine runs that were this long, or snow this soft and forgiving. I have been skiing on hard packed snow for so long. Let's head up to the next adventure."

Michael notified the agents who were accompanying them on their direction and pointed Marie toward the series of lifts they would have to take to reach peak six. Soon enough they arrived at the base of the final chairlift. Marie had been looking at the steep trails as she had glanced toward the mountain from other vantage points, but there was no easy way down so she would just have to find her courage if she had second thoughts at the top. Watching the chair swing around the terminal wheel, they soon sat on the chair and headed for the top.

Perhaps a third of the way up Michael pointed to a small forest of trees and said, "That is where they found Joseph."

Marie nodded and made a mental note to stay out of those trees. The lift continued its upward journey and they were soon hitting the wall of wind towards the top.

"At the top of the lift, we can go one of three ways. We could take off our skis and hike up to that peak," said Michael pointing to a still taller peak. "We could ski that bowl to the left of the lift which is a lot of fun, but is steep. Or we could take the run to the right at the top. I recommend we go right as the ski runs are less steep."

Marie had followed his description of the three routes and affirmed "let's take the right side."

She followed Michael down to the first ridge and stared at the steep run. Taking a deep breath, she proceeded to ski the slope taking lots of breaks and lots of turns. With just one fall she made it to the bottom. As they got ready to board the chairlift a second time, Marie looked at Michael and exclaimed, "Okay that was a lot of fun! I love that I was challenged, but I didn't kill myself. That one fall was because I had my weight on the back of my skis. This time I want to do the run and not fall at all with perhaps a few less stops. If I can keep improving, I want to try the left side."

"Sounds like a plan; let's go!"

They rode the chair and skied down the same trail a few more times and then Marie declared herself ready to tackle the left side of the lift.

"Okay, we're going to go off to the left this time at the top. Head for the center of the bowl as that is the easiest way down a steep slope."

"Okay, you haven't steered me wrong so far."

They both heard a ping at the same time. Then the chair came to a stop. Then a second ping bounced loudly off Marie's helmet.

"Crap, someone is shooting at us," said Marie trying to duck on the chairlift.

Michael was talking to the agents ahead and behind them on the chair. They had spotted the shooter in the woods to the right. They were about halfway up the seven minute lift ride.

"Marie, stay down and try to use me for cover. My agents know where the shots are coming from and they are going to fire back."

Then they heard another ping hit the back of the chair. The two agents followed with shooting a couple of smoke grenades to the woods where the shooter was. The shots stopped as a wall of smoke appeared where the shooter had been sighted.

"We'll need to exit this chair right now! The smoke will give us cover for about five minutes, but let's get down and off the mountain."

Michael pulled out his ropes. As he quickly knotted them to the chair, he asked Marie to pop off her skis to drop them to the ground.

Marie's heart was palpitating, she had never been shot at before or tried to get off a chair in this manner. Just like skiing the steep mountain, she grasped her courage just long enough to go over the chair to the ground which was about thirty to forty feet below. She was relieved to touch the ground and move out of the way of Michael. She looked over at the smoke and it looked like it was starting to get a bit thinner. Seconds later Michael dropped beside her, and retracted the rope. They put on their skis and took off down the mountain. Marie in the lead, Michael on her heels; he had turned on a radio receiver in her helmet directing her down the mountain at a speed she could maintain without falling, while insuring that no wrong turns were made that might not lead to the exit from the resort.

His fellow agents were still keeping watch from the chairlift. The smoke had cleared and no further shots were fired. The lift was still stopped, and they could see a pair of skiers exit the bottom of the trees where the shots had come from. They had taken pictures of the skiers and they seemed to be on the path of Marie and Michael even though they were far enough ahead so as not to be seen by the shooters.

Michael had Marie continue skiing all the way to the gondola. Her legs were burning and she was breathing as though she had just run a sprint 5K road race. She practically collapsed into the gondola car. She leaned against the glass walls panting, while Michael spoke with various agents. Finally, between calls he paused to have a word with Marie.

"Has this still been the best ski day ever?"

Marie just grinned and as she caught her breath said "Yes it was. My son would have loved to have been on this last run between the beauty of the mountain, the smoke bomb, the chairlift shots and then the descent to the ground followed by the race to get off the mountain. In fact, I am ready to go up and be your decoy again."

Michael just shook his head and proceeded with his next call. He was thankful that she had a calm head on her shoulders. He would have hated to spend the past fifteen minutes with a shrinking violet. He had informed his superior, Agent Porter, of what had happened on the mountain and the fact that they were on their way back to the hotel suite. A few minutes later and they were riding the elevator to the hotel suite.

Marie used her card key to enter where she was immediately surrounded by her hugging friends asking if she was okay.

"I just had the best day skiing ever. I'm not sure I'll ever be able to ski in the Midwest again."

"Are you nuts, my friend?" asked Jo. "We just heard that you had bullets fired at the chairlift you were on."

"Yes, but before the bullets were fired, Michael had taken me on one wonderful ski run after another. It was like nothing I have ever skied at home. Then once the bullets started flying, I felt pretty good, sliding down a rope from the chair to the ground and then racing off the mountain. Of course the fact that I had Kevlar on just about everywhere went a long way to that feeling of invincibility."

"I am woman, hear me roar," suggested Jill. She was glad to see her friend was taking the event in stride.

"Yes, something similar to that. I even volunteered to be a decoy again."

"So while we were all worried to death about your safety, you were tightening up your gloves for round two in the boxing ring," noted Angela with obvious admiration for Marie's sense of fun that was shining through.

"Sorry you guys were worried; I was in excellent hands for protection. The agents got pictures of the shooters. Have they made it off the lift yet? Was anything left behind at the scene?"

"Our agents emailed us the photos," replied Jake. "They are still stuck on the lift, and the ski patrol is going to manually move the cable flywheel until all the passengers are returned to the bottom. The lift will remain closed for the day. They should be back here in thirty minutes. We should go examine where the shots were fired from. Michael, is there any way you could take a snowmobile up there and look? I would like to keep this whole thing low-key if we can. Can you quietly examine the shooter's spot in your ski patrol apparel?"

"Let me go look now while everybody's distracted getting skiers off the lift."

"I just got an e-mail from Henrik," noted Nick. "He says the resort has contracted with his company to get the virus out of their lift computers and protect them in the future. It seems this second stoppage on the chair was enough for them to recognize the threat."

"Ask him if there is any way to preserve the evidence of this virus so that we can use it for prosecution of these criminals," requested Jake.

"Will do; I'll let you know if he thinks it can be done."

"My sister is due to arrive here at any moment," observed Jo. "I don't think I want her staying with us as we seem to be attracting violence at the moment. I would like to dine with her in private so that we can catch up. Then I would like to have an agent escort her home, making sure she arrives safely without anyone following her. Jake, can you arrange that?"

"Yes the two of you can have room service in my room which is located on this floor. When you're ready we will have an escort for her to Leadville."

"Thank you. My sister is such a gentle soul I think she would likely freeze in any dangerous situation rather than using her own wits to get out of it. I'll make another trip back to see her later in the spring."

As Jo's voice died down, the suite was called by the front desk notifying them of her sister's arrival. Jo left the suite, an agent in tow to go greet her sister and implement the plan she had outlined to Jake. About two hours later, they expected Jo to be back at work following the money, while her sister would be doing some grocery shopping and then heading back up into even higher mountains.

Nathan had arranged a make your own sandwich set up for lunch for the remaining occupants of the suite. Nick had identified the two shooters from the photos taken by the agents as Sundin and Bogachev. Michael was on his way via snowmobile to the shooter's site. Jill and Angela were about to depart for Denver to interview the two CEOs.

Then Jake got a call from Michael. He had taken the snowmobile to the site where the shooters were located. In addition to the three smoke bomb canisters, there was a dead body. He took a picture of the crime scene and the victim's face from the side and transmitted it to Jake. Everyone in the suite jerked their head toward Jake when they heard him say, "Can you tell what killed him?"

Jill nudged his arm and asked him to put the call on speakerphone and he complied.

"Can you see any visible wounds?" asked Jill.

"No. There is no blood on his body or in the snow."

"Does he seem to be clutching his chest?"

"He's facedown and I don't want to turn him over. We need a crime scene team up here."

"He may have been shot by a poisoned dart, similar to my client, Joseph," observed Jill. "He would have asphyxiated face down in the snow. I wonder if he's an accomplice or an innocent victim that happened upon the shooters."

"Let me see if he has any identification on him."

After a brief pause during which they essentially heard nothing but wind noise, Michael came back on the phone.

"No identification. No wallet. No cell phone."

"Is he wearing a ski pass?" asked Jill.

"Good question; let me look." After another brief pause, he said, "he's wearing a multi-day pass. We may be able to get his name from it."

"Michael, take a picture of the ski pass and send it to me," directed Nick. "I'll send it to Tom who is a local contact for the resort to see if they can identify the skier."

"Jake and Michael, you now have a different problem on your hands. You can call the local cops and see what they direct you to do, or you can go in with full FBI identification, admit to being involved in something going on at the resort and take the lead from the local cops," Jill proposed.

"That's a good point Jill," contemplated Jake. "The locals didn't do a credible job investigating Joseph's murder. On the other hand we don't want anyone alerted about our operation. So far your team knows about us and our suspects, but no one else does and I would like to keep quiet. Nick, can you identify this guy by his picture before you ask the resort about his pass? Knowing his identity will change how we approach the notification of this death."

"I'll need a frontal of his face, Michael, to run it through the software, so I think you'll have to turn him over and disturb the crime scene."

"Ok I'll do that, I think that is our best route to finding out who he is which will determine our next steps."

Angela looked at the clock and said to Jill, "We had better leave; otherwise we'll be late for the appointments according to my traffic app."

"Let's go then, and perhaps someone in the room can keep us updated?"

They got nods that someone would keep them posted and they left, a protective detail actually would do the driving, so Jill and Angela could organize their thoughts and questions on the way. Soon afterward, Nick received the photo of the dead guy to run through Henrik's facial recognition software.

Minutes later, he identified the dead man as Robert Fisher.

"Hey! Jake, we're going to make your career with the FBI. This guy is also on your Most Wanted list. He is wanted for murdering his family then blowing up the house to hide the murder. He is a sharpshooter and thought to be armed. Wow, I wonder if the other guy killed him for missing Marie."

"Michael, please hang out there a moment longer. With the lifts closed, I don't expect that there are other skiers that will come across your path. Let me check with the home office as far as next steps, this is getting really complicated. Rats, I hate to bring Washington into this situation, but we have guys on the Most Wanted list dropping out of the sky."

Jake borrowed one of the bedrooms, and put the call into headquarters. In the end, they thought it best if Michael collected all the crime scene information that he could before calling in the local cops to handle the case. He would remain undercover, representing himself as a part of the ski patrol and not FBI. He took many pictures and Jill had suggested before they left the hotel that he look for a tiny hole in the victim's jacket suggesting the dart. He thought he found one, and took pictures and used a collection kit that he had carried in his backpack to swab the jacket. He also took fingerprints to verify the victim's identity. Finally he ended by doing a thorough walk around the crime scene to make sure that there were no discarded cell phones or other personal items. There were none. He then repositioned the body as he had found it.

Local law enforcement requested that the ski patrol bring the victim down off the mountain. Michael had requested another ski patrol person assist him by bringing a basket and lifting the body into it, attaching it to his snowmobile and bringing it to the base. The medical examiner was on their way to pick up the body and the officer left word that he wanted to speak to Michael the next day about his discovery. That low key exit of the body from the mountain suited the FBI perfectly.

Michael had never seen such disinterest on the part of law enforcement as he had here. Maybe that was one of the things they could fix as a side benefit to this case. Later when Jill heard Michael's assessment she was glad she had stayed out of the discussion for the most part; she wanted them to find out for themselves just how bad the local law enforcement was and they did not fail to disappoint. It wasn't that they had disliked David; they were ill-suited to do investigative work.

When Jill had packed her bags for Colorado, she had included the ingredients she needed to test for curare in case she came across any additional victims. After she returned to the hotel she would run tests on the swab that Michael had collected from Mr. Fisher's jacket.

Jo returned to the suite after lunch with her sister. After learning the shooter was yet another person on the FBI's most wanted list, she was even more relieved her sister wasn't staying any longer. It was just too dangerous for anyone on Jill's team at the moment herself included. She and Morgan would have to take a quick detour to look at Mr. Fisher's finances. They were making real progress on delving into what was appearing to be the shady dealings of RMCT.

The report out of Jake's cabin was interesting as well. Joseph's access to his email on the company server had been terminated about an hour after his death, two hours before his body was discovered. Now they were trying to track down who had cut the access. David really was brilliant with the computer and had found a way to restore and review all of Joseph's emails stored on his phone or computer. They thought they would be working into the night on this and he was going to continue to dine with the nerds and then return to his cabin when he was too exhausted to continue with the emails.

Marie was back at work collecting what she could find on Mr. Fisher. She was sorry to have her ski day cut short, but in those few hours on the slope she had got more skiing in than her average day on a dinky hill with slow chairlifts in the Midwest.

Nathan, having ended his cooking duties decided to work on some designs in the hotel bar. The suite was filled with too many conversations about the details of the case and what everyone was working on. In his mind, there was nothing like swirling a glass of wine to motivate your creativity for label design. He had blocked Jake from sending an agent with him to the bar. Instead he had his back to the wall in a corner so he could watch anyone entering the bar. He had memorized their pictures and felt prepared. His hapkido skills were too slow to save him from a poisonous dart, but he would take his chances there.

Jill and Angela were on the outskirts of Denver heading for their first appointment. Marie had been updating them with texts. David's findings on the deletion of access to Joseph's company computer account, was information in their possession that they might reveal to Broomfield's interim CEO. They would have to judge how the conversation went. They also had some background information of each company's financial health that they might choose to ask about. Angela would drive almost the entire conversation with Jill taking notes and watching for nuances. She would only ask questions at the end, if anything had been missed during the conversation. This way they reduced interruptions and maintained a rhythm of questioning.

Shortly, they were seated in the interim CEO Peter Garrett's office at Joseph's old company. After introductions and offered condolences, they got down to the interview.

"Can I ask why David hired you? Isn't a murder investigation the purview of law enforcement rather than a private citizen?"

"I wouldn't want to completely speak for David," replied Angela, "but I know he was concerned with his interaction by local law enforcement."

"Okay, I must say I find it odd that the police have not shown up on our doorstep. I would have thought they would make a visit to a murdered person's place of employment."

"I really can't comment on the activities of the police. I am not in the loop on their investigation, although it seems odd behavior to us, too. Thanks so much for taking time to meet with us today as we try to learn more about Joseph. What can you tell me about Joseph Morton?"

"I worked with Joe for at least fifteen years. We were both scientists when we started working together. I think he had been in the lab for a few years when I arrived. Then both he and I moved through the management ranks, with him always a few steps in front of me. I was his number two person when he was murdered," Peter paused getting a pained look in his eyes. "Gosh, that feels harsh to say that. I hope I never have to use that word again in relation to someone."

"Can you tell me what kind of leader he was? Did staff like him? Was he well respected? Was he liked by the board of this company?"

"Joe went back to school to get his MBA about a decade ago and he continued always evolving in his leadership skills. We have good staff satisfaction, and low turnover. The company has been growing its revenues every year, and our R & D has found a blockbuster product to launch about every four years. So yes I would say that the company was well run. Our margins are solid and we are sufficiently capitalized to fund our R & D, and pay our shareholders a dividend."

""Sounds like a successful business. Now, tell me about the company you collaborated with for the clinical trials of the drug that doesn't have FDA approval." Angela requested.

"We collaborate with lots of companies. Which company and what would you specifically like to know?"

"Oh! Sorry! How long have you collaborated with Rocky Mountain Clinical Trials? What exactly did they do for Broomfield Pharmaceuticals? Did you have any issues with them?"

"Ah yes, RMCT - we have worked together for perhaps five to seven years. Often we outsourced clinical trials to them. Do you know anything about clinical trials?"

"Not really. I know they are necessary to be able to gain FDA approval."

"Yeah, that is the end goal. Each trial has different phases that have to be tightly controlled and based on the earlier studies; you may be required to study one nuance of the first study. Trials are very expensive and you hate to have any failure due to poor study design."

"Did they do trials on animals as well as humans for you?"

"Just human trials, we do the animal trials ourselves. As to whether we had any problems with them? No we didn't."

"Did any of the trials fail due to poor design or execution?"

"I can't recall any trials that failed, but I'll check my records and get back to you," said Peter writing a note to follow up.

"Is that unusual to have no failures in the clinical trial stage?"

"Now that you ask, it seems unusual but I'll take a look at our failure rates among the various companies we use to perform our clinical trials."

"How do you determine which trial is performed by which company?"

"We may use a different company for different geographical locations or for specialized group trials like children or pregnant women or cancer, for example. Why all the questions about our clinical trials? Do you think that Joseph's death is related to his job?"

Angela and Jill had met each other eyes and decided they could both trust this man and be mostly assured that he had not wanted Joseph Morton dead.

"Yes, we do think his death is related to this company," said Jill. "We would like you to keep that in confidence, even from your board at this point. Do we have your agreement to keep what we are about to tell you in confidence?"

"Why do I need to keep it a secret? Shouldn't the police know that and investigate it?"

"Look your very meeting with us today may put your life at risk and you could end up just like Joseph. But for our safety, the capture of the murderer, and likely your own safety, we need to be assured that you will not share this information with anyone."

"Now you're scaring me. Where is law enforcement in this case?" asked Peter stubbornly wanting some verification that the two women in front of him were not wackos.

Jill sighed as she realized that they had hit a stand-still.

"How about if I call the two FBI agents that provided us with a safe escort to this meeting with you, would that convince you of our legitimacy?"

"The FBI? I thought you said law enforcement wasn't involved?"

"We either need to end this conversation or move on. I repeat do you want to meet the FBI agents which will lead to you agreeing to keep the details of this case a secret?"

"This is about as strange a conversation and situation that I have ever experienced. Yes I will agree to your confidentiality requirement if I can view the credentials of your FBI agents."

In less than five minutes, they were able to move on with Jill giving Peter an overview of the possible problems with RMCT. He looked stricken at the end of the conversation, deeply worried that his company might be providing patients with unsafe or ineffective treatment regimens.

"At this moment in time, there are people across the country swallowing a pill that we completed clinical trials on. I wonder if I should issue a recall on all of our drugs that underwent trials conducted by RMCT. What would that mean to patients that are in treatment for some cancers? I know that not all of our drugs might be questionable. I really need to consult with someone else at the company to decide what to do."

"Peter, I am a physician, perhaps I can be your sounding board to reason this through. Let's eliminate your panic over any drugs that had clinical trials performed by anyone other than RMCT. What percent of your drugs would that eliminate from a recall?"

"Perhaps seventy percent."

"Okay, let's talk about the remaining thirty percent. If you have had medications out on the market for say two years that were bad, don't you think you would have gotten reports of harm by now? They may not be helpful drugs, but at least they are not causing harm. Would you agree?"

"Yes", reasoned Peter some of his panic lowering.

"Let's focus on the treatment regimens trialed by RMCT in say the last nine months - would you have gotten FDA approval and would they be fully marketed?"

"I'll have to check on our records, I can't remember this information off the top of my head. Give me thirty minutes to figure it out. Thanks for talking me off the ledge."

Angela looked at her watch and said, "We need to head over to RMCT to interview their CEO."

"What! I thought you said this was top secret and now you're going tell them what is going on?"

"No! That is not the plan at all. When we requested the interview, our request was to understand the relationship between the two companies. Nothing more. Mostly we are trying to figure out if the CEO knows or condones the presence of a FBI most wanted criminal on its board. We won't be speaking of any of the information we have shared with you. Please email us as soon as you have an answer on that clinical trials data. I'm always available to advise you on the statistics of the situation and if at some point you determine a recall is necessary, I can help craft the message to the board on where your concerns are without calling out RMCT which might be detrimental to your own health."

"Ok. Thanks," murmured Peter. "I am starting to get nervous about this entire situation. Do you know if anyone followed you here? Did you tell RMCT about the appointment with me when you set it up?"

"We made no mention of it and our escorts were looking for a tail and didn't see one. We made a bunch of unnecessary turns on the way here, so I think you're safe. If you're really nervous, I'll make a call from the car to the agent who is leading this investigation. If you have a security guard on the premises, you could move him closer right now. If you're really unnerved, you could come with us and you'll be included in our FBI detail," said Jill generously sharing the FBI's resources. "Just giving you some options."

"I have never been known for my backbone. I'll call my security guard now and if you wouldn't mind, I'll travel with you up to Breck. I've stayed at Joseph's cabin before and I'm sure I could call David and hide out there for the time being."

"We have to leave to get to our next appointment on time. We'll be back to see you soon."

Jill and Angela hurried to the car and left for RMCT. They called ahead and warned the CEO's assistant that they might be a few minutes late.

"Jill, do you really think he could be in danger?"

"I think that soon after he looks at the data to compare the clinical trial outcome data and sees zero failures of the drugs only on the part of RMCT, that the computer hackers involved in this case, will notice his interest. Once that notification goes through to whomever, then I think that Peter will be in danger."

"Yikes this is fast getting out of control," remarked Angela.

"Yes it is and I can't tell how much money is at stake," remarked Jill. "I do think that might be the root of the problem with this case - severe falsification of clinical trials data. I think it will be bad enough so that they are permanently suspended by the government from ever performing this service again. This trial company has total revenues of over a billion dollars. I think there is sufficient financial incentive for some criminal types to kill for. RMCT is not the biggest player in this space but it has been on a huge trajectory of growth for several years. I briefly looked at their website and they mention having unique partnership arrangements with drug companies. They charge far lower fees for clinical trials in return for a small percentage of ongoing revenues once the drug is approved by the FDA. They also assist companies with getting that FDA approval."

"Based on what we heard from Peter, I can't think of any additional questions to ask the CEO of RMCT. I'm afraid if we ask anything about the accuracy of their trials, we'll be overwhelmed by their defensiveness or poison curare darts."

"I was also thinking of implying that there was something wrong with Broomfield's manufacturing just to throw him off the trail."

"I don't like telling lies," said Angela "and what if that came back to haunt us in terms of stimulating these crooks to do something foolish."

"Good points. We'll just stick with our script."

Soon they were at the second company, meeting with the CEO and going through the routine questions of what he knew about

Joseph, what were their companies collaborating on, who was the main point of contact between the two companies. Soon they were wrapping up the interview and back in the sedan with their escorts.

Angela asked Jill, "So what did you think of our interviewee?"

"He was lying through his teeth."

"Yeah, I would have to agree with your assessment. When he never asked us why we were asking the questions we were, it said to me that he was just blowing us off waiting for the interview to end with no real intention of helping us solve this crime. What I really want to know is if he was already on the phone to Mr. Brown."

"I think we have to assume he was and just let it go. Why don't you call Peter and let him know we are on our way to pick him up."

Jill dialed the number, Peter had given her. The phone went to voicemail, which Jill saw as a problem. She leaned forward to the front seat and asked that they hurry in their return to Broomfield. She called the main number and asked to be transferred to the company's security department.

"Hello, is this the security department?" asked Jill.

"Yes ma'am, how may I help you?"

Jill felt like she was overreacting but oh well, "I had a meeting with your CEO about an hour ago. My name is Dr. Jill Quint. He had some security concerns and indicated that he was going to call and request security come to his office. I just tried reaching him on the phone number he gave me and it went to his voice-mail. Can you check on him?"

"Yes ma'am, I was in this office when he called asking for help. I'm going to put you on hold while I try and contact the officer that went to his office."

They heard silence as their car got closer to Broomfield's headquarters. Then the security guard got back on the line.

"I am unable to reach either the guard or Mr. Garrett." He

indicated he would be ending their call and heading up to the CEO's office.

"We're on our way back to your building, can you have someone let us inside the gates?" requested Jill.

"Ma'am, I hope nothing is wrong here. I'll notify the front gate guard to give you entry. See you soon," said the guard as he disconnected the phone.

Unfortunately they hit a snag in traffic and it took ten minutes instead of five to reach the front gates of Broomfield. Jill had not received a call from Peter - probably not a good sign.

CHAPTER 13

They parked and entered the building and the security guard approached them.

"Ma'am, sir, I'm sorry but this building is closed, you need to leave."

"I spoke with security a few minutes ago - I'm Dr. Jill Quint. I had a meeting earlier today with Mr. Garrett. Were you able to contact him?"

"Hi Dr. Quint I spoke with you earlier on the phone. We haven't located Mr. Garrett yet and my guard is missing. I don't have any other manpower to help me conduct the search. I need to protect this building and so I would like you to leave and return to your car so I can lock the doors and keep any strangers out."

"These two men with me are with the FBI." Gesturing at Angela, Jill added "We are private investigators. Can we help you with the search?"

"FBI? We didn't call you here to this building."

"Sir, we are here providing protection for Dr. Quint and Ms. Weber. We are not here for any business purpose with this company. We could split up into two groups, an agent with each woman and that will give you three people including yourself conducting the search. Are you interested in our help with the search?"

"Yes, unfortunately you don't have keys to this building and so it really won't do much good to split up into three groups since you can't get through locked doors. I have not unlocked Mr. Garrett's door yet and I would appreciate some company when I do that."

"Let's go. We will follow you."

They rode the same elevator that they had earlier and returned to the suite that they had sat in less than two hours ago. The security guard knocked on the door. There was no answer. He pulled out a ring of keys searching for one particular style and inserted the key into the lock. He swung the door open and the room was empty. This was where the assistant had sat earlier. Jill looked at her escort and noticed they had both pulled their guns out of their holsters and were holding them against their leg. The assistant's office was empty. The guard repeated the knocking procedure on the door to Mr. Garrett's private office. Again, silence. Using a key from that large collection of keys on the ring, he opened Mr. Garrett's door. The agents had made sure that Jill and Angela were behind them and so they couldn't see what was in the office when the door swung open.

They heard the security guard rush forward and say, "Mr. Garrett, are you okay?"

Jill and Angela's view was blocked by the agents and so when they heard the guard's words, they were hopeful that the question meant that Peter Garrett was in a position to answer it. Once the agents stepped into Peter's office, they knew Peter would never again answer another question. Like Joseph had been, Peter was laying on the floor arm outstretched with a pained look on his face. Between the bloodless color of his skin, the eyes fixed and seeing nothing, they thought it very likely that he was dead.

Jill approached his body and checked his pulse. As she had suspected he had none. She felt the skin temperature and tested the rigidity of his fingers. Her superficial examination suggested that starting CPR would be an exercise in futility. Peter had likely been dead at least an hour. His body was cool and his fingers had some rigidity in them already.

Angela performed the sign of the cross and offered a silent prayer for the recently departed Mr. Garrett.

"He has been dead for a while. I would suggest you call the police and request their assistance. While on the surface his body has no marks of violence about it, I'm guessing that the medical examiner will find curare poisoning in his system."

The guard went over to the phone and made the call to the police. They arrived at the company in less than five minutes. The scene was complicated by the presence of the two FBI agents. Homicide detectives arrived as well and each of the five witnesses were individually interviewed by at least two different officers or detectives.

They noted the absence of the security guard that had been sent to guard Mr. Garrett. A detective returned with the security guard to his office so he could pull the training file on the second security guard. A search of the premises failed to locate the missing guard. The police issued a bulletin to be on the lookout for the missing security guard.

Eventually Jill and Angela were allowed to leave the scene with their escorts. Adding another law enforcement agency into the mix was going to make this case even more complicated. These detectives were smart and interested in understanding the big picture. Jill thought that there would likely be a joint meeting of DPD and the FBI.

It was cold and dark when they reached their hotel. Jake had been briefed by his agents as well as the DPD about Peter. He had also informed the rest of Jill's team, as well as David.

Nathan knowing his woman, had dinner ready for them

shortly after they arrived. From her years as the medical examiner seeing a dead body never destroyed her appetite. Angela, always a light eater, might have had her appetite destroyed by Peter's death. Having said a few prayers over his body she seemed at peace with the situation and dug in to Nathan's delicious dinner.

Jill wanted to update her murder board and refocus everyone on RMCT. She was convinced that they had created massively false clinical data for the trials they conducted. She also wondered about their influence with the approval committee at the FDA. Over the last two decades, huge strides had been made to keep committee members ethical and objective about decision-making for drug and device approval, but there were occasional ethical failures.

After dinner and with a glass of wine, they all gathered at the suite's dining table to discuss theories. Jo and Morgan had compared RMCT Corporation to other clinical trials companies. Many smaller companies were not traded on a stock exchange. RMCT had gone public several years ago and its initial public offering generated $56M. Since that IPO, the company had a growth rate of over one hundred percent every year.

"Have you found another company with this same growth trajectory?" asked Angela.

"We haven't even found a company that had sustained growth over multiple years of twenty percent let alone one hundred percent. So this is so unusual it should be sounding warning bells everywhere," remarked Jo.

"Did the management narratives add any new information? As I recall you said these are usually the most valuable part of any report," Marie asked. "Have they had the same management team in place this entire time?"

"The reports are interesting," Jo commented. "I wish I could have seen a similar report before they went public. They have had the same management team in place this entire time and unlike many similar companies, upper leadership doesn't have an advanced degree in science, medicine, or even business. Only their requisite clinical employees have degrees. They had replaced their chief medical officer about four years ago. The previous physician died from a drug overdose."

Marie queried, "What kind of drug?"

"I don't know, I didn't look that far, but perhaps you could find that on the social media side. If we think that this company has totally falsified data, then they had to have the clinical employees on board for that falsification, right? I don't know the FDA rules for drug testing, but it seems like you would have to conduct some tests under the supervision of a physician and nurse. I would bet that reports submitted to the FDA would require their signature. So how would you go about hiring clinical employees that are willing to falsify data? How would you test for that during the interview without giving the game away?"

"From my point of view, I would study them on social media first. I might purposely look for drug addicts as long as the firm wasn't involved in testing narcotics or other drugs of addiction. " Marie predicted, "You would be amazed at what you can tell about someone - drunken antics or huge tirades and pictures forever capturing their personality. Many addicts have financial problems as it takes money to feed the habit. If you're trying to care for patients with your nursing or medical license while addicted, then you're already breaking the Hippocratic Oath, so that is a vulnerability to exploit. Once you worked for the company, they could control you by threatening to report you to a board that might cause you to lose your license for a while or forever. If you paid them a good wage - slightly above average, then your only worry would be an employee overdosing and killing themselves. Their death would result in paperwork for the company, but really RMCT would likely just move on and find another employee."

"Yikes, that is a cynical point of view," said Angela.

"Just trying to think like a criminal and how you go about exploiting people, which is what you would want to do to gain their silence and acceptance for an illegal operation."

"Jo, what else did you find in the management reports?" asked Jill. "Do they spend much of the report speaking to their drug regulatory approval consultancy? Can you tell what portion of their revenue is due to this division of the company?"

"It seems like there are three pots of money: clinical trials, regulatory approval assistance, and ongoing drug royalties post approval. The first two sources account for perhaps twenty percent of revenues, the ongoing royalties is by far their biggest revenue source."

"It feels like there is a neat little package here," Jill speculated. "The clinical trials company falsifies data, uses its influence to gain FDA approval, than sits back and enjoys the royalties for years to come. If they are a one billion dollar company then roughly eight-hundred million of it is due to ongoing revenues. How many total employees are there? It must be in the thousands for a company this size. I would think at least half would know the results of the clinical trials. That has to be a lot of employees to be judged lacking ethics. Do we have a sense of how well employees were paid? Is that in any of the annual reports or in company gossip? What is the relation of Sundin, and Fisher to the RMCT Company? Is there any relationship or are they just hired guns of Brown? Finally, who was the security guard sent to protect Peter? These are the unanswered questions for me."

"Jake, what have your people found in Joseph's electronics?" asked Marie.

All eyes moved over to Jake, leaning against the wall while he had been listening to Jill's team discuss motives and approaches. He straightened up and said, "As was noted earlier, someone turned off his account before his murder was discovered. David

Gomez was modest in describing his computer talents as good. He can run circles around my guys and we should all be grateful that he has never turned his skills in an illegal direction as I bet he would be successful. He was able to find all emails and other files deleted from Joseph's accounts. In those emails are a series of communications between him and RMCT. They were seeing problems in terms of efficacy with a new treatment that had been on the market for two years. Patients were dying of their cancers at far higher rates than the published studies. Joseph initially thought he had a problem in manufacturing, so he evaluated that first. However he began receiving test results from cancer patients - a cancer marker. He could see from these patients that the therapy failed to impact the cancer antigen. Then he pulled up the test results generated by the RMCT trials and the antigen went to zero in several test patients, who died of diseases other than cancers."

"That is highly unlikely," stated Jill. "Cancer rarely behaves in that manner. Tell me more about patients dying from other causes; explain what you mean - what other causes?"

"There were a lot of accidents. This was attributed to the harsh side effects of cancer drugs. Some patients were accidentally hit by cars, fell off of cliffs, a few overdoses, falls in their homes resulting in brain bleeds, etc."

"I would like to look at that data," directed Jill. "During my career, I participated in several research studies. Usually I would be looking for pathological changes resulting from different therapies. I may have been involved in say thirty to fifty studies, so it was significant. I can't recall in any of those studies accidental deaths being a part of the equation. People undergoing chemo, generally that are weak enough to fall, are not out hiking paths with cliffs. I'll give David a call and see if he'll move over to this suite now. I want to study the data with him. Even though it is getting late in the evening, I would like to look at that now."

Jill made a call to the lobby to see if there was additional space on the hotel floor for another guest. They were again happy to accommodate as the hotel floor was filling up fast with people connected to Jill. She then called David and explained her questions and the hotel room availability. He agreed and the agents made quick arrangements to move him and his technology. More chairs were added to the suite along with another table. It was becoming quite the busy hub of the investigation.

After David and his fellow nerds were set up in the space, he took another look at the updates on the murder board.

"I knew Peter for at least fifteen years including his wife and kids. This killer has got to be stopped so that we bring justice to Joseph, Peter and perhaps even patients from some of the drugs that Broomfield Pharmaceuticals created. The deaths weren't their fault rather it was RMCT Corporation. I understand why you don't want to announce that you are on the trail of these killers, but we need to stop Broomfield from appointing another CEO and putting his or her life at risk. We may also need to recall some of the drugs manufactured by Broomfield."

"David, based on my experience of how these cases go, I think we may have it solved in the next twenty-four hours and at the latest forty-eight hours," Jill predicted. "It's then up to the FBI to find these suspects and arrest them. Broomfield will have to name an interim CEO for regulatory reasons. Angela and I will not interview them so I think they will be safe for the time being. As to the patients, it is unlikely that forty-eight hours more of ineffective therapy will make a clinical difference. If there are dangerous side effects demonstrated in those clinical trials or that have happened since by the data in Joseph's computer, let's find it tonight and then we will assess our risk with patients. Does that sound like a plan?"

"Yes, I really want these bastards that have killed Joseph and now Peter."

Nathan offered everyone a late night sugar boost in the form of a triple layer chocolate cake with vanilla ice cream. It was much appreciated by all and everyone got back to work building the case for the FBI. Jake had his own people working as well, but he secretly thought that Jill's team would win the race on this investigation. They really had sharp and unique skills. His team did not include a physician or a social media guru like were in this room. He could offer a profiler, but that wouldn't likely solve the case any faster. They thought they had their man and motive. They just needed a few more pieces of evidence to lay it out for an arrest warrant. Jake knew he could arrest Jason Brown simply because he was on the Most Wanted list, but he wanted to send him to jail for the rest of his life based on the criminal activities he had been involved with over the last decade. Since Mr. Brown seemed to have a lock on following the four women, if they could gather enough evidence tonight he would need to use them as decoys in the morning the flush out Brown and Associates.

With David's help, Jill poured through the data that Joseph had saved on his computer. Joseph had been reviewing clinical trials data going back six years. Broomfield pharmaceuticals had many drugs on the market. Only about a quarter of them had been tested by RMCT Corporation. That went a long way to reducing David's anxiety about getting drugs off the market.

"Let's focus on these ten drugs," said Jill. "Which is the biggest blockbuster?"

"I know Jo and Morgan are following the money, so it would be good to get their opinion on which is the biggest blockbuster. I have spreadsheets going back a decade on the various drug revenues." Pointing to a column labeled with a drug name David said, "I think this drug would generate the largest royalties for Bloomfield Pharmaceuticals and RMCT Corporation and perhaps RMCT would put the greatest effort into falsifying data for that drug."

It took Jo and Morgan less than five minutes to verify David's assessment, and they both agreed. That really helped Jill focus on the one drug trial. The royalties of this one drug over the years of the relationship was fifty million dollars paid to RMCT.

"I think I would like to verify the safety and efficacy of this drug from the RMCT clinical trials," Jill proposed. "David can you find that spreadsheet first? I would then like the reports that Broomfield has kept for the years since the drug has been on the market. By the way, when did the FDA approve this medication?"

"Jill, here is the RMCT trials results as well as drug incident reports sent to Broomfield after the drug was on the market. As you can see from those dates, the drug went through two years of trials and it took a year beyond that to gain FDA approval. It has been on the market now for six years."

"I would think that it would have been cheaper for Broomfield to hire its own clinical staff to do the tests," Marie surmised.

"I think that is the reason that only twenty-five percent of the drugs went to RMCT," agreed Jill.

"Yeah, I remember Joseph griping about the cost of the royalties and how that was motivating him to start his own in-house trials unit," noted David. "When Broomfield was growing its business in the beginning the company tried to put all of its cash into R and D. So an offer from RMCT to have significantly lower clinical trial costs in return for a share of future earnings would have caught their interest."

"What is this drug used for?" asked Marie. "I am amazed at the royalty payments."

"This drug is Broomfield's most successful drug ever and it is used to boost the energy levels of patients undergoing chemotherapy. Energy level is important as it can boost mood and make a cancer patient more likely to exercise," Jill explained. "Mood and exercise greatly contribute to the healing process. I would guess that this drug has become part of a standard cocktail of drugs used to treat the side effects of patients undergoing chemo or radiation therapy. Since it is not cancer type specific and can be used on all cancer patients, I would guess that usefulness is responsible for creating the huge revenues involved."

"So it sounds like there is a downside to this drug." Angela suggested.

"That is what I am searching for," replied Jill. "I don't remember hearing anything about it in my medical journals, but I don't follow cancer research announcements that regularly."

"We had better all be quiet and let you start looking for the source of the problem," said Marie. "Besides we all have our own work to do."

Silence reigned in the room for a while. Then they all nearly caused themselves neck muscle injuries by jerking their heads around when Jill muttered aloud. "I got it". This was followed by a babble of "what?" from nearly everyone in the room.

"So this drug does exactly as it says. From all reports it elevates mood and patients do report being able to do nearly all of what they want to do. There were one or two marathoners who couldn't run for twenty-six miles while undergoing chemo-therapy, but some patients even took up with more rigorous fitness programs after they started the drug. Alas there are a couple of problems with that level of happiness. The drug is highly addictive and has such a high rate of suicide after its abrupt withdrawal that it deserves at the very least a black box warning and perhaps it would even warrant pulling the drug off the market. Few patients after ending their cancer treatment have been weaned off of it. I think most physicians seeing the depres-sion and perhaps suicidal ideations of patients were afraid not to keep the patient on the drug."

"So why wasn't this additional element discovered during the trials, I would have thought that they saw the problem six months into a trial?" queried Jo. "I thought Jake mentioned cancer antigens."

"The cancer antigens were from a different drug study provided by RMCT for Broomfield," replied Jill. "While it is likely problematic, it generates one of the smallest sources of royalties for RMCT. As to why the element wasn't discovered during the trials, I think it was discovered, but RMCT covered it up by one of three methods. Either they made sure they lost the patient to follow up because their cancer treatment was complete. You expect some of those patients in every study, but I have never seen such a high proportion. A second group of patients were victims of accidents. Again I have never seen such a high accident rate in a study group. This is not my area of research expertise, but I am amazed as to the number of patients that died of accidental causes - it is like perhaps thirty. The third group had the drug continued to be prescribed to them by a RMCT physician, but since the study ended, they didn't have to report that to anyone. So they hid the addiction from Broomfield by continuing the patients on the medications. There were a few suicides, but they were attributed to the general suicide rate of cancer patients.

"In the last twelve months, there were whisperings that turned into louder conversation within the cancer community about the drug. Patients had such a feeling of euphoria that all they wanted was to continue the drug, so they actually wanted the negative side effects to be hushed up. In chat rooms and blogs, patients would talk about how wonderful the drug was which caused many entrants into a cancer regimen to ask for the drug. I think it reached Joseph's level after he spoke with a cancer researcher at a conference. The researcher was highly pleased with a different therapy of Broomfield Pharmaceuticals, but made remarks about the "happy pills" as they liked to call this problematic drug. When Joseph returned from the conference he started reviewing data on this drug. He saved a few spreadsheets last week. One spreadsheet was an analysis of all drug incidents reported to Broomfield. Another spreadsheet contained the names of the original study participants and where they were now. Some were dead as their cancer killed them, but what had really concerned him was the number of study participants still taking the drug six years later. It was unlikely that they had remained in cancer treatment for such an extended time."

"Joseph had a meeting on his calendar for first thing Monday morning when we returned from vacation to meet with the CEO of RMCT. We located the calendar entry as a part of recovering his company communications," explained David. "I keep searching my memory to think about what Joseph may have commented on this issue, but I think he was still in a fact finding mode. He had a habit of not saying anything until he thought he had all the facts and he was probably waiting to hear what the RMCT CEO's explanation was."

"Interesting that the CEO of RMCT didn't mention that meeting when we asked him about Joseph," remarked Angela.

"Yes, isn't it interesting," agreed Jill.

"Okay we have found a motive," said Jake. "There is likely a big problem with any or all of the drugs that RMCT performs clinical trials on and it impacts patients. How do I connect these suspects to the murder? Where is my proof as to who fired the curare dart gun? What is the role of each of these Most Wanted suspects and where can I find them?"

Jake said these words more to his own agents than to Jill's team, but they could all tell he was frustrated. It was getting late, it had been a very busy day and the chocolate cake had long worn off.

"Those are all very good questions," agreed Jill. "You have your suspects so close and yet so far away. I am tired and unable to offer answers to your questions. Actually with the exception of Nathan, everyone in this room may be too tired to think. Let's call it quits for tonight and start fresh in the morning."

Shortly thereafter, her team and David filed into their respective bedrooms or suites. Jake and his agents were left with Nathan who looked at them and said, "Don't worry, she does her best work early in the morning. You'll all figure this out tomorrow. If you would like to depart for your rooms, I'll lock up behind you."

With those words of advice, the agents left the suite and Nathan did indeed lock up for the night and entered the room he and Jill were sharing. As usual, she did her rapid drop-off into sleep. She seemed to drain all of her considerable thinking resources on a case like this such that when she saw her bed, her brain snapped off and it was lights out.

CHAPTER 14

*N*athan was relaxing in bed thinking about Marie's adventure on the chairlift, when he thought he heard a noise in the suite. He held his breath and listened again. Then he was sure there was someone out there. He woke Jill up, quickly told her what was happening and dialed Nick. Jill then called Jake to let him know what was happening. She hoped it was all a false alarm. She hadn't called her friends for fear that their ring tones would make noise in the suite. They could see the occasional light under their door like someone was walking around with a flashlight.

Nathan and Nick had both peered into the suite's living room to see someone taking flash photos of Jill's murder board. That was the light they saw and the sound they heard - he had been snapping pictures and moving papers on the board. He had his back to the suite's bedroom doors, so Nick held his hand out as he counted one-two-three, and both men ran toward the photographer. He heard the noise and, startled, he ran for the suite's door and opened it to find Jake standing there. He started backing away from Jake and ran into Nick, who grabbed his arms to restrain him, hoping that Jake carried wrist ties with him. Nathan had stood back turning the lights on once the intruder was detained. Jill was right on his heels knocking on the doors of the other three women. She heard Jake talking in the suite's living room.

"Bjorn Daniel Sundin, you're under arrest for various cyber-crimes including ones that you have likely committed tonight in this suite." Jake proceeded to give him the Miranda warning, and called his team members from the cabin to assist him in escorting Mr. Sundin to an interrogation room at the FBI building near the airport. They would arrive there about two in the morning and Jake made arrangements to have another agent take charge of the operation in Breck while he accompanied Mr. Sundin to Denver. Two Most Wanted criminals dead or arrested in the past sixteen hours and now he was on the hunt for Bogachev and Brown. He might bag four people off of the Most Wanted list within a week. If he wanted a job at Quantico, he would bet it was his for the asking after this case. Of course he couldn't take all of the credit. Jill's team was the best set of private investigators that he had ever worked with.

After Jake left with his agent escort and prisoner, it took some time for the suite of people to relax again. Before any of them could go to bed, they discussed what the likely next steps were when Sundin didn't show up or contact Brown. Nick would review the room key system in the morning when they awoke. They agreed that it was likely that nothing would be tried in the suite again this night. They might know some new information after Sundin's interrogation so they may as well all get some sleep. Again the suite was quiet, but this time Nick was taking a sofa in the living room to be the guard for the night.

Despite the interrupted sleep, Jill was again up early. She sent Nick back to his room to get a little more sleep as she guessed the sofa was not the most comfortable spot for a tall guy like him. He hesitated than agreed he would be a little better with some sleep.

Jill was sitting at the dining room table staring at the murder board. Fortunately, last night's intruder had not destroyed her board. While she was sitting there, she got texts from both David and Morgan to see if she was awake. Morgan knew of last night's adventures; David did not. They soon joined her in the suite.

"Good morning, David. We had another adventure last night with someone breaking into our suite. Mr. Sundin is now down in Denver being interrogated by the FBI. Morgan, have you heard any news from Denver yet?"

"Who was Mr. Sundin again?" asked David.

"He was on the FBI's Most Wanted list for cybercrimes," replied Jill. "We think he may have been either solely responsible or part of a team that shut down the lifts. I am referring to the sixteen minute stoppage that occurred about the time that Joseph was murdered. He may have been the person that wiped Joseph's computer drive and cut off his access. He got access to this suite last night and he was taking pictures of the murder board at the time of his arrest. Nick is following up on the room access card, but while you are in your suite, you should have an agent guarding you."

David looked at Jill with concern. "Wow, you had a busy night Jill. I'm glad that of the four criminals, one is dead and the other in custody. Perhaps this case will get solved today like you said. I thought you were being optimistic yesterday when you gave that timeline."

"Yes I am a little short on sleep, but as a morning person, I can never sleep late no matter how poor my sleep was the night before. So I have been staring at the board thinking about Jake's question on how we tie the clinical trial problems and Joseph's murder with Jason Brown."

"Jill, didn't you say that Jason Brown worked as a manager while the company was growing and that he was the supervisor of clinical trials at the time the falsified data was created," asked David.

"I did say that. However, how do I get from there to sitting next to Joseph on the chairlift, injecting him with curare?"

"Have you tried to track down the purchase of the curare or the dart gun? Or how about asking Mr. Sundin where did the order to stop the chairlift come from?"

"David, those are great suggestions. I'll chase down the curare source. We still don't know who actually pulled the trigger of the dart gun. It could have been Mr. Fisher since he was a sharpshooter. I remember from our viewing the woods where Joseph was located that I decided the dart gun shooter had to be good. He would have had to stop on a dime and take perhaps fifteen seconds to calm his breathing down and fire accurately. A sharpshooter would have the ability to do that. While we don't know if our sharpshooter was a 'skier', he was found dead on an expert ski run so I think we can assume that he might be Joseph's killer."

"What kind of slope was he found on? Just because he was found on an intermediate slope doesn't mean he was advanced enough to ski the slope where Joseph was murdered."

Morgan joined them, having ended her conversation with Denver.

"I spoke with Jake and he'll return here later this afternoon. As you can imagine, he wants to drop by his own home, see his family, and grab some sleep and a shower. They aren't finished interviewing Mr. Sundin, but they do have some new information for us.

"Mr. Sundin understands he is going to jail and he'll be without computer access for a long time. Jake said he cried when they told him he wouldn't have computer access while he was in prison. Computers seem to be his obsession, passion, and addiction. He didn't cry about going to jail, he cried about the lack of access to computers. Throughout their interview, he asked each agent at different times if he could play with their iPhones. If an agent took it out of his pocket to check a text, the interview stopped until it was out of sight. They are going to have a psychiatrist evaluate him today, since his behavior was so strange. Jake also mentioned that he and Bogachev, at Mr. White's instigation, were experimenting with the ski resort's computer systems. Sundin only knew Brown as White and had never performed an internet search on him to know his criminal background. It appears that in addition to just stealing from skiers' credit cards, they planned to hold the resort hostage through a series of planned chairlift failures. He seemed to be totally exploited by Brown, and had no perception that his activities with computer systems might be illegal. He doesn't understand the concepts of legal versus illegal; rather for him, it is just what he can do with a computer. The criminal justice system will have a hard time dealing with this gentleman as he seems so brilliant in his understanding of computers and yet he has a childlike grasp of right and wrong. Jake is not sure we could even use his testimony against Brown."

"Wow! What an interesting individual," exclaimed Jill. "I think we can cross him off our list of murder suspects. I sort of get the picture of his mental brilliance and deficits, so I can't think he'll lead us to Brown. Thus, we still have Bogachev and Brown running around out there. I think our next focus is three areas. David, see what you can find in Joseph's email. When you recovered Joseph's communications, did you recover just for the date and time that the computer was wiped around his death? If so, I would like to see if you can recover any emails for the month leading up to his death. These would be emails that Joseph deleted so I anticipate there will be a lot of junk mail in his trash. The second focus will be the video camera footage around the resort of Joseph, and the third will be tracking the curare purchase."

"Hey guys, good morning! Let me get some coffee and I'll hear what you have been up to," said Marie.

Jill gave her a quick overview of Sundin and her plan for the morning. They agreed that she and Jill would go skiing in the afternoon. When all else failed, try the decoy method for smoking out Brown. Jo and Angela would pass on that adventure and likely Nick and Nathan would want to join Michael and the other agents in protecting them. She would check with Michael to be sure there was enough Kevlar for all of them.

Once Nick and Angela were awake, she would have them work on the video identification, and she, Jo and Morgan would work on the curare and dart gun source, with Marie assisting David in going through a ton of emails. Nathan as always was expected to be their chef. Jill had a real urgency to solve the case today as she was losing most of her team tomorrow. Nick was heading back to the Netherlands aboard Henrik's plane; Jo and Marie were going back to Wisconsin. Angela had an extra day and so if they solved the case today, they would spend some time together enjoying the ski town. The weather was expected to be good for the next three days after an overnight and early morning snow storm which was perfect for skiing and for Angela to take photographs. Morgan coordinated the agents for the afternoon ski excursion, keeping Jake informed of their activities.

As each of them awoke and entered the suite's living room, they were quickly brought up to date on the game plan, and Nathan was of course the last to make an appearance. Michael was bringing in additional Kevlar from Denver to protect the four civilians and working out a protection detail. He wanted to put every available agent on the mountain so they would capture Brown.

Jill was researching curare. Did a killer have to buy a commercial preparation, or could they make it themselves? She discovered in the end that a killer could make the solution, and load the dart canisters without sophisticated equipment. This made it likely that the killer had an unlimited supply of dart syringes.

Next she looked for a signature of the gun or the canister. With a gun, each bullet had a unique marking from the barrel causing markings as the bullet left the chamber. Could the same be said for a safari gun? It didn't look like it caused much of a marking on the syringes and since they hadn't found a syringe;

they had nothing. Sadly it seemed that they needed to catch this guy in the act of shooting the gun.

She would follow that by looking at curare. It had to reach the bloodstream and it would take a fairly large quantity. However, there were multiple outlets to buy it so that would take more time to run that down. The paralytic agent required a prescription from a veterinarian to order the product. She would look into whatever records she could find. She wondered if David had any hacking skills. Since the FBI was in the room, she would wait until she had David alone to ask if he could and would hack into the purchasing system of RMCT. Of course since they lacked a search warrant it was an illegal search, but if they did find a purchase of paralytics by RMCT, they probably could go get a warrant for the vet supply that was used. She decided to take a break and see how the others were doing then it might be time to change into her ski gear to go up the mountain to ski. She hadn't figured out yet the perfect tactic to use to connect Jason Brown to Joseph Morton's shooter and that gap was driving her nuts. Perhaps the pristine air of the mountain would give her some inspiration.

She invited David out on the balcony and he nodded as he noted the hand sign she gave him that she wanted to chat with him. He stood up and followed her outside to admire the view.

"David, how is it going?"

"This work and your team are interesting; thanks for allowing me to join in."

"You have been a real help and in fact I was hoping you would agree to do something more."

"Sure, how can I help?"

"You seem to be very talented with computers, I have been wondering if you could take it a step farther? Do you have the ability to hack into other companies' computers?"

"That is illegal."

"That is not my question. Do you know how to do that?"

"Of course," David replied with a smirk as if that was ever a question.

"I have been searching for a way to tie Jason Brown to Joseph's killer. In looking at the agent used - curare has several sellers. It has to be a veterinarian supplier as it is not used on humans anymore in the United States. So if I could find that RMCT bought that product from an animal supply house, it would help establish a link. Do you think you could hack into the RMCT purchasing system?"

"Is that all you want? That small bit of information will be easy to find inside their system. I could do the reverse and check out the supply companies, but I think going to RMCT will be faster."

"If you find the data with RMCT, I think it will be easy for the FBI to get a warrant for the vet supply businesses. Since we're extracting the data illegally, they won't be able to be use it as evidence against Mr. Brown. You could also be prosecuted for hacking into their system. No matter how good you are, it is not worth that risk. I know I seem to be giving you conflicting signals here but while I really want you to hack something, I also really want you to consider the downside of my request."

"Okay. Once everyone clears out for the afternoon ski adventure, I'll hack into their purchasing system at that time."

"Just be careful. Remember they, and I don't know who the "they" are, had some kind of warning that Peter was digging into company data and about forty-five minutes later he was dead."

"Thanks for the reminder and I will be careful. Most companies don't put as much security and encryption on their purchasing side so there may not be any monitoring at all."

"Have you found anything usable in the email or files you restored on Joseph's drive?" asked Jill as they returned to the suite's living room.

"Yes, I can see some of the conversation between Joseph and the RMCT staff concerning the data from the trials. It points to motive but I don't think it is incriminating - at least what I have found so far."

"You know the general theory of what we're chasing here so let us know if you find anything definitive."

"Will do."

Nathan prepared them all a high carbohydrate lunch to fuel those that would be on the ski slope. Then Michael assisted the four civilians in putting on the Kevlar protection. They got very hot very quickly with the extra layer of protection and Jill went outside on the balcony to cool off while the others finished getting dressed. Soon Michael deemed them ready. He went over some self-protection moves and had them all practice. Then he had a conversation on how to get off the lift in an emergency. Again they proved to be excellent students. Jake wanted to be on the mountain in hopes of taking down Jason Brown. After a little sleep, he had left his home in Denver and driven up the hill to the ski resort. Through walkie-talkies, Jake would make sure that he was always on the ground while they were on the chairlift.

The group was quiet as they left the hotel for the gondola. On one hand, they were excited to be up on such a superb mountain, on the other hand, they traveled to the lifts not knowing if they were being followed or not.

"I wish this guy would shoot and miss us so we could get this cat and mouse game over and just enjoy the mountain," Marie declared. "I am going to try and come back every year now that this mountain has spoiled me for the local resorts. Michael, with your help I feel very comfortable on the mountain."

"How long had you guys been skiing yesterday when shots were fired at you?" asked Jill.

Marie looked to Michael for an answer, "About two hours. They are obviously following you and it takes them time to not only follow you up the mountain but to make arrangements to shoot you. They have to be in the perfect position which is not easy with you guys constantly on the move. This time if I were them I would shoot you from the ground and I would use the dart gun rather a gun. I would aim to take us down with paralytic agents."

"OMG!" exclaimed Jill. "I should have brought an antidote for us as well as an Ambu bag in case any of us gets hit."

"Not to worry, I have the antidote in my backpack as well as a manual resuscitator. Besides you're all wearing Kevlar so unless a dart hits an uncovered part or at a particular angle, you should be safe. All of you avoid taking off your helmet and gloves except inside a bathroom stall and I think you'll be protected. Gentlemen, for any bathroom larger than a single, avoid the urinal and use the stall for all business. Jill, if I should be the one to go down, let me tell you what I carry in my emergency pack." Michael listed off a series of first aid supplies plus a few additional items unique to skiing and high altitudes.

"What did you mean that the dart could get through the Kevlar if it hit a certain angle?" asked Marie.

"Kevlar is best known for protecting law enforcement from bullets. The way it does this is by the Kevlar fibers locking and repelling something hitting them. They spread out the force of a bullet across the fabric. However in the case of knives, there is a cutting action that allows you to get through the fabric. Darts fall somewhere between the two. If the dart is fired from some distance and comes at you with some force, your Kevlar will repel it. If the killer should engage in close range knife or dart combat, where the motion is much slower, you may be vulnerable," Michael disclosed.

"Do you have enough antidotes for all of us? I think the guy could get one or two of us at close range, but not all of us," asked Nathan. "How does the antidote work in case you or Jill are incapacitated? How fast does the paralytic agent work? Would we have time to inject the antidote ourselves?"

"Good questions Nathan. I have about ten antidotes with me. In addition to you four there will be other agents on the mountain. Each agent is carrying an antidote in addition to my stock-pile and I'll give each of you an antidote to carry. The drug works quickly so you will have one to two minutes to self-inject at the most. The antidote works in two-three minutes, so it is quite possible for you to have complete respiratory failure even if you get the antidote injected. Stay in pairs so that one of you can give mouth to mouth while waiting for the reversal-agent to work."

"That's a grim thought," exclaimed Marie. "I think I like the threat of guns more."

"You and me both," agreed Jill. "We just need to make sure that no one gets close to us. I have a sixth sense for bad people getting close to me, so we have that in our favor. Michael, do you have pictures of the other agents so I know who the good guys are up on the mountain?"

Using his phone he brought up pictures of the agents. Then while pointing out the chairlifts and discussing which ones they should take, he managed to identify for the group all the agents in his vicinity. The chairlifts generally seated six people on each chair. The agents were going to rotate and ride the chairlift as that sixth person. Michael took them through a series of warm-ups on easy slopes getting to know everyone's strengths on skis. They were all advanced intermediates probably willing and able to ski anything on the mountain except the double black diamond rated slopes.

Nick was amazed with this ski resort. It was as good as any resort in Europe that he had skied. He liked the atmosphere in this American resort and wanted to return sometime for a vaca-tion rather than work. Maybe instead of looking at towns with medium populations around half a million, he should concentrate on resort areas where the rich played, but still wanted security protection.

Marie was looking forward to another wonderful few hours of skiing with Michael, even though the threat of the paralytics hung over them. She had loved the few hours of skiing she had enjoyed the previous day with him as a guide.

Jill had mixed emotions. On one hand she was going to enjoy some time with her friends. On the other hand she felt guilty for not doing work to solve the case and she was worried if any of them should be hit by the paralytic agent and they were alone, they could die. She was going to work hard to make sure that none of them were alone at any time.

Nathan was tense. He just had a feeling that something was going to go wrong this afternoon. They were out on the ski slopes inviting trouble and the hair on the back of his neck had been up for the past fifteen minutes. He was freaked about anyone getting close enough to touch any of them. It was still early in the ski season so the lines were light, but it was now the week-end and so the day skiers from Denver had arrived and both the resort and the town were busier. It seemed the only place they were safe from the killer was on the chairlift. It was really wrecking his enjoyment of the snow, his friends, and the beautiful day.

Michael was not wearing his ski patrol jacket today. He had too many people to guard and couldn't afford the distraction of a skier in distress that he would normally stop and assist. He was carrying his ski patrol first aid kit and the antidotes. His fellow agents were doing a great job rotating and keeping a net around the group. He had set his phone to vibrate at the time that marked when they had been attacked the previous day. He figured that it took time for the killer to determine where they were skiing and perhaps get in-sync with their speed on the mountain. Since it was busier today, people were just standing closer together which made it worrisome. Someone could just walk by them and stab them with a poison dart and they wouldn't see it until they collapsed to the ground. If one of them got hit with a dart while on the chairlift, that would be even more dangerous. He shuddered inwardly as he imagined someone being paralyzed on a moving chairlift high above the ground; not only would their 'partner' need to administer the antidote, they would also need to keep the victim from falling out of the chair. In addition, someone would likely have to ventilate the paralyzed person. He would just keep his fingers crossed that if an attack came, it would happen on the ground.

The group each with their own occasional worrisome thoughts, continued to enjoy the day despite the risks. Michael was able to coordinate all their bathroom and water breaks to a ski hut that he could watch anyone entering and exiting. It was getting down to the final thirty minutes that the lifts were open and everyone had begun to relax that an attack wouldn't be coming that day. They had been on the T-bar for the past three runs and were taking advantage of Michael's ski knowledge to improve with each run down the mountain. The lift came to a halt which it had done several times throughout the day. They all chatted expecting the lift to start at any moment.

CHAPTER 15

*E*xcept this wasn't any ordinary stoppage. This one was planned and executed by Bogachev. He and Brown were tired of this lady and her team getting too close to the secrets of their little arrangement with the RMCT trials. They could tell based on where she and her friends were looking in their computer searches that they likely understood their scheme. The two planned to end their relationship with RMCT and disappear. When they were ready to resurface again they knew they could set up a new scheme to make money by hacking into computers from anywhere on earth. Bogachev was tired of the snow in Denver; it was too similar to the cold of Russia.

Brown knew Jill Quint was about to expose the illegal scheme he had been working for almost a decade. Oh well, it was time to move on. He had been watching the four skiers with their FBI escorts all afternoon. He had a new dart gun that allowed him to fire more darts quickly. He had been close to the T-bar lift when it stopped. In fact, he had been speaking to Bogachev to make sure the lift stopped at the right moment where he would have perfect aim and execution. He planned to pick off the two women first followed by the two gentlemen, and then he would take down everyone around them as he thought they were all FBI or some such agency. He had a snow berm and tree to duck behind and then he planned to ski quickly off the mountain, head for his car, and leave the state.

He had been lying on his side as snowboarders were wont to do on the mountain, looking like he was taking a rest. He had managed to get his dart gun out of his backpack and assembled, loading it with ten rapid fire paralyzing darts. He had just been waiting for the lift to stop. He aimed and fired from behind the tree.

Marie was on the lead bar with Michael as her partner. Jill was looking straight ahead when she saw the dart hit Marie. She yelled at everyone "take cover". She released the bar and dove to the ground while still more darts were being fired. Skis still attached to her feet, she used them to block an incoming dart. She heard a gun-shot ring out behind her.

"Nathan, are you okay? Have you been hit?" Jill asked from where she was taking cover.

"Need the antidote" was all he weakly managed to get out.

She had been crawling on her belly to reach Nathan. She pulled an antidote out of her pocket and injected Nathan. She watched his respirations, glad for the smoke screen. Additional darts had been fired and had struck some of the agents. An agent had popped off his skis and taken cover behind the wide metal pole that supported the T-bar cable. He was keeping constant fire aimed at where the darts had come from and then he threw a smoke grenade in the vicinity of the shooter.

Taking a quick look around her, she saw Marie being bagged by Michael's manual resuscitator and Nick assisting the agent with him. She got to her knees above Nathan and started to do mouth to mouth resuscitation. She had been giving him air for about two minutes, when he started to breathe a little on his own. Again looking around, she saw that Marie was doing better as was Nick's agent.

Just as she was saying a silent prayer for all of them, first a body, then a face appeared through the smoke screen and ran at her. It felt like slow motion, because he was moving slower due to his heavy boots and she was breathing hard from the horror of the last few minutes. The man running at her looked crazed. Jill had a few seconds to remember her martial arts teacher telling her how to shift her own weight to throw someone heavier away from her. She saw another dart clenched in his hand. She judged his shoulder, put her head down and managed to redirect his momentum to the ridge edge.

Before he could stop himself he went over the ridge. Michael believed Marie was on the road to recovery and, therefore had stepped towards Jill to assist. After her brilliant move, he instead focused his attention on Mr. Brown's journey off the side of the mountain. He lay below, faintly asking for help, his knee and opposite shoulder at odd angles. Michael looked at the group to assess their recoveries.

"Marie, are you still doing ok? Having any trouble breathing on your own?"

Marie nodded and managed a small smile.

"Jill, how is Nathan and how is your shoulder?"

"He is breathing on his own," said Jill in a strained voice. "We're going to need baskets to get these folks off the mountain. They're too weak to ski down."

"I'll get help," replied Michael in full control of the situation. "Just checking in with my fellow agents. Nick, how is my agent doing?"

"Ditto, Jill's response. We need some help up here."

"Yes, I know. Our killer is over that ledge yelling the same thing. Let me just check that we had only one shooter." He radioed his agent at the bottom of the chairlift pole; and the agent had only seen one shooter. Then he called Jake.

"Jake, we got your man and I have several of our group recovering from the paralytic agent. We need help now."

"Got it, I'm coming up the T-bar path right now. We'll send ski patrol on snowmobiles your way to get people off the mountain. Where is Jason Brown?"

"Jill assisted him over the ridge beneath the T-bar so he is lying on that slope with a broken or dislocated leg as well as a dislocated shoulder. We have not yet confirmed that there are no other shooters in this area since the smoke hasn't cleared yet, but once we confirm, I'll send an agent down to Mr. Brown immediately."

Jake requested "Can you keep an eye on him or is that dangerous in your current position?"

"Dangerous until the smoke clears. Half the group here is recovering from paralytic agents and would be unable to help the other half if they get hit by a dart or bullet. Like I said Mr. Brown is too injured to go anywhere and even if a friend rode up to him on a snowmobile, the pain of moving him would likely render him unconscious."

"Okay, I understand your critical situation. Help is on the way."

Michael ended the call, assessing the situation again. Everyone was breathing on their own and able to move fingers. After updating a barely moving Marie, he walked over to Jill and Nathan, and then Nick and one of his agents. He heard Jake's snowmobile head over to where the smoke was clearing.

"I should warn you that you'll be receiving special recognition from the FBI for saving one of our own," said Michael. "This may be a first as I can't recall any non-US citizen saving one of our agents. We'll likely have our ambassador speak to your government to make sure they know what a hero you are in the eyes of the Americans."

"I'd like to avoid all of that," replied Nick. "I just did what any decent human being would do."

"Sorry it is out of your hands. We really do appreciate you saving our agent's life and we must recognize you in public to express our gratitude. Perhaps it will help your business or your expansion into the US. All wit aside, I really do appreciate from the bottom of my heart your saving my agent's life."

Then Michael turned around and admonished, "Folks, the smoke is clearing, so we are all vulnerable again, so stay down until I yell 'clear'. Jake is over at the site now checking it out."

The smoke had nearly dissipated and Jake and another agent searched the area and came up with nothing. The group was safe.

"There appears to be just this one shooter so we are clear. I'm heading down the hill to check on our shooter," said Michael as he soon disappeared over the ridge.

Jill yelled at another agent standing by, "Don't let him go by himself! The guy could shoot him with a dart. We're safe here; all capable agents should rush down the slope and assist Agent York in arresting him."

After a few seconds, they agreed that their boss might need help and they went over the ridge.

Jill paced back and forth checking Marie, Nathan and the agent. All seemed to be recovering, but none had enough muscle control to even lift their heads off the ground. She soon heard snowmobiles coming their way. One able bodied agent was still with them, so she asked him to pass the downed agent's weapon to her in case she needed to use it. The agent would check for ski patrol identity.

It was soon clear that these were friends. All three recovering victims soon had oxygen going and were placed in baskets to be hauled off the mountain. They all appeared to be slowly recovering but at this altitude a little extra oxygen never hurt.

Jill looked over the ridge as her friends were being loaded. It appeared that Mr. Brown was not moving, and neither Michael, nor any of his agents, was in any danger. She caught a ride on the back of the snowmobile that carried Nathan. She would just bet that when he could talk he would be proud that she had used her martial arts skills to defend the two of them. Nathan had taken her to a martial arts competition after her first dangerous case and from that experience; she had begun learning Tae Kwon Do. Soon all three of them were in first aid being checked out by a doctor. Their control of their muscles was slowly returning and they were able to stay upright in a wheelchair. The doctor made a call to an anesthesiologist friend who gave them a timeline on a full recovery of three more hours. All three victims returned to the hotel suite in wheelchairs to be made a fuss over by Angela and Jo.

"Nathan, how are you feeling?" asked Jo. "I understand you will be able to walk again in an hour or so. I guess that means you won't be cooking us dinner?"

"Ha ha. Why don't I supervise Jill cooking dinner?" suggested Nathan.

There was a chorus of "no's" from her friends and Jill.

"We all know that even with your keen supervision, I'll still not win Master Chef," lamented Jill. "I simply don't care to learn how to be a good cook. If you guys become steady on your feet in about ninety minutes, we'll go eat out. Otherwise, we will order in pizza. Michael, we should be safe now that Jason Brown is in custody, right?"

"Jake has officially arrested him for the prior murder a decade ago as well as the attempted murder of all of you. Since one of the paralyzed skiers was an FBI agent, he'll do extra time for attempted murder of a federal agent. Jake may be able to charge him in Joseph Morton's death eventually. Remember though that Bogachev is not in custody and he may have been behind either the snowplow or snowmobile attacks."

"I think our chances are better with him than with Jill's cooking, so let's go for dinner in town if you guys get steady on your feet," said Jo.

"I would be hurt by all of your disparaging remarks about my cooking except that I agree with you," said a smiling Jill. "I'm going to give David a call and check on his progress and invite him to dinner with us. He was working on identifying the dart gun drug source for us, but since we caught Mr. Brown holding the smoking gun, we may be able to link him to Joseph's murder without additional information."

Minutes later David arrived in the suite amazed at what had happened during the past hour or so. He was glad to see Nathan, Marie, and the agent taking tentative steps signifying that they were nearly at the end of working the paralytic drug out of their systems. It also pained him to think of how Joseph died when he heard about the rescue operation up on the mountain. They had Joseph's likely killer in custody. They had a call scheduled in an hour with Jake to get an update on his conversation with their suspect. Jill suspected that the FBI might stay in the area for a little longer in hopes of capturing Bogachev, but she would see what Jake said.

David had found the purchase of the veterinarian darts on the supply ordering computer system of RMCT. The delivery location was Jason Brown's office. This would add weight to his conviction. They all wanted to ensure that he would be locked away for life.

Jo and Morgan completed the trace of the company's and Brown's financial records including some that were off-shore. The man had amassed a fortune he could not spend in his lifetime and yet he was still greedy for more. He should have walked away when Joseph started asking questions; instead he let his greed, ego, and psychopathic killer instinct rule the day. Now he was in custody, hopefully for the rest of his life.

While Nick was out skiing, Angela had been reviewing a series of photos of the hotel lobby and the ski resort to see if she could track Bogachev. She couldn't locate him in the lobby shots but she had located him up on the mountain. She had found him on beginner rated ski slopes and at two different ski resort lodges. With the interior shots, he was often seen using a computer tablet. She had wondered if that was what he was using to stop the lifts. She went back and looked at the time on the photos and

A BRECK DEATH

decided that it was likely what he was using. When she had heard about the trouble up on the mountain, she had requested video feed from the resort for the two ski resort lodges for an hour before the incident. They had willingly sent the footage. She located him in the lodge, but since the resort had closed by the time she looked at the tapes, there was no reason to send any agents to that location. Therefore, they would discuss options for finding him after they spoke with Jake. They were curious as to whether or not Jason Brown had given up any information on Bogachev.

After watching Marie and Nathan each do a light jog around their suite, it eased everyone's mind about their recovery. Then they gathered around a speaker phone for the call with Jake.

"Hey Jake, it's my team plus David and your agents. What is the news out of Denver?"

"First let me ask - Marie, Nathan, Agent, how are you doing?"

"We just did a light jog around the suite so I think we are fully recovered," replied Marie looking at the other two and getting nods of agreement.

"Nick, you will be receiving an award from the FBI honoring your actions that saved the life of an FBI agent. I want to thank you for your actions."

"He would have done the same for me," said Nick simply.

"Yes he would have, but we don't expect civilians to save us," commented Jake. "I'll move on to my interview with Jason Brown. He is quite a piece of work, and resting uncomfortably at St. Louise Medical Center, thanks to you, Jill. His journey off the ridge caused him to break his tibia and tear nearly every ligament in his knees. He also has a concussion and broken ribs and collar-bone. He is presently flying high on narcotics and under heavy guard."

"Did you have a chance to ask him about Bogachev?" asked Jill.

"No, he was under heavy sedation. David, he did confirm that he killed Joseph. I can't use his confession because he could easily claim his brain was fuzzy from the drugs and maybe the concussion, but we'll get it from him eventually."

Jill put her hand on David's arm and gave it a squeeze as he said "Thank you, Agent Porter."

"The hospital believes he'll be reasonably coherent later tomorrow or the next day and he'll be ready to be transferred to the infirmary at the jail. I'll keep you posted on any updates. We have also entered the offices of RMCT and seized their records. We have asked the FDA to appoint a panel to review any patient harm from the falsified trials. It will be slow going but we don't have the expertise to do anything else but ask for outside assistance."

"It's important that someone focus on any harm that is occurring today with patients. From what I learned in looking at the studies, they were not so much harmful drugs as ineffective drugs," Jill observed. "It will delay treatment for some patients and some may have passed away by now since some of the products go back five years. Broomfield Pharmaceuticals has a need to be briefed on the problems with RMCT's work so that they can begin looking at their records and notifying patients where necessary. Fortunately we noted in our research that this was twenty-five percent of their portfolio in terms of revenues but only ten percent of their portfolio in terms of patients using these drugs. I would think that while this will be a financial blow to Broomfield, they will survive due to successes with other drugs."

"RMCT has relationships with other pharmaceutical companies so there may be other drugs and other patients at risk at the moment," noted Jake. 'We're looking for our experts to help us with that. Tomorrow a press release will be sent out and a press conference will be held about the deaths of Sundin and Fisher, the capture of Brown, and a 'be on the lookout bulletin' for Bogachev. We will be making an announcement of the problems with RMCT during that press conference and will be distributing the press release to all major pharmaceutical companies which will serve to put them on notice if they used RMCT."

"Do you know where Bogachev is presently located?" asked Angela.

"No I don't," replied Jake.

"I saw him on camera at one of the resort lodges at the time the T-bar stopped. That was about two and a half hours ago. He could be in Denver by now boarding a plane to Bimini."

"Bimini?" questioned Jake as though Angela had said 'Mars'.

"Doesn't Bimini sound like a place you should hide if you're wanted by the FBI?" reasoned Angela.

"Bimini is owned by the Bahamas and we can have you arrested and held for our arrival. If I were Bogachev, I would head home to Russia, stop off in Cuba, or drop in on the Middle East. We don't have extradition agreements with most of those countries. Do you think he knows that Jason was arrested? What do we know about their relationship?"

"We don't know much about their relationship other than we saw them together in the one bar and they seem to be working in tandem with one stopping the lift while the other was doing the killing. He had to have perfectly timed the lift stoppage so that we were in close range of the dart gun. Perhaps when we return from dinner, we'll put our brains to work to solve this question," suggested Marie. "We don't even know if he is a very misdirected computer nerd or if he has been an active participant in any of the murders committed by RMCT."

"If I recall, most of you are leaving tomorrow," mused Jake. "Is that still the game plan?"

Jill replied, "I think everyone is leaving except me, Angela, and Nathan, and we all leave the following day. I was hired to find Joseph's killer and we think he is in custody. I would argue Bogachev should be charged as an accessory. I assume, Jake, that you'll be able to confirm Jason Brown's role tomorrow?"

"Yes, I should be able to confirm that. Jill, would it be possible to hire your team to find Bogachev? You have greatly aided in the capture of two most wanted criminals and I agree he is an accessory to murder; I would love to get Bogachev as well."

"I'll have to talk it over with David and then my team and I'll let you know later tonight," replied Jill.

"Thank you, Jill, and again thank you, Nick, for saving an agent's life today." And the call ended.

"David, I'd like to chat with you on where we are in this investigation and your level of satisfaction with our performance so far. But let's do that after dinner. I suspect the restaurants will be full tonight so we should get a move on. Thoughts on where we should eat and if we should drive - David, I assume you have your car here at the hotel and I have my car as well."

"Is the restaurant far?" asked Jo.

"No matter which restaurant we pick it will be about a seven to ten block walk," Jill estimated getting a nod of agreement from David. "I'm concerned with Marie and Nathan having the stamina to make it there and back. Taking a quick jog in the suite is one thing, walking that distance is another."

"I would welcome the opportunity to walk that distance. You have no idea what a privilege it is to be able to do a light jog after those terrifying moments up on the mountain when I couldn't move my lungs to breathe at all. Walking is sort of a celebration of life for me," mused Nathan. "Marie, Agent, are you two up to a walk?"

Marie looked at the agent before confirming Nathan's statement with a nod, "It is a celebration of life! Let's walk."

"Ok that is settled. David, you know this town best, why don't you pick a restaurant and we'll start walking," Jill advised.

Shortly thereafter the group set off for the downtown area. David surprised them with a sushi bar. There was enough variety in the menu for everyone to enjoy and be filled up. A couple of bottles of warm Sake disappeared while the group dined. In total there were three agents, David, Jill's team of four and Nick and

Nathan. The group of ten had a large table with their own chef. It was a great night with good food, drink, and conversation.

The bill arrived and most of their credit cards were rejected for insufficient funds. At first it was embarrassing, and then Angela had an idea: "Was this Bogachev hacking into our credit cards?"

Fortunately, they all had enough cash to pay their dinner bills. The agents were able to use their credit cards and everyone speculated it was because their names were not known. They each called their credit card companies to find out that someone was making a run on their credit cards. Jill was most concerned that the hotel they were staying in would get paid and her bank promised to contact the hotel to guarantee those charges.

"Aarrgg, that was a hassle, what other computer surprise does he have in store for us?" said Marie.

Jill decided she would notify Jake only to find her cell phone had quit as had everyone else's in the group, including the agents. Bogachev must have gotten their names when they paid their bills.

"Wow, this guy is one of the best hackers I have come across," exclaimed David. "And I should know since I have entered and won several hacking contests."

"We're lucky that you have a desire to teach kids rather than using your computer skills illegally," teased Jo. "I can't begin to imagine what else he can do but we will need someone to counter attack for us."

David speculated, "I wonder where he is? Most hackers have to be within a range of so many feet to hack into your stuff. In the case of your cell phones, he likely masked himself as the telephone company and accessed your phone that way. He must have a portable cell tower - it is something you can buy for about a thousand dollars. Then he uses that fake cell tower to make contact with and control your cell phone like a routine refresh that occurs throughout the day."

"So you're saying that this guy is such a good hacker that he can get in just about anything that is operated by a computer," Angela inquired.

"Yes, that is correct."

"Hmmm, we will have to keep our eyes open for problems," noted Jo.

"I think I see the first problem. My phone is working again and I received a text from my airline that I am on the FAA's no-fly list, so they have canceled my travel plans for tomorrow," announced Marie. "What a pain this is going to be trying to resolve this issue so I can fly again. We may need the FBI's help on getting this cleared. Granted if I have to get stranded in some random location, this is not a bad choice."

"I just got a notice that my passport has been revoked and that I will have to visit the Embassy of the Netherlands in San Francisco or Chicago to leave this country. I would definitely appreciate help from Agent Porter to see this resolved," said a worried Nick.

"The question is, are these notices real or fake?" probed David. "A good hack could fake a notice and an awesome hack could get into all of these computer systems. Since he got into so many while we were at dinner, I would guess that the notices are fake."

"We're lucky to have such a computer whiz in our midst, especially one that thinks like Bogachev does. First thing when we return to the hotel will be to determine real or fake," declared Jill.

They had been walking toward their hotel during this discussion. They could hear the sound of more than one snowplow in the distance. After their previous experience, no one could be faulted for looking for places to run and hide from the plows; everyone picked up their pace. It was soon apparent that Bogachev had taken over the plows like remote control Hot Wheels cars. Unfortunately these were twelve foot by twelve foot tall plows rather than the two inch by three inch cars. They could see no drivers in any of the three plows coming from different directions towards them.

"David, doesn't this guy have to be near us to see where he is driving the plows?" asked Angela.

"No, if he has an accurate GPS, he could drive them remotely; in fact it would be easier to do that given that he is trying to track all three. He must have hacked into one of our cell phones to know where we are. Why doesn't everyone turn off their cell-phone after they put it in airplane mode. That may block him from figuring out our location. Then we need to turn away from this path and see if the plows follow us."

Everyone quickly followed David's instructions and after a short debate, they agreed on a different path to the hotel. Sure enough, the plows didn't make the same turns and follow them. Still, everyone would be more comfortable once they reached the hotel. In another few minutes, they heard silence. The diesel snowplow engines were turned off.

"Before we pat ourselves on the back, let's see what else he has in store for us," suggested David as everyone was grinning.

"I would rather go on the offensive," said Jill. "How can we figure out his location and let our FBI friends take him into custody."

"Let me think a moment," replied David as the group was entering the hotel and continuing to their suite.

"How about if we move out of the hotel and go to either my cabin or Jake's. I have a landline there that we can use, since there is a great need not to turn on our cell phones. This will hide our location and give us phone use. I'll have to think about computer usage. I wouldn't trust any of the computers in our hotel rooms. I also think any other computers attached to the internet will be a problem. At the same time, we need the internet to identify physi-cally where this guy is hiding. Does anyone have suggestions on how to accomplish that?"

"Sorry David, but I don't understand how we leave a trail on the internet to give someone the opportunity to monitor our activity. Maybe if you explained in layman's terms how you would personally track my activity on the internet then I might have a suggestion for you," offered Angela.

"Okay, here goes. A hacker could implant a piece of software like a virus on a computer using remote access or by intercepting a shipment of new computer supplies and implanting spy software which will then notify another computer of activity whenever a computer is powered on. Also your IP address identifies your longitude and latitude settings."

"So with the implanting of spy ware, that would be dumb luck for Bogachev if such malware was implanted in advance of whenever he needed to use it," replied Angela. "It sounds like there is no way to stop that kind of location knowledge if indeed it was planted on all of our computers at the time of manufacture. So the latitude/longitude measurement - can you turn off that feature or remove the GPS widget from our computers while we are in this hotel and then we will move the computers to another location? It sounds like if as long as we keep those location features turned off, that we would be safe at your or Jake's place."

"Yes, you are right and thanks for being my sounding board. That will work for our purposes. I wonder if we should try to go to a different location from our homes as Bogachev likely knows those locations. We could try another hotel or late night restaurant with Wi-Fi access."

They were disrupted by smoke alarms going off in the suite, followed shortly by sprinklers. Jill made a dash for her computer, notes, and murder board. The noise from the alarms was so loud that they couldn't communicate with each other. Everyone started picking important things up and covering them in ski jackets, plastic bags and anything else they could think of that was waterproof. The agents assisted them by grabbing their belongings and getting them out of the suite. No one saw any flames or smoke and many of them thought of Bogachev. This seemingly false alarm and subsequent water mess had his computer hacking skills written all over it. They sent one agent in the elevator with their luggage while the remainder of the party exited via the stairwell carrying purses and computers.

The lobby was calm and silent when they reached it. There were no smoke alarms or sprinklers going off. In fact the person at the front desk was unaware that there were alarms going off in their suite and looked very surprised to see all of them wet from the sprinklers. One of the agents walked security staff back to their suite so he could see the damage. Meanwhile the agent with their luggage was stuck in the elevator. She might be there for hours since a repairman had to come up from Denver. The local fire department was going to try and get her out but there were risks to that if someone else was in control of the elevator.

The hotel meanwhile had offered to switch their rooms, but Jill was afraid that Bogachev would find them and do further damage to the hotel.

"Well, where to now? I'm wet as is everyone else and my dry clothes are in the elevator," stated Jill. "None of us can take much exposure to the outside cold."

"Does anyone's computer work?" asked David. "If our technology is working, that gives us many more options on where to go. If we don't have internet access, I would suggest we go to Silverthorne or perhaps Denver."

Everyone took a moment to check their technology and fortunately about ninety percent of it was working. So now they just needed to find lodging. Fortunately Jake came through; he had a cabin that belonged to a friend that had conveniently left the key close to the cabin.

"How is the agent doing?" asked Jo. "Are they going to be able to get her out tonight?"

"Yes, actually the fire department thought they would be able to release her and the luggage in the next fifteen minutes. They are bringing the elevator to the ground level," Nick explained as he had been keeping tabs on the effort to release the agent. Since he managed hotel security in Europe, he had often dealt with stuck elevators.

Marie commented, "So now we need transportation to the new cabin and we need to make sure that we can't be followed."

David announced, "I have that covered. I have a friend who is in town at the moment and he is going to make as many trips as necessary to move us to the new space. I warned him that we would need some evasive driving and he was looking forward to the challenge. He understands and is relishing the risk with transporting us."

"That sounds like a plan. Are you sure he understands that his own safety is not guaranteed? We had several team members nearly die this afternoon," noted Jill. "Does he have a computer with him? We are one short, at this point thanks to the sprinklers."

"Yes he has both a laptop and an iPad so he can make up for that shortage and he does understand the risks. He is appreciative as am I, for what you have done for me in bringing Joseph's murderer to justice, and wants to help your team."

Just then the agent that had been stuck in the elevator strolled toward them with several pieces of luggage in tow.

"Glad to see you free!" exclaimed Jo. "Was it scary being stuck in there?"

"It wasn't scary once the elevator stopped," the agent replied. "I don't know if you realized, but he sent me on a ride to the top of the building and then to the bottom about ten times. If he had kept it up for another few minutes, I might have had to vomit on your luggage, but fortunately it didn't come to that and thankfully, we are only in a four story building."

"Yikes I would have felt claustrophobic so I guess I would have been happy with the distraction of the elevator movement," declared Jo.

"Is everyone ready to move to a new location?" asked one of the agents. "There is room for all of us to have a bed at Agent

Porter's friend's cabin. I would advise you to leave your luggage here in case there is anything implanted in it and take your night-clothes as well as clothes for tomorrow."

After a few minutes of everyone sorting through their belongings and grabbing the essentials to put into plastic bags provided by the hotel, they were ready to go and the remainder of their belongings was put into storage. David's friend drove a massive SUV that was able to take seven of them at a time. With an agent watching out the back of the car, and with the driver taking several unnecessary turns, they were assured they were not followed. A second trip in the same manner saw all of them ensconced in the large cabin of Agent Porter's friend, and as promised, everyone had a bed.

CHAPTER 16

*A*fter losing an hour and a half of research time due to the problems at the hotel, they were all back at trying to find Bogachev. Jake had meanwhile sent two more agents to the cabin in case they were needed to apprehend Bogachev.

"Let's talk about where Bogachev might be from a location prospective," suggested Jill. "David, with the credit cards, snow-plows and now sprinklers events, could Bogachev have been in Denver conducting these computer malfunctions?"

"Yes and no. Yes they could be directed from anywhere on the planet with a high speed internet connection. However my mathematical mind tells me that the timing has been exquisite on these events which makes me think that either he has a camera trained on one of you at all times or he is in the area for some of these events. The credit cards and snowplow events could have been coordinated through the GPS feature in your phone. The moment you walked into the restaurant, he likely cut off the credit cards, he could have played at any time with your travel arrangements, and I think the snow plows were chasing our phone signals. The hotel smoke alarms and elevator stoppage required a little more coordination. Plus this has a revenge feel to it. What is his motivation for messing with you? If indeed anger or revenge is his motivation wouldn't he need to be around to enjoy your misery?"

"Those are all good points," said Jill thinking aloud. "What is his motivation for messing with us? Perhaps he is on a power trip showing off his prowess with computer systems. Does he care about the arrest of Jason? Is he knowledgeable about Henrik taking over the security at the resort therefore blocking his access to all those credit cards? I would ask if he is any good at hiding, but clearly he is since he has been on the most wanted list for almost five years. How would we determine his location?"

"Let's start with where we have seen him," stated Nick. "When I worked with the Belgian police and we were looking for a criminal, we would look first to where we had sighted them previously as that was a good predictor of the future. David, would you be able to write a program that searches all the footage we have from the resort and identifies every time he is visualized on the tapes. I would also look to our FBI agents to see if they could hustle up the film from cameras around town by contacting the local police."

With those suggestions, they set to work. Marie was looking at what she could find on Bogachev on social media. Nick, Angela, and David had their heads together on what was the best way to find all of the pictures of their suspect. Nathan and Jo were trying to figure out the travel problems to see if they were real or fake. The agents were working their channels to gain access to any around town cameras. Jill had taken her temporary murder board with her when they evacuated the suite. Now she was staring at it while pacing - trying to think of any other avenue to track Bogachev. She didn't understand computers, but if the FBI had been able to crack his Zeus and Gameover programs why couldn't they take it a step farther and infect his computer? Perhaps the agents in the cabin could connect her to the agent or agents that had discovered Bogachev's thieving ways. She walked over to where the three of them were conferring with Denver and the locals.

"I have another idea on how to locate Bogachev that I would like to discuss with your cyber experts. Specifically I would like to speak with the programmer that worked on the Zeus and Gameover software detection. Can you connect me to him or her?"

The agent that had listened to her request looked thoughtful. Then she began scrolling through her phone and dialed a number.

"Before I call, let me warn you that the FBI programmer, the cyber expert, is a teenager by the name of Sophie. She resists all efforts to be called an agent. She may be the most abrasive and bright FBI employee you will ever meet."

"Sounds interesting I can't wait to speak with her," replied Jill.

"Sophie, it's me Agent Sanders. How are you doing?"

After a pause in which Sophie must have provided a decent answer to the question, Agent Sanders continued.

"Look Sophie we are all huddled together in Colorado reviewing data on your friend Bogachev."

Sophie must have responded with some rather colorful language, as Agent Sanders held the cell phone away from her ear for a few seconds wincing.

"Yes that is all true but I have a non-FBI person that wants to speak with you. Before you ask me a hundred questions, I'll warn you that she is standing next to me and can hear my end of the conversation."

Again there was a pause on the part of Agent Sanders while she listened to Sophie with patience; then without a word she handed the phone to Jill.

"Hello this is Dr. Jill Quint, I'm a private forensic pathologist. You must be Sophie."

"Yes this is Sophie, what is your question about Bogachev? I don't have much time to talk to you."

Jill had spoken with many abrupt people in her career. She

wondered what lay behind Sophie's unconventional behavior.

"I don't know how much you know about what is happening in Colorado with Bogachev, but I wanted to pick your brain for some ideas on how to locate his position," said Jill deciding she had better keep talking before the woman cut her off or hung up on her - all a possibility. "We have sighted him via cameras up on the mountain and around town. We even were face to face with him in a bar here, although we didn't know it at the time. Tonight he has managed through his computer to cut off our credit cards, cancel a passport and airline tickets, chase us with snow plows and turn hotel smoke alarms and sprinklers on us. So let me fire away questions to you - would he need to do that from this town, what are the ways he could have tracked our locations, is the passport and airline ticket cancellation likely legitimate, and can you create a virus that would infiltrate his computer system to tell us where he physically is hiding?"

"Well those are the most interesting questions I have heard all week. I hate to say this but I admire how Bogachev has caused you problems tonight. Explain what happened with the snow plows."

"Snow plows in this town are large and sophisticated and there is software that operates the big machines rather like the large combine used in farming. He remotely hacked into the plows, started them up and tried to mow us down. Then we powered off our cellphones, putting them on airplane mode so he could no longer locate us. His timing in the hotel was excellent such that we think he had to be close by to watch his handiwork. He hacked into the resort computers, stopping chairlifts at the perfect time so that his friend could attempt to kill people with guns or poisonous darts."

"So you know he is connected to the internet while he is carrying out these various deeds and you want to use that to tract his location. Yes?"

"Yes that is correct," said Jill deciding to play to Sophie's tech knowledge ego. "I figured that since you solved the

Zeus/Gameover software problem that you might be our best source for solving Bogachev's location. Can you do it?"

"Hmm let me think, then I will call you back on Agent Sanders phone," said Sophie ending the call before Jill could respond.

Jill looked over at Agent Sanders and shrugged handing her the phone, "Well Sophie has a different personality. I think she will call me back on your phone sometime in my life."

Agent Sanders just grinned at her. "She is very good at what she does. She can work magic with computers, but not with humans. If she said she would call you back, she will do so likely in the next hour. I would bet that she is experimenting with computer code right now, thinking about the challenge you launched at her."

"Good." Unable to think of anything else she could do to solve this crime she checked in with the various groups to see if they were making progress.

David had written a program that had located all of Bogachev's images and now they had them lined up by date and time with the camera that had caught him. They could use this same program on the city's camera feed if the agents succeeded in gaining access to the footage. By the sounds of their conversation, they were close. They were speaking with the employee that knew how to obtain footage from the system and it sounded like he would forward them the last forty-eight hours of footage within the hour.

Nathan and Jo's search of the passport and airline ticket situation was proving interesting. Bogachev had managed to cancel their tickets and Nick's passport, but by working with the airlines and explaining the hacking situation they were getting reinstated. It helped that there had not been an approval from any of them agreeing to the fees for a cancelled ticket. Nick's passport situation would be handled by the Dutch embassy and Nick didn't need to appear in person.

Marie was developing a profile on Bogachev that said a lot

about his personality. He didn't use any of the typical social media sites she searched and she couldn't remember looking into a Russian applicant in her day job. The Russians used a site called VK rather than Facebook, but the effort of translating everything into English made it a time consuming proposition. Instead she had found some computer hacker chat rooms that yielded far more interesting information on their suspect. He had clearly been in the U.S. for several months and had entered through Canada by walking over an undisclosed, unguarded border.

"What kind of things does he talk about in the chat rooms?" asked Jill.

"Bogachev and the other computer hackers communicated with each other by logging onto a restricted online chat room and sending messages to each other," Marie explained. "As reflected in the chat room messages, in the months prior to a hack of the FDA servers, he bragged to the other hackers in the chat room that he was searching the Internet for computer servers that were running a particular software program. He was aware that the program contained a vulnerability that he could use to gain unauthorized access to those servers and manipulate the data seen by the FDA. This hack and the other actions that he and Jason took allowed them to get approval for several pharmaceuticals that brought RMCT millions of sales revenues. In the chat room, he mentions moving on to exploit the credit card data of the ski resort, but needing to manipulate the chairlift system as leverage against the resort. It's all data that likely the FBI can use to prosecute, but I haven't come across anything that gives us his location."

It was getting close to midnight. Maybe they should all get some sleep and hope that Jake got something out of Mr. Brown in the morning that they could use to pinpoint his location.

Then Jill heard Agent Sanders' phone ring and she looked over at her hoping that Sophie was calling back with a solution.

"Agent Sanders," said the agent as she listened to whatever the caller said.

"Hi, Sophie. Just a moment and I'll put you on speakerphone."

Jill had a brilliant thought and asked David to join them as their resident on-site computer expert.

"Okay Sophie, you are on speakerphone with me, Dr. Quint, and David Gomez. He is a private citizen involved in this case who happens to have a hobby of entering hacking contests. So he may understand you best. The rest of the cabin may be able to hear you but they are not participating in this call."

"Dr. Quint, I did some experimenting with what you suggested about inserting a virus into Bogachev's computer and I could kick myself for failing to think of that solution earlier. You are pretty good for not knowing much about computers."

Sophie continued, "Can you tell in your photos who the manufacturer is of the computer he is using in the footage you have of him?"

"It's a Lenovo laptop," said David remembering from the multiple frames he looked at.

"Awesome, I thought it might be since they're the number one company in Russia. I know exactly how to exploit his vulnerabilities. Give me an hour and I'll call you back." Just like the last call, Sophie ended the call before giving them a chance to say anything in response.

David looked at Agent Sanders and asked, "How old is Sophie?" He had missed the earlier conversation between Jill and the agent prior to the first call with Sophie.

"Nineteen," replied Agent Sanders. "She has worked for us since she was fifteen when we found her doing illegal things on the Internet. Now she takes great pride in trying to bring down hackers worldwide. She looks at it as a hacking competition that she is determined to win."

"I had guessed that was her age," mused David. "As you can imagine as both a school teacher and a hacker, I've come across students like her. I guess I should be directing them to my local FBI office for safe-keeping and employment."

"I'll leave you a pile of business cards so you can connect the kids to me," noted Agent Sanders.

Jill's eyes felt gritty as it was well beyond her usual bedtime, but she was on the hook for Sophie's call in an hour. Nathan had noticed her flagging energy and murmured to her, "Why don't you go lay down for a nap and I'll come get you when Sophie calls back."

Jill looked around the room and had to agree that not only she, but most of her team should head for bed. Nick and Angela had finished tracking Bogachev in pictures; Marie had been going blind waiting for the translator software to translate Bogachev's messages from the Cyrillic alphabet into English. Jo and Nathan had resolved the travel arrangements.

"I think I'll do that," Jill said to Nathan. Then turning up the volume of her voice she said to the group at large, "I'm going to go and try to get a little nap. Nathan will wake me up when Sophie calls back."

She heard a chorus of "goodnights" and "sweet dreams" as she left the room. She lay on top of her bed with the comforter covering her and quickly nodded off. She was awakened forty-five minutes later by Nathan's voice telling her that Sophie had called back.

Jill joined the speakerphone conversation tossing a "hi Sophie" at the phone.

"Hi, Dr. Quint. I was just telling them I designed a virus that penetrates a vulnerability in Lenovo's operating system. Each time he logs on to an internet connection, the virus will send me his geographical coordinates - latitude and longitude. I've set up a system here so that each ping I get of activity goes to Agent Sanders."

"Where is he now?" asked Jill.

"I don't know, the computer is turned off," observed Sophie.

"So then you haven't actually infected his computer yet? You don't actually know if your virus will work?" challenged Jill.

"Pleeaaasse, I know what I am doing and I am sure this will work. Bogachev has gone to bed and that's where I'm going, too," asserted Sophie and she ended the call.

Jill found herself grinding her teeth. She knew the FBI was lucky to have this young hacker and that she was brilliant, but the absolute confidence in her virus creation was astonishing to hear. She looked to Agent Sanders and raised her brows in question.

"She hasn't failed yet for the FBI so I am sure the program works. I recommend we all head for bed. We may have our answer early in the morning depending on whether he is an early riser or not."

The cabin contained several bedrooms with multiple beds. So Jill and Nathan were quiet as they entered the room they were sharing with Angela and Marie. Jill was as always lights out in no time, waking five hours later due to her body clock.

She had been awake for awhile when Agent Sanders entered the living room carrying her cell phone.

"Sophie was correct, her virus did work. Bogachev must be awake and connecting to the internet. Do me a favor and start monitoring these coordinates while I wake everyone up and we put together a plan to capture him. Jill, your idea of speaking to Sophie was excellent. We now have the means to capture our fourth Most Wanted suspect in a week."

"I'll study his position and see if I can get a view of where he is staying from Google earth. If you need help from my team, feel free to wake them up."

"We don't need them yet. I may wake David up since he is the most knowledgeable about this area," commented Agent Sanders.

Soon Jill had the coordinates entered into Google Earth and she had a picture of the building he was staying in up on the screen. The other agents were soon dressed and would be shortly joined by additional agents from Jake's cabin. They were watching the screen as they were dressing in bullet proof vests and weapon holsters. An agent from Jake's cabin would lead the operation.

The building that Bogachev appeared to be holed up in was an unpretentious A-frame ski house. Court records showed that it was likely a rental as the owners had been in the area for twenty years. A Hummer was parked in the driveway, but there was no activity outside. There were homes in the area but they were at least a hundred yards away. A winter storm was expected to hit the area in about two to three hours and there was light snow growing heavier by the moment. Within the hour, two agents were doing surveillance outside of Bogachev's house. Each was hunkered down examining the trees for any security cameras, but they didn't locate any. Hopefully that was because Bogachev had believed he couldn't be found, and therefore had no need for additional security rather than they missed sight of a camera.

The agent running the Operation soon mapped out a plan. This left Jill and her team back in the cabin with three agents. They all piled into a few cars and left for the cabin where they thought Bogachev was hiding. The snow was getting heavier; the visibility worse.

Agent Pugh, located in the cabin with Jill and team kept them informed of the Op. By now, Jill had been joined by David, Nick, Marie, and Angela. Nathan and Jo were still asleep. About an hour into the Op, they got word that when they entered the cabin, Bogachev was not there. It was clear he had been there at one time, but sometime before the FBI had organized their resources on-site, he had escaped out his back door on cross country skis, based on a trail that left the cabin. Unfortunately, no one in their party had the skill to follow Bogachev and they had no snowmobile at their disposal. One could be delivered within an hour, but the tracks were fast disappearing under the weight of new snow from the storm which was picking up. Initially they had concluded that Bogachev would likely die in the storm given the level of snow and backcountry trees that his tracks hinted he had skied towards. Then Marie put an end to that conclusion.

CHAPTER 17

"*I*nteresting that he took off on skis," remarked Marie. "I remember somewhere in all of the research that I did on him that he had been a member of the Russian World Championship team for cross-country skiing, so he must have some serious ability to ski and likely survive in this snowstorm. Just a reminder, Jo and I have about six hours before we have to leave for the airport. I am hoping this storm passes through by then or the shuttle operates in snow storms. Nick, you were heading back to the airport about that time as well, I think?"

"Let me get word to our team leader of Bogachev's skiing ability," declared Agent Pugh. "He may want to go after him with a snowmobile. As for your travel, I would think we would have you well out of here by your deadline."

"How long ago was Bogachev detected in his cabin? I think we could do a calculation of how far he could have skied. I might shave twenty-five percent off the top assuming he is no longer in competition shape. That should give you a radius of where he is," David suggested.

"Yeah, but he could have picked up a car along the way," said Angela.

"True, but". Jill didn't get any more words out of her mouth because bullets started flying through the front door. They all dropped to the floor, crawling behind large pieces of furniture for protection. One of the agents had been hit, as was David. Fortunately, both were superficial wounds. They made a big mess dragging their bloodied bodies across the floor.

Jill looked around her and saw the two agents in a shooting position on their bellies. Angela, Marie, and David had all taken cover. Who was shooting and why? She had a fleeting thought about Nathan and Jo, maybe still asleep if they were able to sleep through the noise of the bullets striking things.

The front door sat ajar on its hinges. Bullet holes everywhere around the door frame. Snow was blowing through the opening in great gusts. Then something else came through the door, and Jill saw it was a grenade.

She yelled at everyone.

"Run toward the kitchen and take cover; it's a grenade!"

But no one had time to get to the kitchen by Jill's count the grenade detonated three seconds after it came through the door. Thankfully, the heavy furniture they all took cover behind saved them from most of the explosion. Everyone had ringing in their ears and cuts wherever their skin was exposed from flying debris.

The cabin's living room looked like a tornado had gone through it. Then she heard some grunts from the front porch along with another explosion outside which was muffled thanks to the heavy snow.

She looked over at Marie and Angela and said "Should we move toward the kitchen or head outside to see what is going on?"

And then the decision was made for her as one of the agents raced to the doorway, peered outside, and then exited the cabin. Jill headed in the same direction when she heard a gunshot sound outside.

Jill looked outside then and was startled to see Nathan taking heaving breaths, and the FBI agent standing over a man on the porch, who was bleeding heavily into the snow around him.

"I think this is Bogachev and he took a bullet to the stomach. Call 911 and the other agents, and then come back here and care for him. Nathan is fine, he just can't speak at the moment."

The agent's comments about Nathan caused her world to balance again. She had been momentarily frozen when she saw Nathan lying on his back taking deep gulping breaths. She stuck her head back inside the cabin.

"David, call 911 for an ambulance for a male wounded in the abdomen by a gunshot and get the other agents here. Marie and Angela, can you come outside with me and help?"

Everyone hurried to follow Jill's requests.

Jill knelt by Nathan's side and asked, "What happened? Where are you hurt? What happened to your throat?"

He whispered in the smallest of voices, "snuck out bedroom window, circled to porch to stop him from throwing another grenade," he paused for a few moments then added, "Bastard knows Sambo, had me in a choke hold when the agent finally got the opportunity to shoot him."

Jill puzzled over the word Sambo. She at first thought he said Samba but couldn't figure out the connection between dancing and choke holds. Seeing that Nathan was ok, just recovering from having the air choked out of him, she moved quickly over to Bogachev.

"I can verify this is Bogachev. His pulse is fast and faint. Fetch me some towels so I can apply pressure to this wound," commanded Jill.

She could hear a siren in the distance but, with the snow, wondered how long it would to reach this cabin. She wanted to move the man inside but didn't want to risk moving the bullet; instead she asked Marie and Angela to set up a makeshift tent over him and to throw a comforter around him. She really didn't want to do CPR on this man so she kept talking to him demanding he keep his heart going. Meanwhile, Nathan was making a strong recovery and had been able to move indoors out of the snow.

The ambulance turned into the driveway. Jill told one of the agents, "Go get a paramedic over here quickly with some oxygen and a mask. Tell him we'll need to do CPR in about a minute."

The agent returned in about thirty seconds, paramedic in tow with the necessary equipment in hand.

Jill looked up, "I'm a doctor. This is an abdominal gunshot wound. We need to get him out of the snow and into your ambulance for treatment and move towards a hospital."

The paramedic nodded and went to work. The other agent came on a run with the other paramedic with the stretcher. Between the three of them, they were able to move Bogachev onto the stretcher. It was getting really slippery with the snow and moving a stretcher now weighted down with a two hundred pound man was tough going. As soon as he was in the ambulance, they spent a minute trying to get an IV started before taking off. Jill and two agents accompanied Bogachev in addition to the paramedic. In this weather, the hospital was a twenty minute ride. His heart rate was poor and Jill conferred with the paramedic. "If you'll get me the supplies for a venous cut-down, then we'll stop this ambulance for less than a minute while I do the procedure to get fluids going into him. I have not done this procedure on a live patient in about fifteen years, so I am really open to other suggestions."

"Dr. Quint, I am worried about the condition of the roads making this trip longer, I agree we need to make an attempt to start fluids as soon as possible. I'll get the supplies ready then have Aaron stop the ambulance. If you can't succeed in two minutes, I would suggest moving on."

"It's Jill, and I like your timeline. Let's do it," said Jill quickly reviewing in her head the steps to get an intravenous line going in this man.

A minute later the ambulance came to a stop and they had a go at starting a line. Forty-five seconds later Jill had the line inserted and taped in place and the ambulance began rolling again. She took over at the head of the gurney and began ventilating Bogachev manually. The paramedic was in touch with the base station and had started fluids to support their victim. Their ambulance was now being escorted by a state trooper who was trying to clear the path for the ambulance to keep going. They were barely able to avoid doing chest compressions on the man and Jill was thrilled to see the lights of the hospital come into their snowy view. The weather was probably too bad to get a helicopter here to take the patient to a trauma center in Denver, so it would be up to the emergency room and surgical staff to keep him alive. She had done her part.

After the stretcher was removed, the two agents accompanied the man inside the emergency room. Jill was left alone in the lobby and began to shiver when the state trooper approached her.

"Hello ma'am, I'm Trooper Hanson. Do you know why the FBI is involved with the man from that ambulance?"

"Hello, Trooper Hanson. I am Dr. Jill Quint and thank you for the escort today. That man is on the FBI's Ten Most Wanted list and one of the agents shot him in the stomach as he tried to kill all of us."

The trooper looked at her as if accessing whether she had been drinking. She could swear he even sniffed her breath looking for fumes. She decided to take mercy on him.

"Trooper Hanson, let me give you my business card. I was called into the investigation to assist a family member of someone who was murdered. During the investigation of this case, it was discovered that three of the players involved were on the FBI's Most Wanted list. That was when I called the Denver FBI office to involve them in this case."

The trooper looked even more skeptical with her choppy

explanation, so she decided to call Jake to see if he was available to speak with the trooper.

"Let me call Special Agent in Charge Jake Porter in the Denver FBI office and you can speak to him instead of looking at me like I am a crazy woman."

"Ma'am I didn't mean to offend you, but you have to admit your story sounds far-fetched," said the trooper apologetically.

She dialed Jake's number and was pleased when he answered the phone. She provided a quick update to Jake on Bogachev's actions and condition then asked him to speak to trooper Hanson and explain the case in cop language. Ten minutes later the trooper ended the call and handed her phone to her.

"Let's go check on Mr. Bogachev and see if the Agents need anything. If they don't, I'll give you a ride back to your residence."

"Thank you. I would very much appreciate a ride."

Three minutes later they were on their way out of the hospital. Jill had no coat and was covered in Bogachev's drying blood. Yuck. On the up side, the man was still alive and well guarded by the agents.

The storm hadn't let up yet so the ride was slow. Trooper Hanson asked her numerous questions all the way back to the cabin. In theory he had no official role in the case, but it was so unusual he couldn't resist asking questions about it.

When she arrived back at the cabin, there was a swarm of local law enforcement as well as FBI agents documenting stuff. Jake's friend, who had lent them the cabin, was also there, amazed at the destruction, which he was documenting for insurance purposes. He was making arrangements for an emergency shipment of plywood so he could close up the cabin while he worked on remodeling it back to its original beauty before bullets and a grenade had changed its face.

Jo was also walking around the scene amazed that she had slept through it all. She had emerged from her bedroom after the ambulance had left chagrined that even a grenade in the next room had not shaken her out of her dead sleep.

Jill was looking for Nathan wanting to see how his throat was. She found him inside a warm inner bedroom lying on his back, ice around his throat. Jill went over to kiss him softly and check on the swelling and bruising.

"Hey babe, how are you feeling?"

In a hoarse voice he responded, "Like a two hundred pound man tried to choke the life out of me. What does the bruising look like?" and he lifted up the ice bag.

"Well, you have bruises around your neck, but the most important thing is that you can breathe. I performed my share of autopsies on people choked to death. In some cases their windpipe is smashed. I think your throat is swollen and it will stay that way for a few days until the bruises start going away. Thank you for going out the back window and circling around to get this guy. He was pretty close to blowing us all to bits. You saved all of our lives."

"You're welcome, but I am going to avoid talking if you don't mind. Did he make it alive to the hospital?"

"Yes, I left him with two agents at the hospital and they were taking him into surgery. We need to move everyone back to the lodge so that Jo, Marie, and Nick can leave as scheduled. The lodge had a spa with a steam room that might feel good for your throat. You just stay and rest here and I'll organize our team outside and come and get you when we are ready to move. I just need to change out of these bloody clothes," so saying she kissed him again and did a quick swap of her clothing, taking the bloody ones with her to toss in the garbage.

"We need to get back to our lodge as this one is not habitable," remarked Jill. "Also our luggage is there and Jo, Marie, and Nick are leaving for Denver in three hours. Is everyone ready to move and who can give us a ride?"

David responded that the same friend who had transported

them last night was available. He added that his friend was very curious about the all the activity that morning and he would be there within half an hour.

"Great! I want to settle Nathan in at the lodge and see my friends off to the airport. So if you don't mind David, I would like to send my team back to the lodge first as it seems that the roads are still open, although the driving will be slow. They are on a tight time frame if they still want to make their flights."

"Jill, that is fine, and I'm sure it will be fine with my friend. I'll walk him through this scene and that should put both of us in his good graces. We all want to thank Nathan for saving our lives, but we quickly left him alone when we saw it was too painful to converse."

"He knows and perhaps the steam room at the lodge will do wonders for his throat."

Soon they had piled into David's friend's massive SUV for the ride back to the lodge. They would be in different rooms since the clean-up of their suite had not yet occurred. Jill was sure that the lodge would be thrilled to learn that while they had the sprinkler damage, at least they didn't have the bullet and grenade damage. She hoped they would continue to view her as a good customer.

There was no need for a hotel room for Nick, Jo, or Marie. Angela was staying with Jill and Nathan for her final night in Colorado. They used the bathroom to get refreshed while Jill took Nathan down to the steam room. The bruises were beginning to look really bad around his throat and she was extremely grateful that the FBI agent had shot Bogachev when he did.

Jill said to Nathan, "This steam will either make you feel better or worse, I really can't guess, but we'll leave quickly if you start feeling worse."

Nathan nodded in agreement as they settled into the warm foggy interior. Jill added eucalyptus oil to the steam and Nathan nodded his agreement that it improved his throat. They stayed there for a half an hour then returned to the room to say goodbye to Marie, Jo, and Nick. Hugs were exchanged all around.

"Jill, you are going to have to increase our contracts soon for hazardous duty pay," declared Marie. "The chairlift and grenade events were more excitement then I wanted in a second job!"

"Next time, get me out of bed so I don't miss any excitement! I never used to be a heavy sleeper; I am still astonished that I slept through a grenade blast," said Jo.

Jill was laughing when she said, "That is exactly why we don't get you out of bed - not even a grenade wakes you up when you're in a deep sleep!"

"Most of all we need to thank Nathan. He saved all of our lives by having the smarts to sneak around back and stop Bogachev from tossing that second grenade at us. I am so sorry your throat is so sore," said Angela, her voice a mixture of awe and concern.

Nathan then whispered slowly, "You're family - what else would I do but try and save you?"

Marie added, "You know they say 'when you save a life, you are responsible for it.' So it is a good thing that we're family."

Nathan just smiled and nodded.

"Jill, thanks for asking me to join you on this case," said Nick. "I thought the violent criminals and adventures in your last case in Belgium and the Netherlands was just a unique experience. Now my conclusion is that seemingly quiet murders hide the most heinous criminal minds."

They all left and soon it was just Angela, Nathan, and Jill sitting back in the steam room, glasses of wine in hand, relaxing and enjoying the quiet companionship of friends, mountains, and the satisfaction of taking down murderous villains.

The End

If you liked this story, please leave a review on Amazon by clicking here

ALSO BY ALEC PECHE

ABOUT THE AUTHOR

I reside in Northern California with my rescue dog and cat. I love to travel, play sports, read, and drink wine and beer. I enjoy the diversity of the world and I'm always watching people and events for story ideas. In a prior life, I worked in healthcare which powers my medical knowledge for Dr. Quint.

If you would like to sign up for my monthly blog and announcement of new books, please follow this link: https://www.alecpeche.com/

Amazon Author Profile

Author Profile on Goodreads

Author Profile on BookBub